"TURN AROUND . . ."

Slocum nodded and made as if to turn to his left. Instead, he crouched, spun, and threw himself to the right. The Henry's muzzle blast deafened him. He kept spinning. Zeke had to swivel his whole torso to the right to bring the Henry to bear on him. There was the sound of the lever jacking a round into the chamber. Slocum saw him and released his thumb from the held-back hammer. The .36-caliber Colt spit flame, the grip rolled back in his hand. The bullet hit Zeke in the belly and doubled him over.

Zeke, face working in shocked disbelief, struggled to one knee. Slocum fired again. The bullet slammed Zeke backward and down. He lay, heels drumming the ground in the throes of death, with his gaping mouth black with blood vomit.

JAKE LOGAN

SLOCUM'S GRUBSTAKE

J

JOVE BOOKS, NEW YORK

SLOCUM'S GRUBSTAKE

A Jove Book / published by arrangement with
the author

PRINTING HISTORY
Jove edition / October 1996

The Putnam Berkley World Wide Web site address is
http://www.berkley.com/berkley

ISBN: 0-515-11955-5

A JOVE BOOK®
Jove Books are published by The Berkley Publishing Group,
200 Madison Avenue, New York, New York 10016.
JOVE and the "J" design are trademarks
belonging to Jove Publications, Inc.

PRINTED IN THE UNITED STATES OF AMERICA

10 9 8 7 6 5 4 3 2 1

1

Slocum set his pan on a rock and climbed out of the icy water of the California Gulch. He'd worked his way downstream from the Greenhorn Gulch to the California, and was nearly to the junction of the north fork of the Palouse River. So far, he'd gotten little for his efforts. A few scads and some dust. And feet and calves numb from prolonged hunkering in cold water. March still saw patches of snow on the ground. His horse followed him, grazing on what grass was bare. The Hoodoos, part of the Clearwater Range and bordering the territories of Washington and Idaho, still wore their winter coats.

He climbed on to the muddy bank stiffly with legs so numb they felt like stilts. His aching hands rolled down his canvas trousers and tugged on his wool socks. He grunted. Pain shot through him when he straightened up after having been bent double most of the morning. He threw more wood on the embers of his fire.

In the middle of the coals sat his one indispensable connection with civilization—a coffeepot. He grimaced from the ache of sore joints when he pulled on his coat against the chill and tugged on his waterproof boots. All the while he sniffed with anticipation the brew's aroma coming from the enameled pot whose lid chattered from escaping steam. He stretched his tall, muscular frame, pulled off his hat, and ran long, thick fingers through his rough tangle of hair, black as a raven's wing.

He was reaching for his tin cup when the shout rang out.

"Hallo, the fire!"

Startled, he unhooked the hammer thong on his Navy Colt.

"Step ahead!"

Two scraggly, scrawny men approached, their boots crackling like gunfire in the underbrush. He stiffened in alarm when he saw neither carried a panner's equipment—shovel, pail, gold pan, and pickax. And no packmule. Both carried Henrys, wore bandoliers heavy with .44s, and had skinning knives stuck in their belts. One was tall and skinny, too tall for his shoulders, the other medium-tall and stocky, like a bull. Muley hats hid their faces in shadow. Dried food and spittle matted their rough-trimmed beards. He smelled their stink seven feet away. They were the first men he'd seen in a week.

Slocum's coat covered his cross-draw holster.

"How's it goin', pardner?" the tall one asked, his face—what Slocum could see of it—showing beady, gleaming eyes that reminded him of a weasel's. Greed had etched the face with grim lines. That wasn't unusual. A man couldn't live the raw life of a gold prospector without greed chousing him. Greed was natural in a grubstaker. Like eating. Or shitting. It was when greed became all-consuming and drove reason from a man that trouble followed as it all too often did in the gold camps.

"Find any color?" the shorter man asked, his broad face friendly except for the eyes. "Heard this gulch pans out real good."

"No better'n the Beagie and Cleveland Gulches south of here." Slocum, alert now, wiped his face with his bandanna, taking his time doing it so he could study the two without appearing obvious about it. His danger sense prodded him, a hammer of alarm beating at the base of his skull.

The shorter man asked, his tone more an eager demand than polite curiosity, "Find much?"

"Few scads."

"Big 'uns?"

" 'Nough to pay for a room and a bottle. Why?"

"We's tryin' to figger if the Palouse is worth fishin'. Tha's all." Their greedy gazes shifted to Slocum's plunder bag and his horse and stayed there.

"This isn't exactly a safe place to do anything," Slocum replied. "Found two men dead up on Eldorado Gulch day before yesterday."

"Dead, ya say?" The taller man licked his lips. "What kilt 'em?"

"Somebody murdered them."

"How 'bout thet, Zeke? Poor fellers murdered. All fer crass gold. Whatchya think about thet now? The law know?" The shorter man, his thick lips pursed, eyed Slocum intently.

"Nearest law's at Palouse Flats," Slocum replied. "This here's Idaho."

Zeke shook his head in what Slocum reckoned was supposed to be a gesture of sorrow. But he was no John Wilkes Booth.

Zeke clucked his tongue and shook his head again. "Bead—thet's plumb *tir'ble!* No law. Jus' think! Man dies—an' no soul 'roun' to bring the killers to justice."

Bead nodded his agreement, his smile climbing no higher than his mouth. His eyes reminded Slocum of the twin muzzles of a Greener scattergun.

"Didn' ketch whither you said you bin makin' the riffle here, pardner," Zeke said.

"Probably because I didn't say."

Zeke pouted. "No call to get frothy, friend." His grin

with its missing teeth reminded Slocum of the crenellated battlements of a castle wall.

Bead managed to look hurt. "We wasn't pryin' none, friend."

Slocum considered the two from beneath the brim of his hat and decided he definitely didn't like what he saw. Couple of ill-mannered types, he thought. Don't know when not to ask questions. Or how to ask them when they do. That can get you killed out here. Aloud, he asked, "Where've you been panning?"

"Placer minin'. Near Gol' Creek." Bead shook his head with contrived sadness. "Didn' pan out none. We're so plumb broke, we're fixin' to sell our saddles so's we kin eat."

"Hear they're paying twenty dollars a day wages in the Hoodoo Mine."

Zeke shook his head. "Won' last. It's eighty miles to Lewiston. Nearest trading post but hard to get to. Mine's 'bout played out anyway."

Bead, his broad smile wooden, asked, "How long you bin panning, friend?"

"Long enough to get chilblains."

He deliberately turned his back on them to reach for the coffeepot. His right hand slipped under his coat. He was taking a chance that could get him backshot, but he remembered the murdered men. He figured whoever had killed them enjoyed killing their victims slowly. The killers had shot out their kneecaps, then mangled their shoulders with bullets. Helpless, the two had then been butchered with knives—fingers and noses hacked off, ears sliced, eyes gouged out. He'd thought of Indians, but the Coeur d'Alene Indians weren't kill-crazy.

"Don' move, mister!"

Slocum straightened slowly, back muscles tensed to receive a round. Though he'd expected something of the sort, his stomach muscles contracted with sickening force, and his blood emptied from his heart with chilling swiftness.

For one panicky moment, fear prevented him from acting with reason. A Henry being levered sounded as loud as an avalanche in his ears. He fought to keep his voice even. "What do you want?"

Zeke cackled. "Hey, Bead! Id'jot wants to know what we want."

Bead's guffaw sounded like a grizzly's growl. "Why— yer poke. What else? 'Less ya got a bitch stashed nearby." Bead's laugh was an insane cackle.

"You killed those two men, didn't you."

"Yup."

"Why? Why didn't you simply take their pokes?"

"They was right unfriendly. Had to larn 'em some manners." Zeke prodded Slocum with the muzzle of his Henry. "Whir's yer dust?"

"What I got's in my plunder bag." Slocum half-turned.

"Search it, Bead!" Slocum heard Bead rummaging through his bag and bedroll.

"Lookee here!" The sound of Bead standing turned Slocum's danger sense to full throttle. The blood rushing, heart pumping brought him to full alert like an animal.

Bead did a quick dance. "Who-ee! Lookee! Gold! Bags of it!" Both men jumped up and down like children in their glee. "The preacher don' know what he's missin'."

"If I iver finds thet lily-livered skunk, I'll bore him! Flyin' off an' leavin' us here in the middle of nowhir!" Zeke's voice trembled with outrage, and his features twisted with hate.

Slocum, ready to grasp at anything to distract the two, asked, "Flying off? What do you mean? Flying off. How? Where?"

The laughter of the two, as if he had intruded on some private joke, sounded insane. He reckoned he was dealing with men touched in the head.

"Want's to know 'bout flying, Zeke. Gonna git the chance whin we bores ya. Fly right up to heaven."

"Or straight down to hell! We got yer grubstake. An'

the grubstakes of thim others.'' Bead's guffaw wet the back
of Slocum's neck with spittle.

"Only, the preacher ain't a-coming down to git us this
time.'' Zeke's voice echoed a note of tragedy. "Left us
here to rot, he did.''

"Shoot thet bastard fuller of holes than a Swiss cheese
if iver I finds him!''

"Turn 'roun'—id'jot!'' A carbine being raised rustled
against Zeke's canvas trousers.

Slocum nodded and made as if to turn to his left. Instead,
he crouched, spun, and threw himself to the right. The Henry's muzzle blast deafened him. He kept spinning. Zeke had
to swivel his whole torso to the right to bring the Henry to
bear on him. There was the sound of the lever jacking a
round into the chamber. Slocum saw him and released his
thumb from the held-back hammer. The .36-caliber Colt
spit flame, the grip rolled back in his hand. The bullet hit
Zeke in the belly and doubled him over.

Bead was bringing his rifle up when Slocum's second
round hit the receiver and drove the weapon back into his
chest. His face flashed surprise and shock. Slocum's third
round bloodied his right shoulder, the fourth, his left. The
Henry clattered to the ground. Bead stared in bewilderment,
then sank to his knees, both arms dangling as useless as
sticks.

Zeke, face working in shocked disbelief, struggled to one
knee. Slocum fired again. The bullet slammed Zeke backward and down. He lay, heels drumming the ground in the
throes of death, with his gaping mouth black with blood
vomit. Slocum tossed the two men's rifles aside and
whipped the knives from their belts.

The picture of the brutalized dead men fresh in his mind,
he aimed at Bead and pulled the trigger. The hammer fell
on a bad cap. Well, he was in no hurry. Neither man posed
a danger.

Seating himself on a log, he removed the cylinder from
the Navy, used a pick to punch out residue in the nipples,

then poured a measure of powder from his powder flask into the five empty chambers. Next, he placed lead balls in each chamber. He put the cylinder into the frame, locked it in place, then cocked the gun to rotate it. When each chamber lined up with the rammer, he rammed home the charge. Caps went on the nipples last. Using his knife, he pried the splintered cap off its nipple. He then took his can of bear grease and carefully daubed grease into the ends of the chambers.

He hefted the gun and studied the finished operation as he debated whether to finish off the two. They would both die—eventually. Just as the men they'd tortured had died. He holstered his gun and stood. No point, he thought, in wasting powder and shot. Zeke made a death rattle, Bead passed out.

He found their horses a hundred yards away in a gully. The two animals looked worse off than their erstwhile owners. He unsaddled them, patted them, and turned them loose to graze. He then went through the men's saddlebags.

He hefted the four leather sacks of scads and dust, which he figured they'd taken from the dead men. Around two hundred dollars worth, he figured. Value depended on the purity, of course.

He'd found nothing on the murdered men—no letters or papers—that told who they were. Only two unused dance-hall tickets in their pockets for some hurdy-gurdy hall in Oregon. In all likelihood, from the look of them, they'd been part of the army of men following the lure of gold from Nevada to California to Idaho like the children of Hameln had followed the Pied Piper. He placed the sacks in his saddlebags and rode northwest toward Palouse Flats.

He'd come to the Hoodoos to disappear long enough for the sheriff hunting him from Oregon to give up. While hiding out, he'd busied himself by panning for gold. No one had seen him arrive. No one saw him leave.

The dead men could cause trouble. He hoped whatever law stumbled onto them found the murdered men first, then the murderers. He sighted on Kamiak Mountain from eyes perpetually squinted from staring at too many horizons. He would have to cross a broad valley through heavy stands of pines. The rugged Hoodoos faded into a dark skyline behind him. Tired and hungry, he rode into Palouse Flats two days later.

2

As he rode, Slocum surveyed the settlement that clung to the banks of the Palouse River. Groves of cottonwoods and alders bordered both sides. He'd ridden past Perkins's sawmill and Cox's flour mill. A few houses stood clustered near the wood bridge spanning the river. The wide main street glistened with mud from a recent rain. Several log and clapboard buildings with faded facades fronted on the single boardwalk. He was quick to notice the jail. The town didn't appear to have two hundred people in it.

He hitched his horse in front of the saloon, a massive rough log structure. Two lanterns that guttered and smoked in the close air lit the cave-like interior. Two barrels supported a plank for a bar. Rough tables and benches sat on a dirt floor. He sniffed the pervasive smell of stale tobacco, beer, and food. A meager fire in the big stone hearth battled the damp chill. The place reminded him of a root cellar. He half expected to see mushrooms growing from the dirt.

"What's yer pleasure, friend?" A small, wiry oldster wearing a dirty white apron too big for him appeared from a door behind the bar.

Slocum dumped three scads on the plank. The saloonist scooped them up and set them on a scales as if he was used to the procedure, which he probably was. "Ten dollars," he announced.

Slocum nodded. He was in no position to argue. Gold was the barter of exchange, but he had the suspicion the only ones getting rich were the saloons and stores. The barkeep handed him ten silver dollars.

"What's your whiskey?" Slocum asked. He absently unbuttoned his coat to reveal the Colt. The barkeep glanced at it but didn't react.

"Depends on how drunk you wanna get. And how quick." He turned and motioned to the sparse row of bottles on the shelf behind him. "The usual phlegm-cutters—flavored with genuine tobacco, gunpowder, and old nails outa Sam Cox's burnt barn. Gives it a special boo-kay. Then we got the better item." He fingered a dark bottle. "Genuine blackstrap. Guaranteed to soak the stain off your teeth."

Slocum snorted. "Rum? That the best you've got?"

"Ain't nothing wrong with rum, mister." He handed Slocum the bottle. "Made in Cuba. Goes down nice'n easy."

Slocum wasn't certain about rum, but it was probably to be preferred to the rotgut on the shelf. "How much?"

"The bottle? Five dollars."

He again snorted his disgust. "Give you three. Take it or leave it!"

The barkeep looked about the empty room. "This here's gold country—"

"With the gold played out and the land in the grip of a depression. Bet I'm your only customer so far today." He slapped three silver dollars on the bar.

The barkeep hesitated, then nodded. He wiped a glass with his apron and laid it alongside the bottle. Slocum took both and walked to a table to clear the dust from his throat. "Where can a man get something to eat?"

"What're you hungry for?" The voice, female, turned his head. The woman was maybe eighteen, slim, and garishly made up. When she came closer, he saw that under the paint she had a hard prettiness to her. She sashayed up to him. Her dress, little more than a sack, was filled out pleasingly by the body beneath it.

Slocum sighed. Whores came in all sizes, shapes, ages, and looks. But they seldom varied their routine. He steeled himself for the encounter, knowing exactly how it would proceed and how it would end. He was too spent to engage in a mating dance. A closer look showed him that she appeared clean enough.

"Barkeep!" he called. "You got a wet rag? A clean one?"

"Reckon so. Why?"

"Give it to the lady."

The old man frowned, puzzled. Fumbling beneath the bar, he handed the girl a sopping towel.

She grinned to show teeth slightly uneven but healthy-looking. "What you want me to do with it? Clean your table?" She snickered and glanced at the barkeep.

"Wipe your face with it!" Slocum said.

Her grin faded. "Do—*what*?"

He stood and approached her. Holding her by her thick mane, he took the towel and scrubbed her face clean of powder and paint. His action so confused her, she failed to react but stood helpless in his grip. Done, he released her and stepped back.

She spluttered, "Wh-What was *that* for?"

"Want to see what I'm buying." He made a point of walking his gaze up and down her. "Reckon, you'll do. How much?"

"Don't you want to know my name? Aren't you going to buy me a drink?" She shot him a rueful look.

"Okay. What's your handle?"

"Rose. And I'm not sure *you'll* do." She angrily shook her dark hair loose where he'd bunched it.

He fished five dollars from his vest pocket, took her hand, and pressed the coins into it. "You'd better be worth it! You got a crib here?"

She gave a sullen, half interested look. "Room in back."

"Rustle me up some grub." He looked over at the oldster, who watched the transaction with detached interest. "How much for a tub big enough for me to sit in and enough hot water to fill it?"

"Three dollars," the man replied. "Go on back with Rose. I'll send back a chateaubriand for you." He chuckled in a dry voice and called out. "Jess! Come in here!"

A boy Slocum reckoned to be fourteen came in. He seemed all arms and legs topped with an unruly mass of orange hair. "Yeah, Dinty?"

Dinty relayed Slocum's request. Slocum slapped a five-dollar gold piece on the bar and followed the girl through a dark, narrow tunnel-like hall to a small, dark room. When Rose lit two candles on the bed stand, it surprised him to see that the place was neat and clean. A pitcher and bowl stood on a small table at the end of the bed, a four-poster. A clothes press stood against one wall, and a window looked out into an alley. She pulled the curtains. The place smelled of lye soap and cheap perfume.

A noise alerted him. His hand moved to the Colt. A knock, and Dinty and the boy shuffled in with a zinc tub between them.

"Food's coming up," Dinty announced.

"If Hank shows, you ain't seen me," Rose whispered. Dinty nodded. Slocum, wondering who Hank was, tugged off his boots and coat, made certain his Colt was where he could reach it fast, then stretched out with a sigh of contentment on the bed. Rose opened the bottle and poured him a drink. He sat up, bolstered by pillows, and drank, the rum burning his throat, then settling in his belly like fire.

The boy made six trips with buckets of water, half of them steaming. Slocum stripped down and climbed gingerly into the tub, then settled himself in the hot water.

Aches he'd forgotten he had were soothed. He closed his eyes and tried not to think of anything but the animal comfort enveloping him.

"Rose. Get my razor out of my bedroll. You got soap someplace. Can smell it. Start earning your money. Shave and wash me."

Rose, who was staring with unabashed admiration at the muscular torso of the big man, opened her mouth—probably, he thought, to protest being put to work on her feet instead of on her back. But she saw something in the hard, bony face framed in lank black hair that warned her to do as he asked.

She washed him, shaved him, and frayed a twig so he could brush his teeth and gums. The bottle was a third empty when he stepped out a half hour later. She dried him off, her hands lingering longer than they needed to on certain parts of his body as she dabbed at him with the towel. His erection made her blink in surprise. She muttered something that sounded like, "I sure didn't bargain fer no horse."

"You're next," he announced. "Peel down and get in there."

She went through what was probably meant to be an erotic undressing. Other than her sack dress, she didn't have much to take off, but managed to wriggle her hips and undulate like a snake shedding its skin as she pulled the garment up her body and over her head. Next came a petticoat. She hung the garments on the post to cover Slocum's gunbelt, holster, Colt, and ammunition bag hanging there. She stood before him in a hipshot stance, a look of both defiance and shame coloring her thin face.

He wondered how long she'd been in the business. Not long enough to completely lose her innocence, he thought. Long, slim legs, taut belly, a swatch of dark fuzz at its base. Breasts small with dark, nipple-tipped aureoles. Shoulders thin and rangy, long neck, and small, compact head. At first glance, she gave the impression of being all hair and eyes.

He felt a surge of remorse that he was buying her for the night. She could be his daughter. But, he thought, anger surging up in him, no daughter of his would ever sink to selling herself. He'd see her dead first.

But, he reflected, there was no worry on that score. He would die, and his line would die with him. As far as he knew, he'd never gotten a woman pregnant.

He soaped her down, his hands exploring her, fingers searching as he scoured those parts of her he wanted especially clean. She bent her head and submitted to having her hair washed, grunting at the strength of his hands. He helped her stand and toweled her dry. Picking her up, he carried her to the bed. He was about to climb in beside her when a knock on the door sounded and Dinty's muffled voice announced, "Grab on a root 'n growl! Come'n get it!"

It was a steak big enough for three men, with fried potatoes, greens, and hot-buttered biscuits. Slocum, naked, tried to remember his manners as he wolfed down the food. Rose, also naked, stuffed her mouth and chewed, trying to be dainty and ladylike about it. He wondered idly if she got enough to eat on a regular basis. Business was obviously slow in 1873 Palouse Flats.

The candles had burned low when they lay in bed together, panting heavily. Slocum had to remind himself that his 190 pounds probably felt like three hundred to the girl pinned beneath him. She relaxed her legs and withdrew her heels from the small of his back.

"Whew! Ye're somethin' else, mister!" She pushed him gently off her as her breast rose and fell in raucous breathing. "Looks like I'm gonna earn thet five dollars—and then some. Took you a long time to come thet last time. Ye're like to bury me in the mattress."

"Running out of steam. What time is it?" He sleepily tried to focus on his turnip. "Three in the morning? Reckon, that'll do." He fell back and stared at the low-beamed ceiling. "Blow out the candles, Rose."

She blew them out, and the cool darkness took over. She settled against him and let her fingers stray to his limp penis. She took his scrotum in her small hand and worked his balls with her fingers as if they were marbles. He grinned in the dark. Rose had proved to be a pleasant surprise.

He dozed off, then came jarringly awake when Rose, bending over him, nipped the head of his semi-erection. He almost balked, but let her go ahead. Her oral ministrations were bringing him alive. She had to work at it because he'd already taken her twice during the night. His orgasm building to a crescendo, he lurched and spasmed under her as she drained the last dregs from him. He settled himself in the feather tick, pulled Rose to him and let her squirm and settle herself against him, and fell asleep to dream he was floating on a cloud.

He dreamt that Zeke and Bead were coming down on a huge thunderhead to snatch him, kicking and screaming, into the air. He shot up in bed, cold sweat drenching him as he fought to orient himself. When the girl stirred beside him, his panic left when he realized where he was.

3

Slocum eased back in his chair in the saloon and stretched his legs while he studied the few men in the place. The smell of wet wool and unwashed bodies hung heavy in the close air. Stale smoke from quirlies gave the atmosphere a murky bluish hue that burned the eyes.

Miners, most of them, he judged. A few prospectors. Down-on-their-luck men. Talk buzzed like a distant hive of bees, words registering as a discordant hum to his ears. However, the muted conversation between two men at the bar caught his interest.

"They hit the Hoodoo again."

"Who'd they git this time, Hank?"

"Couple of prospectors. On the north fork of the Palouse. Over to Idaho. Found four dead."

"Takin' to murder now, are they."

"Don' know." The man Hank slowly shook his head. "They ain't kilt before. Bead Maleau an' Zekial Scroggins was the other two we found. Mean as skunks, those two." Hank downed the shot of whiskey and wiped his mouth with the back of his hand. "Looks like mebbe they kilt the

17

first two, then tried robbin' somebody else. Picked the wrong man, whoever he was. Done fer 'em both, he did.''

Alert now, Slocum studied the speaker. He was heavyset, a mite shy of six feet, and about forty. He wore a four-point and heavy boots. His flat-brimmed black hat hid his face. Slocum's gaze fixed on the star pinned to his coat lapel. His coat barely hid a Colt strapped to his waist. He looked cold and tired.

The other man was young, tall, and lean, corn-yellow hair shooting out from under his hat like sticks of straw. He also wore a badge. "Long ride over to the Hoodoo," he observed.

Hank nodded. "Wish they'd git some law here. Joe Davis bein' sheriff of this whole county with only us an' three other deputies jus' ain't workin'.''

"Not whin we gotta cover Idaho too. How much they git this time?"

Hank tapped his glass for Dinty to hit him again. The barkeep poured, his eyes fixed on Hank.

"Six prospectors was robbed, Bill. Two kilt. Can't figger it. Zeke an' Bead done the killin'. I'm sure of thet." Hank threw his drink back into his throat. "We didn' find any dust. Whoever walked away after the shootout walked away with thir pokes." He signaled Dinty for another hit. "Bin any strangers in here lately?"

Dinty didn't look at Slocum. "What you mean by strangers, Hank? Most everybody passing through's a stranger these days."

Hank looked about the room. Slocum stiffened slightly and unbuttoned his coat to free his Colt. Hank's gaze drifted across him with no visible interest, then fixed on Dinty. "Where's Rose?"

Dinty licked his lips. "Out."

"Whir?" Hank straightened. His face and tone took on a hard edge.

"Don't know. She ain't mine."

"She with a man?" Hank's knuckles glowed white in clenched fists.

Dinty took a swipe at the bar with his rag. "Like I said—don't own her. Long as I get my ten percent—"

Hank's hands fastened on Dinty's lapels like talons. His face was pure fury. "Thet woman belongs to me! I tol' her no more men!" He probably would've shaken Dinty's teeth loose had Bill not pulled him off.

"Hank! Fer Chris' sake! It ain't Dinty's fault!" He removed his hands to let Hank simmer down. Hank fought to catch his breath. He was huffing like a bull. Silence hung over the room like a pall.

Bill said, "Jesus, Hank! Rose's a whore."

"She ain't no whore, dammit!"

"Then what the hell would you call her?"

"Don't want to talk about it!"

"Come on! Let's get outa here. You need sleep." He managed to steer the deputy from the saloon.

When they were alone, Dinty made an exaggerated gesture of whipping his brow. "That Hank Yetty's a real snuffer when he's riled."

Slocum eased the hammer thong back on his Colt. "Rose his woman?"

"She don't know it if she is. Yetty thinks she's his, though, and since he's the big augur hereabouts—I reckon she is." He gave the plank another swipe with the cloth. "Take my advice and head outa here."

"Not too good at taking advice. Who's this Yetty?"

"He's a sheriff's deputy out of Walla Walla. No law here. No law along the Idaho border either. Hank Yetty and Bill Pietch cover the whole territory. Rough job."

"You been getting killings here?"

Dinty shook his head. "Usually claim fights. Somebody always gets hurt. Month ago an outlaw gang bushwhacked a gold shipment coming out of the Hoodoo district over in Idaho." Dinty pulled out the makings and expertly rolled a blanket. Striking a lucifer, he took a drag and blew smoke. "Hank and his posse found the three guards and driver bound and gagged, and the freighter gone. They chased the gang into a box canyon. Figured they had 'em cold." Dinty shook his head.

When he made no attempt to continue, Slocum figured he was purposely driving the story to the edge of the cliff and putting on the brakes. Probably counting on curiosity to get his customers to buy another beer.

Slocum tossed three nuggets on the board. "Give me another bottle of that rum." Dinty set one on the bar.

"What happened?"

"Well—when Hank and his men rode into that box canyon, they found the wagon, the eight-up, six saddled horses—but no robbers. And no gold."

Slocum cocked his head slightly, his eyes narrowing in skepticism. "Where'd they go?"

Dinty shrugged. "Never found hide nor hair of 'em. The horses were stolen. That much they knew."

"Must've had a hideout close by."

Dinty shook his head. "Covered the area for two miles around. Nothing. The shipment weighed three hundred pounds. That's a lot of weight to lug on foot with a posse dogging you."

"No idea of how that happened then."

"That Bead Maleau and Zeke Scroggins the sheriff mentioned they found shot? Horseback opinion has it they were left over from some gang that operated in California, then in Oregon a few months back. Specialized in robbing gold shipments. Bead and Zeke used to come in here to get roostered occasionally. When they were drunk, they'd talk about how the gang they were with flew from one job to another."

"Flew?"

"That's what they said. Couldn't get 'em to talk about it except when they were skunked—and then they didn't make any sense. Claimed the gang flew off without 'em. Left 'em stranded here."

Slocum smiled. "Sounds windy to me. Let me know what brand of piss they drank." He winked at Dinty and went through the door leading to Rose's room in the back. His smile faded when he was alone. The nightmare came back to him. Zeke and Bead's story of the flying bank robbers. "Burro milk!" he muttered.

Rose, naked, lounged on the bed. He undressed absently, his mind unable to shake Dinty's story.

Soon he was rutting on her, one hand under her shoulder to hold her, the other full of her left buttock, pulling her up to meet his hard, demanding thrusts. Her left leg was over his back to force him deeper into her. He grunted and panted as he neared orgasm, and buried his face in her neck. Rose, teeth clenched, breathing like a steam engine, arched her hips upwards to match the increasing tempo of his rhythm. "Oh, God. John! Do it! *Do* it! Faster—"

The door crashed open.

Startled, Slocum, ejaculating, withdrew to spill his sperm on her belly. "Damn it! What the *hell*!" He scrambled to pull the sheet over them. Rose's wide-eyed ashen face stared over his shoulder at their intruders.

He flopped onto his back in a flurry of naked legs—his and Rose's—and tried to focus his eyes in the crib's dingy gloom.

"Don't move! Don't even breathe!" Slocum stared into Hank's gun muzzle. "Bill! Hobble him!"

Bill moved his tall, lanky body to the side of the bed.

"Put out your right wrist!" Slocum eyed the bedpost where Rose's drawers were draped over his gunbelt. Too far. He held out his wrist. Bill slipped a thong loop over it. "Now, the other!" Slocum struggled to find an opening but didn't see one. Hank's look said, "Go ahead! Try me!" He stuck out his left wrist.

Hank, however, ordered. "Pull on your long underwear!" He pulled it on while Bill held on to the wrist thong. When he had his left arm in the sleeve, Bill placed the other loop on his left wrist and took off the right pigging strap. When Slocum's right arm slipped into the right sleeve, Bill replaced the loop on his right wrist. Hank's gun muzzle rested against Slocum's temple the entire time.

"Where's yer irons?" Hank jabbed the gun at him.

Slocum didn't look at the bedpost. Shock, then pain shot through him when Hank buried his fist in his belly. His insides felt as if molten lead was pouring through him. Hank gripped his hair and shook him fiercely, his face a mask of hate. "I asked ya. Where's your rig?"

He muttered, "In my boot holster."

Bill pick up the boot with the derringer and removed the stubby piece he kept in his boot holster along with fifty dollars in gold. The gun was a four-shot .32 Remington-Elliot derringer.

"Where's your hogleg?" Hank demanded and shook him again. "I know you carry one."

"Lost it in a card game in Lewiston."

"Search his saddlebags!"

Bill rummaged through them. "Look, here, Hank." His grin was triumphant when he held up two canvas sacks. "Dust. Two more in there."

Hank's face lit up in a mirthless grin. "So—you're the one who killed Bead and Zeke."

"Don't know what you're talking about."

"You're the one hitting the prospectors between here and the Hoodoos." Hank hefted the bags. "Not bad. Now. Where's your piece?"

"Derringer's all I got—" Hank's fist exploded fire in his head. He staggered backwards.

Rose screeched and leaped on Hank to drive him back against the wall. Yelling like a banshee, she flailed her fists at him. "I told ya to never interrupt me whin I'm with a customer! You ruin everything—you ape!"

Hank struggled to pull her off him. Naked, she kicked and hit, teeth flashing. She sunk her teeth in his ear. Hank yelped and slapped her. She collapsed in a heap at his feet.

Bill held Slocum, who was trying to put himself between the girl and Hank.

Breathing like blown horse, Hank pulled the dazed girl up and tossed her onto the bed. Jabbing a thick finger at her, he ground out, "Told you—no more men! Told you you're outa business! Happens again and I'll . . ." His face reflected pain, fury, and—here, Slocum had difficulty believing it—love. His features relaxed and he muttered in a sheepish voice, "Didn't mean to hurt you none." He swiped blood from his face where she'd scratched him. "Come on! Let's take this sidewinder to the lockup."

Slocum shot one look at Rose, who lay staring at them, and at her petticoat still draped over his gunbelt. She winked at him and grinned. Hank gathered up Slocum's clothes and followed Bill and his prisoner to the jail.

The jail was a log building with the office in front and the cell behind. A single window, not much more than a slit, let in light and air. The place stank of stale urine and sweat. A plank bed and a slop bucket were the only furnishings. The blanket looked to be alive with lice.

Bill came in, arms full of Slocum's boots and clothing, and stuffed them through the bars of the door. "Better get dressed. Gets cold in here at night."

"Do I get fed?"

"Bring you supper 'round eight."

"What did you do with my poke?"

"Hank's keeping it for evidence."

"I get a trial then?"

"Federal marshal'll be notified. Hank found a flier on you for killing a judge back in Georgia."

"Never been in Georgia in my life."

Bill grinned. "You talk like Robert E. Lee himself." He added, "Reb."

"Take that as a real compliment, friend."

"Grub'll be along in an hour or so." Bill handed him the bottle of rum through the bars. "Dinty says you bought this earlier."

"Thanks. By the way. Where's my horse?" He cradled the bottle to his chest as if it were a baby.

"Hank's got it and your gear down to the stable."

He listened as Bill left the jail. Gloom settled in, then darkness. He pulled on his clothing. Sitting on the plank bed, he debated whether to get drunk to fight off the creeping chill. No, he thought, can't afford to dull my mind with rotgut. Have to be sober in case I get an opening, slim as the chance is of one coming my way. Bill, the easygoing deputy, seemed his only possible bet.

It surprised him that Yetty had the flier wanting him for murdering the judge in Georgia in 1866. It must've been a long time in his desk, first having been circulated in 1867. Six years earlier.

As he absently studied the bleak, stinking cell, he recalled the meeting with the judge back in Calhoun County, Georgia, during that first year of Reconstruction. The judge and a hired gun rode onto Slocum's homestead with an order to vacate the property. The judge gloated how he'd always wanted a horse farm complete with house, barns, and stables—and now he had one. He'd bought the mortgage because Slocum's father hadn't paid taxes on the property during the war.

Slocum couldn't believe it, but the Yankee waved the papers in his face. He'd told him he had until the next day to be off Slocum's Stand. The judge said he would be back with his aide.

When the judge rode in the next day, instead of finding a tired dirt farmer meekly prepared to surrender his homestead, he found a big, hard-shouldered veteran of four years of war and wearing twin Navy Colts. The judge's aide was a hard-eyed gunslinger prepared to kill.

It was a fair fight. The gunslinger drew first. When the smoke cleared and the echoes of gunshots died, Slocum left the judge and his hired killer each six feet of red Georgia earth for their trouble. Before riding out that last time, he'd torched the place, leaving nothing but scorched earth.

He awoke with a start. "Must've dozed off," he mused. He'd no idea how late it was or much time had passed. His turnip, along with everything else he owned, was either in Yetty's office or in the stable. Cold now, he debated using the blanket, but decided he would rather freeze than be lousy.

"John?"

He came to attention at the muted sound of his name.

"John? You in there?" The whispered female voice came from the window slit.

"Who is it?"

"That you, John?"

"Yeah. *Rose?* What the hell're you *doing* here?" Alarmed, he pulled the plank bed to the wall and stood on it.

"John. Got yer rig." She stuffed the Colt and gunbelt through the slit. Next came his knife and the leather pouch containing caps, balls, and tools. Last came the powder flask. Her voice stumbled over her words. "Gotta go! I'm standin' on Suzie's and Belle's shoulders."

"You're an angel, Rose," was all he could say.

"Gotta get outa here! Hank's lookin' fer me."

"If he hurts you—I'll come back and kill him!"

"Don' worry none. He never hurts me."

"He hit you a good lick."

"Kin hardly blame him none. Had my teeth fixed on his ear. John?"

"Yeah."

"Don' hurt him or Bill."

"Try not to."

"He's not a bad man."

Slocum felt his aching ribs and whispered, "I'll try to remember that."

"Bill's comin' with yer supper. Here!" She stuffed a length of rope through the window. It coiled on the floor with a faint plop. "Use it to tie him up."

"Thanks, Rose!"

"Hank's got yer horse. He'll be with me tonight. Keeps his nag in the stable behind the hotel." She reached a hand through the window to give his a squeeze. "Whir will I tell him yer a-goin'?"

"Oregon."

"You be good, hear?" She giggled. "Say good-bye to thet thir corncob of yers fer me, will ya."

He couldn't help laughing as he heard a faint scrambling outside, muted whispers, and a spate of giggling. Then silence.

He drew the Colt, checked the loads as best he could in the dark, then settled back to await Bill.

4

The grating screech of a bolt being drawn and then the door being pushed open roused Slocum from the cold stupor he was in. He put the Colt under him and sat up. A lucifer flared in the office, and voices mumbled. A man bearing a lantern stood silhouetted in the doorway, the guttering flame making weird shadows flicker on the walls.

"I'll unlock the cell, Lin. You stick the tray in."

Relief flowed through Slocum when he recognized Bill's voice. That meant Hank was probably with Rose.

A small Chinese man with a ragged beard and carrying a tray shuffled up to the cell door. Slocum breathed in the smell of steak, potatoes, and coffee. His belly painfully reminded him that he hadn't eaten since the night before. Bill hung the lantern on a hook by the door.

"Stay where you are, Slocum!" The key grated in the lock. The unoiled hinges squeaked in protest as Bill pushed the door open and stood aside to let Lin enter. The Chinese set the tray next to Slocum on the plank bed. Bill hadn't bothered to draw his gun. Probably figured he didn't need to since he was outside the cell. Lin straightened to leave.

Slocum pulled the Navy from under him and cocked it. The noise was as loud as a pistol shot in his ears. Bill was caught cold in the dingy light.

When he made a move toward his gun, Slocum murmured, "Don't!" He shoved an astonished Lin into a corner. "All right, Deputy—get in here!"

Bill hesitated as if weighing his chances. Slocum settled the question for him. "Your boss knows me. Knows my rep with a gun. Believe me. He'd advise you to do exactly what I tell you to do. Don't want to hurt either of you."

Bill raised his hands and entered the cell. Slocum whipped his Remington from his holster and unloaded it. "Lin! Tie him up!"

Lin, his eyes huge, gulped and bound Bill's wrists behind him with trembling hands, then his ankles, while Slocum looked on.

Bill demanded, "Where'd you hide thet thir gun? I searched you—"

"Not well enough. Your trouble is—you're too used to dealing with Saturday night drunks." He didn't like thinking what might happen to Rose if Hank learned she had helped him by hiding his rig.

Holding the Colt on Lin, Slocum marched him into the office where pigging straps hung next to the rack of Henry rifles. He used the straps to bind the shaken Chinese.

"Where's your boss?" he demanded of Bill.

"Reckon he's with Rose."

"At the saloon?"

"Naw. She'll be in his room at the fleabag."

"Where's the gold he took from me?"

"Your pokes're in the strongbox in the office."

"How do I get into it?"

Bill's laugh was a dry snort of amusement. "Same as we do. Kick it. Ain't locked. Ain't got a lock."

Slocum opened the lid of the small wrought-iron chest. His bags of gold were in there with his watch. Several purses chinked richly with eagles and double eagles. He counted eight bags of dust and coin. Hank was apparently squirreling away loot for his old age. Prisoners clearly walked out poorer than when they entered if the cache was any sign. He took only his. Then, remembering he would be riding out with Hank's horse, he took a purse. He somehow doubted Hank kept a record of his loot.

In the cell, he gagged both his prisoners. "Tell Hank that since I'm taking his horse and a rifle, I'm paying for them." He laid four double eagles on the bunk. "Eighty dollars. Way more than the nag'll be worth. Don't want him to think I'm a horse thief."

If he hadn't been ravenous and faced with a long ride, he wouldn't have taken the time to wolf down the meal. He took Bill's keys, unlocked the rack, and picked out a Henry. A drawer yielded a box of .44s. His derringer and boot holster were in another drawer. When he looked in Hank's desk, he saw three Whitman County deputy sheriff's badges and a stack of blank warrants signed by the federal marshal and the sheriff. He took a badge and six warrants. They might come in handy.

He carefully opened the jail door and peered out. Moonlight bathed the empty street in pale lights and sharp black shadows. A light from the saloon told him that probably most of the town's men were in there hurrahing it up. He couldn't chance trying to retrieve his mount from the stable since the hostler probably lived there. A five-minute walk took him to the dilapidated clapboard one-story building that served as the hotel. A horse stood hobbled in the small corral in back as Rose had said it would. The stable threw a long shadow in the moonlight. He wondered how Hank was making out with Rose.

He cajoled the horse in his low, singsong voice. Interested, the gray looked up. Thank God, he thought, Yetty didn't unsaddle him. No doubt he'd been so eager to get into the saddle with Rose he'd neglected his mount. Slocum knelt and gently worked the hobble loose from the gray's front feet, taking his time doing it so as not to spook the animal.

He wished he had his slicker and bedroll, but couldn't complain. Luck had so far dealt him a pat hand. He'd stay with it. He led the gray out of the corral, stopping once to rub the animal's nose when it jerked its head and nickered.

"Easy, boy! You and I will get along just fine."

When he was fifty yards beyond the hotel, he rode south along Main Street. He saw no one. When he was clear of the town, he reined in and adjusted the stirrups.

The moon flooded the land with pale blue light. Kamiak Mountain loomed dark and ominous east of him. He muttered a silent thanks that it wasn't one of those overcast, moonless nights that swallowed up the world in impenetrable black. If his luck held, he'd be on the Snake by morning.

He followed the river south, never letting up, keeping the gray moving. The horse had balance and was collected, his movement behind the bit, his energy under control. Slocum rode with the knees, too tired not to doze off now and again. Dawn showed no one in pursuit. He stopped at ten o'clock to rest for a spell. He watered the gray, hobbled him in grass, and then found a tree to rest against. At best, he probably had only two hours' start on a posse that might be trailing him. He wondered how far he could depend on Rose to throw Yetty off his trail. There was no way for him to trash it other than riding in water. And that would slow him down.

He allowed himself an hour's rest, then rode into Lewiston that afternoon. The hotel tempted him. So did the saloon. Instead, he bought a Bull Durham, slicker, bedroll, coffee, a pot, and jerky at the trading post, and rode on through. Lewiston would be the first place Yetty would look for him if Rose failed to convince him his prisoner was heading for Oregon.

Yetty was no fool. He no doubt knew his business when it came to tracking a man or figuring what he would do.

Slocum rode the Clearwater River east into the mountains. The second day, he spotted the highest rise of land he'd seen yet. If he was right, one of the richest gold areas in Idaho nestled in the shadow of its south slope—Elk City. He waited and rode in at night. Yetty couldn't have alerted the law that John Slocum might be heading that way, but he took no chances.

He stopped in a restaurant run by Chinese and ate his first food in two days. When he walked the single dirt street of the town, he noticed that half the population was Chinese. They paid no attention to him, but scurried past him on the boardwalk as if he weren't there. Mining machinery rusted in piles in the side streets and alleys. Signs were in both English and Chinese.

When he spotted the jail and the light inside, his first reaction was to turn and walk the other way. He wasn't sure where the idea came from—it was certainly stupid enough. But, he reflected ruefully, Colonel Joshua Chamberlain's bayonet charge by his Maine boys against the Confederates trying to roll up the Yankee right flank at Gettysburg had been a stupid idea too. But the sheer gall of it had worked.

He took the deputy's badge from his vest pocket, pinned it on his coat, and went back to the restaurant he'd just left. The Chinese girl who'd waited on him looked up in surprise, then smiled in recognition.

He had to use pantomime to get across to her that he needed pen and ink. That, and two silver dollars. When she understood, she bowed a quick little bow and vanished to the back of the eatery. When she returned, she held an ink pot and a small brush.

He practiced on a piece of paper to get the feel of the brush, then took the warrant from his pocket. He wrote on it that Deputy Sheriff William Bell was authorized to arrest and bring back to Palouse Flats Zekial Scroggins and Bead Maleau, wanted for robbery and murder. An examination of the document convinced him it looked genuine. He hoped the federal marshal's and the Whitman County sheriff's signatures on it would convince the lawman sitting in the local marshal's office. He murmured, *"Seh-seh,"* to the girl, who blinked in surprise, and then he left.

He stabled his horse and borrowed the hayloft for the night. In the morning, he cleaned up at the water trough and headed for the jail.

The man wearing the star was middle-aged, lean, and tough. He introduced himself as Dave Grisholm. He glanced at the warrant. When he didn't question it, Slocum reckoned he was still ahead of Yetty.

Grisholm studied the paper and murmured, "Yeah, know those two. Scroggins and Maleau. Ran with a gang that preyed on prospectors between here and the Hoodoos. Disappeared about three months ago. Someone said they thought they'd spotted them working as roustabouts for an evangelist outfit in San Francisco."

Interested despite himself, Slocum exclaimed, *"Roustabouts?"*

Grisholm chuckled. "Sounds strange, I admit. Don't say much for gold when it becomes so scarce, badmen give up robbing gold prospectors to work putting up tents for revival meetings."

"You sure you got the right two?"

"Like I said, it was what someone claimed they saw." Looking thoughtful, the marshal poured coffee from the pot on the wood stove. "The only reason I mention it is that we've had a series of strange robberies here recently. Gold shipments, mostly. A revival meeting group came through here about the same time."

"Were Scroggins and Maleau with them?"

Grisholm shook his head. "We checked. But no."

Slocum asked on the impulse, "Anything strange about the robberies?"

Grisholm looked up sharply. "What do you mean?"

"Did you run the outlaws down?"

Grisholm wet his lips. "No. Never caught 'em."

"Wonder if same gang that hit us hit you."

"Palouse Flats is a long way from Elk City."

"Yet gold shipments were stolen from both places."

Grisholm's eyes narrowed. "What're you getting at?"

"Did the robbers escape—or did they simply disappear?"

"Matter of fact—we run 'em into a blind canyon. Couldn't believe our luck. Figured they didn't know the country, to make such a stupid mistake. Thought we had 'em cold."

Slocum finished for him. "But when you got there they were gone. Just their horses. I'll bet."

Grisholm's expression was a mixture of relief that what had happened to him had happened to someone else and anger that he'd been second-guessed.

"That's how it happened. More coffee?" He held up the pot. Slocum nodded. "I'm s'posed to be the law, but I let those varmints slip right through my fingers."

"Maybe there's something else involved. Same thing happened at the Hoodoo mine a while back. Deputies followed the robbers into a box canyon and—poof! They were gone. Horses were there, but no robbers—and no loot. Never had a clue." He was about to tell of Zeke's and Bead's insane mumblings about flying, but decided not to. They were buzzard bait on the Palouse River, but Grisholm wasn't supposed to know that. Instead, he said, "If you see those two—hold 'em. I'll be heading back to Palouse Flats."

"Keep my eyes peeled. We got more Chinese now than white men, so a white hoodoo stands out. The Chinks work the placers now. White man'll give up if the color's no good, but a Chink will manage to squeeze a grubstake out of the area if there's anything to squeeze."

"Thanks for the coffee. Be on my way."

Grisholm nodded. "Take care."

When he climbed into the kack, Slocum hoped he'd trashed his trail. He wondered if he should've told Grisholm he was riding east. Yetty—if he was behind him—would assume he'd lied to Grisholm about his destination and follow him east into the Anaconda Mountains. But then, he might figure he was lying on purpose and was actually doubling back to Palouse Flats.

He made the Big Hole River in three days. Two prospectors told him if he followed it south, he would hit Big Hole Pass and flat country south to Bannack City, the only town in the area.

"Not much there," one grizzled old-timer told him. "All played out. Most everyone's left."

Five days later, he rode into Bannack.

5

Slocum woke up to crashings and bangings in the stalls beneath him. A horse whinnied and kicked the side of his stall, which caused the other animals to act up. Rubbing sleep from his eyes, he rolled over and sat up. Sunlight streaming in through the hay door blinded him. He yawned, stretched, and brushed hay from his clothing while looking through the door at Bannack's main street. The Goodrich Saloon reminded him that a hot breakfast and a bottle of good whiskey were all he needed before riding out.

He yawned tiredly as he descended the loft's ladder and saddled his horse. At least, he thought, they were both rested, the horse fed, watered, and rubbed down. He would've done better in a hotel bed, but the memory of Yetty breaking into his room still haunted him. He paid the hostler a dollar and led the gray toward the saloon.

He never got to Goodrich's. When the bullet cracked by his right ear, he threw himself to the ground. Drawing his Colt, he tried to fix the source of the shot, difficult to do while belly-down.

Screams, shouts, and more shots kept him there. For one

panicky moment, he thought, "Jesus! Yetty's found me!"

The ruckus came from down the street. Exactly where, he couldn't see. Then four masked men clad in yellow dusters ran from the Bannack City Bank on the corner. Two masked outlaws stood in the street, one holding six horses while the other yelled and sprayed the area with lead from guns held in each hand. His gunfire emptied the street of people, who fell over one another in their mad scramble to get to cover. Dogs yipped and barked, and raced about. Screaming mothers grabbed their children and ran for safety. Cursing men ducked into doorways as bullets whined.

Four outlaws carrying bulky moneybags slung over their shoulders ran from the bank and paused only long enough to dump the heavy sacks into their saddlebags before swinging themselves aboard. The horse holder and lookout loosed another fusillade of shots to cover them both while they mounted. The six swung their horses about and punched the breeze out of town, galloping around the bend in the main street and heading south, scattering people in their wild flight.

Bank employees armed with guns ran into the street and blazed away with reckless abandon at the fleeing outlaws. The town marshal, pulling his suspenders over his shoulders with one hand and gripping his Henry rifle with the other, loped from the jail, shouting, "After 'em! Mount up!"

Seeing Slocum, he shoved his red face into his and yelled, "Which way they go?"

Slocum, reacting to the star gleaming on the marshal's chest the same way he would react to a rattler, pointed south. When the lawman prodded him wildly with, "Come on! You're posse now!" he figured it would be safer to obey than refuse. He untied the reins of his horse and climbed into the kack.

The marshal led the way, two bank clerks and a dozen other citizens thundering after the bank robbers. The road south led through a narrow valley with high, precipitous hills on either side. There was nowhere for the robbers to go. They had no choice but to outrun the posse.

Slocum had nowhere to go either. He could only follow the mad rush. To break off would draw the attention of the marshal, and the last thing he wanted was a lawman's interest in him.

He figured they'd ridden four miles when they came to the junction of a small trail that led into the hills west of them. "They're a-headin' for Badger Pass," someone yelled.

They reined in their mounts when the marshal held up his hand, stopped and studied the dirt as he leaned down from the saddle. "They ain't a-goin' there. Must've rode up that trail to our left. Followin' thet creek. We got 'em now! It's a blind canyon. Let's go, boys!"

They galloped through a narrow gulch between two brown, domelike hills. The marshal led the way, rifle ready. They rode into an opening perhaps a hundred yards wide and reined in to keep from colliding with six saddled horses grazing. There was no sign of human life. They were in a small blind canyon, steep, rolling hills bare except for short yellow grass.

The marshal pulled his horse about in a circle as he surveyed the surrounding hills. "Where the hell they go?" he demanded, his coarse face redder than ever, mustache quivering.

"You sure them's their horses, Jim?" a white-shirted bank clerk asked.

"They're hot. Been ridden. And just recent."

"Recognize the Appaloosa," put in another clerk.

The marshal peered at the horse from over the ears of his mount. "Damn! Ye're right! That's Jim Yancy's. Reported it stolen only yesterday. Some varmint filched it right in front of the Elkhorn! Them horses is all stolen— or I'll eat my hat!"

"But—where in hell's the bank robbers?"

"Fan out! They can't have gone nowhere. They can't climb thim hills. We'd see 'em! They gotta be here somewhirs."

But the bank robbers weren't there. The posse scanned the bare hills for sign of fleeing men, but saw only the smooth expanse of ochre-hued grass.

Slocum pretended to search. The robbed bank wasn't his concern. Getting as far from Bannack as possible was.

He wondered if Bannack's lawman had a flier on him. He couldn't help grinning at the memory of Yetty and his deputy barging into Rose's room. They'd taken him by surprise.

He reckoned that if he hadn't been rutting away on top of Rose and on the verge of emptying himself into her, he might've gotten to his gun. Women, he thought, smiling, will do you in every time.

An hour's search unearthed no sign of the bank robbers. The posse rode up the smoother hills and peered across the rolling terrain. The treeless hills provided no cover for men on foot. The marshal scratched his thick neck and mumbled. "Beats all! That's the second time this month robbers have simply vanished. Can't figger it! Where in the hell could they go? We could see 'em if they was in those hills. There ain't that much cover."

Another man added, "Why would they leave thir hosses? Don' make no sense."

The marshal turned to one of the men. "Joe. You'n Asa stay here a spell. We'll take the horses. If it's like the other times, they're gone. But no point in takin' a chance they're not still here—someplace." He stood in his stirrups and yelled, "Okay! Let's go home!"

The white-shirted bank clerk objected. "Jim—thim hoodoos made off with the mine's payroll. Two thousand dollars."

"You'll have to settle it with Lawford, Bob. You kin see fer yerself there ain't nothin' more we kin do. Insurance'll cover it."

"That's the second payroll in a month, Jim."

The marshal was sweating despite the cool April air. "I know. Keeps up—an' I'm like to be set down. You don' have to remind me."

Curiosity overrode Slocum's circumspection. He rode next to the clerk. "Tell me, friend, what the hell's going on?"

The clerk, a man of forty or so, lean and tougher-looking than a clerk had a right to be, stared with suspicion at him.

"Ain't seen you before."

"Ain't been here before." He chuckled. "Stopped to water my throat when your bank was robbed. Tell me. What did the marshal mean when he said this has happened before?"

The clerk studied him from hard eyes, then apparently decided to trust him. "A whole raft of holdups. Bold as brass. When the vigilantes light out after the varmints, they run 'em down—only to find their hosses and no sign of the robbers—or the money. Not just banks neither. Gold shipments have simply vanished. Find the Army escorts bound and gagged, the gold gone. In one instance, the packmules hauling the miners' pokes disappeared like smoke in a blizzard. Like one of thim magic acts whir the magician waves a wand and—poof! Gone"

"You're telling me the mules vanished too?"

"Yup! They were carrying panniers full up with grub-stakers' pokes. The only thing the marshal could figure was thet it would've taken too much time to unload 'em. So—whatever it was simply took mules an' all."

"Strange."

"Sure is. Second time our bank's been hit fer payroll money. Last time it happened, the robbers ran outa town in a surrey." The clerk barked a bitter laugh. "Damn wagon! Kin you beat that? Mile outa town we found the team—but no surrey."

Slocum fell silent. He wanted nothing more than to put Bannack City behind him, but the disappearing robbers fascinated him. The mysterious claim by Zeke and Bead of flying outlaws wouldn't let go of him.

He didn't know if the Bannack marshal had contact with marshal at Palouse, but he wasn't going to hang around to find out. He bought bread and supplies at the City Bakery and rode out late that afternoon for Virginia City, south along Grasshopper Creek to where it flowed into the Beaverhead.

Virginia City was over fifty miles east as the crow flew— but Slocum was no crow, and the mountains from the Beaverhead east were rough going. He stayed off the trail because Sioux and Cheyenne still roamed the area, and because he didn't want to leave a trail.

6

The trail led uphill on a long, tortuous climb that soon had Slocum's horse lathering and heaving. The sun beat down overhead with relentless force in a cloudless sky the color of mercury. He reined in and dismounted. The ascent ahead was still a long one, and he didn't want to kill the gray. He filled his hat from one of his canteens, let the horse drink, then walked him. He'd gone about a mile when shots—eight or nine—echoed off the hills. He halted and strained to listen, but heard nothing. He judged the gunfire came from beyond a rise in the trail where a huge outcropping of bare rock loomed.

Heart beating from apprehension of the unknown, he stopped and studied the ground. Ruts had clearly been made by a heavily laden freighter's iron-tired wheels, and the steel-shod hooves of its team had left trails of freshly crushed and scarred rock that gleamed white. He patted the gray's velvety muzzle and murmured, "Easy, boy! Let's see what we're riding into."

He knew road agents on the lookout for prospectors and stages still haunted the trails despite vigilantes who'd hanged dozens of them over the years. He muttered to the horse. "That rock up ahead's a perfect place for a road agent's roost. When the stage or wagon gets to the top, it's going too slow and its team's too winded to do anything. A perfect place to drygulch somebody."

He drew the Henry from the scabbard and levered a round into the chamber. Keeping to the left of the trail, he led the horse up the last five hundred yards to where the huge rock stood guard on the hill. Hawks circled lazily overhead.

He approached with cautious care because he heard and saw nothing unusual. He led the gray behind the rock and tied the reins to a boulder. He then climbed the slanted stone outcropping, its rimrock formation giving him plenty of toeholds. He climbed about twenty feet to the top, then peered over the edge.

What flew to the eye were the four cavalrymen lying bound on the edge of the trail like blue cocoons. He muttered, "What the hell?" and glanced quickly about to see if anyone else was in sight. He quickly descended the rock and cautiously approached the four soldiers. He picked up a hat in the road and examined it. Crossed rifles with a seven superimposed. The Seventh Infantry. He drew his knife and knelt by the first man, a corporal. As he cut him loose, he noticed the nasty bruise on his head. The man groaned when Slocum pulled him to a sitting position and held his canteen to the man's lips. He gulped the water, his eyes fluttering open as he gazed in bewilderment about him.

He muttered in a weak voice, "Thanks." Then, as if just then aware of his benefactor, he demanded, "Who're you? Where'd you come from?"

"Let's get the rest of your men untied. You okay?"

The corporal blinked, ran his swollen tongue over parched lips, then nodded. He held his head in his hands and stifled a groan. Slocum quickly cut the bonds of the other three and gave them water. All had been knocked out by blows to the head and were no doubt suffering splitting headaches, not only from their injuries but from the relentless sun beating down on their unprotected heads. The six-thousand-foot altitude of the High Plains didn't provide much barrier from the bronze-hued disk of fire hanging in a sky as silver as molten lead.

He helped the men into the shadow of the rock. A stream nearby provided water to replenish his canteens.

"What happened here?" he asked.

The corporal, an older man with a big mustache and lean to the point of emaciation, rubbed his head. "Name's O'Reilly. Me'n the boys were riding shotgun on a gold shipment going to Fort Ellis for transfer to Fort Lincoln. We reached Robbers' Rock here and . . ." He shook his head and gave a bitter bark of laughter. "They were waiting for us. Six of 'em. All armed with Winchesters. Us with our single-shot carbines. We were so busy helping the team up that last rise, we didn't see 'em until too late. Knocked us on the head and . . ." He looked down the road where it vanished over a rise. "Must've taken off with the freighter. Had to. Over a ton of bullion on it." He punched his knee with his fist. "*Damn!* The colonel'll bring me up on charges fer sure!"

Slocum shaded his eyes against the light as he stared at the road. "I heard shots. Not more'n a half hour ago. Got here quick as I could. If they took the wagon, they can't be that far ahead."

"Depends where they're going."

"Where can they go? Other than Virginia City?"

"Wouldn't dare go there. Another detachment's expecting us. We're on our way to Bozeman and Fort Ellis. The Bozeman Trail's closed on account of the Sioux. We were to double up the escort."

"Too late now," a tall, lanky private muttered.

"Who shipped the gold?"

"Belongs to William Gramford. Big augur in Virginia City. Mine owner. He was due to follow us."

Slocum sat on his heels and drew in the dirt while he

pondered the situation. He needed to get going. The gold theft wasn't his concern. But he couldn't leave the four injured men in the middle of nowhere. Silently cursing himself for a fool, he said, "Guess we'd better wait for this Gramford." He took the Henry from his scabbard and handed it to O'Reilly.

"I'll leave my bedroll and coffee makings. See if you can get a fire going." He retrieved his horse and climbed aboard.

O'Reilly looked up in alarm. "What do you plan on doing?"

"That freighter can't be that far ahead. Should be able to catch up to it. Maybe get some idea who the road agents are and where they're going." He pulled the reins. "Be back in a couple of hours."

The road led through a gulch and then wound east. He reckoned he'd ridden a little over eight miles when he sighted the big wagon. It stood at the edge of the trail where its six-up, still harnessed, cropped the grass. Six saddled horses contentedly cropped the grass along the side of the trail.

He reined in and dismounted. He wished for his rifle. The Colt wasn't going to do him much good against six outlaws. But he saw no sign of human life. Puzzled, he led his horse off the trail and into a gully to keep out of sight. He approached the wagon from its right side, where anyone seeking to drygulch a pursuer would likely be hiding. Again, he spotted no one.

Convinced he was alone, he approached in the open. The wagon horses snorted and rolled their eyes at him in alarm. He absently patted the leader's nose to reassure him.

"Where'd they go, boy?" he murmured. The horse didn't answer, but only shook his head. Slocum noticed the black maw of an abandoned mine about five hundred yards south of him in the side of a hill. It occurred to him to inspect it, but if the outlaws were holed up in it, he wouldn't get across the stream flowing in front of it.

Using his glasses, he inspected it. Abandoned equipment lay strewn about. The remains of a sluice sagged in ruined disarray. He was convinced no one was inside. The outlaws hiding in a mine would make no sense. Not next to the abandoned wagon.

Next, he inspected the freighter. It was, as he expected, empty—all but for the soldiers' Springfield carbines and field packs. He stood on the seat and surveyed the surrounding land. High rolling hills, gullies, gulches, trees bordering the stream, ochre-hued grass covering everything else. He wondered how six men could carry two thousand pounds of metal by horse? And why they would when they had the wagon and team? Where would they go? Why not stay with the wagon? They could've taken another trail than the one to Virginia City. None of it made any sense.

He gathered up the six saddle horses, led them and the team to the stream, and let them drink. Stringing out all seven saddle horses, he drove the wagon back. It was getting dark when he pulled up at the campfire where the four soldiers hunkered about it. The temperature would drop to around forty when the sun took its last bow.

O'Reilly and his men gathered around him, and expressed both curiosity and disbelief when he explained where he'd found the wagon and the horses of the robbers.

"There's a busted flush somewheres," the corporal observed and shook his head. He ordered his men to break out the rations and make ready to bed down for the night. Slocum debated if he should ride on, but his horse needed grazing and rest, and clouds had moved in to swallow up any light. He couldn't see ten feet beyond the fire.

He was lying out his bedroll when he heard something on the road behind them. He felt for his rifle.

"Hallo, the fire!" The voice came from back down the road.

"What do you think?" he whispered to O'Reilly. It was near ten o'clock.

"Could be Gramford," the corporal whispered in reply.

"You men get up! Be ready!" The three men stirred from their bedrolls and seized their rifles.

Slocum hailed, "Step ahead!"

The sound of hooves, sparks from shoes, then the dim outline of three men. The leader reined in. "Whom do I have the honor of addressing at this late hour?"

"Corporal O'Reilly, Seventh Infantry, United States Army. And who might you be, sir?"

"Bill Gramford." Silence, then: "*O'Reilly?* Is that you? What the hell're you doing *here*? Figured to meet you in Virginia City tomorrow."

O'Reilly wheezed like a broken bellows. "Come on in, Mr. Gramford. And hear the bad news."

7

William Gramford dismounted on the side of his horse facing the soldiers, as did the two men with him. The mine owner's immediate concern for the soldiers' welfare and not for the fate of his gold impressed Slocum. Gramford examined them and inquired how each was. When he shook Slocum's hand and thanked him for being a Good Samaritan, Slocum protested, saying there wasn't much else he could've done under the circumstances. Gramford introduced the two men with him as Angus MacTaggert, his foreman, and David Fotherby, a mining engineer.

In the firelight, Slocum saw that Gramford was tall and straight-backed, and wore plain but good clothing and serviceable boots. White locks flowing from under his hat coupled with his white Vandyke beard reminded Slocum a little of Bill Cody. Both had the same proud, eagle look. Gramford, he figured, was in his sixties, but carried his years better than many men half his age. MacTaggert was in his thirties, tall and muscular. Fotherby, small and slight, was probably fifty.

Corporal O'Reilly tossed more wood on the fire, and a

47

soldier heated coffee. Gramford produced a bottle of Old Overholt and passed it around.

"All right. Let's hear the bad news." Gramford's expressionless gaze studied the unhappy ones around the fire.

While O'Reilly related the details of the robbery, he sat hunched in silence, his large hands dangling listlessly from his knees. O'Reilly finished with: "Mr. Slocum here rode after them. The thieves had the wagon, so he figured they couldn't have gone that far."

Slocum said, "I followed 'em, Mr. Gramford. Rode about eight miles to a pass east of here—"

"Badger Pass," Gramford murmured.

"Found the wagon and team—but no robbers."

"And no gold," Gramford finished for him.

"That's right." He added as an afterthought, "I'm sorry."

Gramford gave a snort of bitter laughter. "Not your fault, certainly."

"There's something else." Slocum nodded to where his horse was tethered to a line with the other six. "Found those grazing by the road near the wagon. Looks like the road agents abandoned them."

The mine owner looked bewildered. "But why? Where would they go? There's nothing out there."

"Thought they might have a hideout. But leaving their horses don't make any sense."

"Well, this has happened before. The robbers simply disappearing. Can't figure it."

Slocum changed the subject. "You say there was a ton of gold in that wagon?"

"Two thousand three hundred pounds. All going to Fort Ellis, then to Fort Abraham Lincoln by boat." He explained, "I not only mine gold but refine it. About half what I process belongs to prospectors and other miners. The government buys from me, usually at sixteen dollars and twenty-eight cents an ounce, though the price fluctuates. I then reimburse the miners and prospectors. So—you see half of the gold stolen wasn't mine." A gloomy silence fell over the group like a pall.

"They'll sure as hell court-martial me," O'Reilly muttered, and shook his head.

Gramford put his hand on the wiry Irishman. "No, Patrick. This isn't your fault. The gang doing these robberies is well organized. If there's any fault, it's mine. I shouldn't have sent the lot in one shipment. Should've had my own men with you as well."

Slocum was curious. He'd hefted pokes before. They were as heavy as the bag of lead balls he carried for his Navy Colt. "How much metal is a ton of color, Mr. Gramford?"

"A cubic foot of pure gold weighs a little over eleven hundred pounds, Mr. Slocum. We're talking about two cubic feet. The volume of a large gladstone traveling bag."

"And weighing as much as the freighter carrying it." Slocum gave an involuntary whistle.

"It was in twenty-troy-pound ingots. A hundred and twenty-eight."

MacTaggert asked, "What do we do now, Mr. Gramford?"

"Sleep on it," his boss replied. "Nothing else we can do." He slapped his knees with his hands in a gesture of finality and stood. "Get some sleep. We'll need it come morning."

O'Reilly and his men managed a breakfast of corn mush and beef jerky. Coffee steamed and spluttered in the pot on the fire. Daylight lifted spirits a little. Between mouthfuls, Gramford questioned the soldiers.

"How many robbers?"

"Six," said O'Reilly. "All masked, wearing yellow dusters and carrying Winchesters."

"Anything odd about them? Anything you'd remember about them?"

The men shook their heads. "We were just topping the

rise,'' said one. "It was a long haul, the horses pretty well blown. We were either pulling or pushing because we weren't sure how long the animals would hold up. The road agents were waiting behind this rock.''

O'Reilly added, "We put up a fight but they had the drop on us. Knocked us out.'' He shrugged. "After, that, don't know what happened. Came to tied up. Reckon it was about a half hour later that Mr. Slocum found us.''

Gramford turned his attention to Slocum. "You're riding to Varina?''

He gave him a puzzled look. "Varina?''

Gramford chuckled. "You're a Reb, if I'm not mistaken. Varina, originally named for Jeff Davis's wife but renamed Virginia by a Yankee judge.''

Slocum gave a snort of bitter laughter. "Yankee judges do have a way. Yes. I am heading for Virginia City.''

"Then I suggest, Corporal, you and your men take the wagon and we'll ride with you.''

It was twelve miles to the Beaverhead River. They forded it and rode east, to follow the level terrain because of the wagon. It was twenty miles and seven hours later that they halted at the entrance to a narrow gorge through which a stream flowed. Gramford called it Sweetwater Creek. They camped the night and were again on the trail by five the next morning.

Sixteen miles later, they rumbled past the mines at Alder where piles of tailings made a small canyon through which the road crawled. Alder Gulch had one street along which saloons, the Cabbage Patch, and stores lined the way. They stopped and had breakfast at a ramshackle structure with a sign proclaiming, "Mrs. Cobb's Home Cooked Food.''

Slocum ate the greasy concoction, wondering if the bull cook who prepared it lived there with Mrs. Cobb. If that were the case, then it was home cooking. The cook, who talked like a Texan with a mouth full of manure, was probably the remnant of some Fort Worth cattle drive, Slocum figured, and by the mean look of him, not a man to mess with and certainly not the man to complain to about the food.

Miners, laborers, and farmers crowded the cafe. Serving women rushing to and from the kitchen in back. Gramford pulled his cigar case from his inside coat pocket and extracted a Havana. MacTaggert held a lucifer for him to puff the end into a red glow.

When Slocum pulled the makings from his vest pocket, the mine owner chuckled, shook his head, and offered him his case. Slocum took a Havana, sniffed it, ecstasy warming his face, and bit off the end. MacTaggert held a light. Slocum nodded his thanks and settled back, the rich blue smoke enveloping him.

Gramford told his foreman, "Angus, get me a fare on the Tracey Dougherty heading for Bozeman tomorrow. Inform the marshal of the robbery. Going to have to figure some way to break the news to our clients. A lot of men were depending on me." He shook his head worriedly.

MacTaggert stood and pushed back his chair. "Should we inform the Pinkertons, sir?"

Gramford considered the question, then shook his head. "Not yet. If news gets around I've lost the shipment, the banks'll be on me like vultures. Got to have time."

"I'll see to it, Mr. Gramford."

Gramford ate his eggs and bacon in that measured, preoccupied way people do something when they're worried about something else. To Slocum, a thousand dollars was almost beyond comprehension. Losing five hundred thousand? Half of which was somebody else's money? Well, he could sympathize with the old man, but that was about all.

Slocum savored his freedom. As far as he knew, no one was after him except maybe Hank Yetty. It was springtime. His poke jingled with a few double eagles. And he had a good horse in the gray. He would buy new boots in Virginia City, soak them, and wear them until they dried to break them in. He could even spring for a bottle of good whiskey.

With luck, he'd be at the Northern Pacific's end of track in North Dakota in two weeks. If he could dodge the Sioux and Cheyenne along the Bozeman. He hadn't seen New Orleans in a coon's age. Maybe, he'd even visit Calhoun County. With a summer name, of course. He wondered if anybody remembered him there. He wondered what new name Slocum's Stand bore now. And who owned it.

Dreams. Always dreams of what lay across the river or on the other side of the mountain. And always the same. Somewhere on the periphery of his awareness, he heard the buzz of Gramford's voice as he talked to him.

Nodding without really listening, he debated the wisdom of getting further involved in Gramford's problem. He admitted to himself that if it hadn't been for Zeke and Bead's insane rambling about flying, if he hadn't seen firsthand that something strange was involved in chases ending with the robbers simply vanishing along with the loot—if he hadn't found Gramford's freighter and team with the cargo gone—if not for all that, he would've shaken the mine owner's hand and ridden away.

But curiosity had dropped its rope over him. The same curiosity that kept him fiddle-footed, kept him riding the rivers, prowling the mountains—that same curiosity gnawed at him to find out more about the mysterious robberies.

He heard himself saying, "If you don't mind, Mr. Gramford, believe I'll accompany you to Virginia City."

Something lit up in the white-haired man's strong, bony features. Just what—happiness, relief, alarm—Slocum couldn't tell. Gramford smiled. "Glad to have you along, Mr. Slocum. Be at Tracey's Cartage Company next to the Wells-Fargo office by six in the morning."

Slocum rode down Jackson Street in Virginia City, past the St. Louis Restaurant on his left and the California Restaurant advertising meals at all hours, on his right. Just beyond was John Dow's Dry Goods and Groceries. He reined in and entered the store, pausing on the threshold to let his eyes adjust to the change from sunlight to shadow.

The interior was dark and cool, like a cave—it was already heating up outside. Counters and display cases held every conceivable household item. Shelves were heavy with airtights and boxes of every imaginable article a householder or farmer might need. A hotchpotch of smells hit him—fresh bread, bacon, gun oil, apple cider. An open pickle barrel exuded an enticing briny smell, another held crackers. A coffee grinder gave off the rich aroma of freshly ground coffee beans. Smoked hams and bacons hung from rafters. Rifles, shotguns, and revolvers of various makes lined the back walls. One counter contained Indian artifacts—moccasins, dresses, blankets—made by reservation Indians.

A tall woman was buying a Cheyenne squaw's outfit—doeskin dress, moccasins, and leggings. She held the dress in front of her.

"What do think?" she asked the proprietress, who tilted her head, studied the woman through half-closed eyes, then nodded. Slocum suppressed a smile while he purchased powder, lead, caps, and two pounds of beef jerky from the owner. The woman didn't much resemble a Cheyenne. She would've looked more at home, he thought, wearing the Norse Valkyrie's horned helmet and breast armor he'd seen pictures of. She had copper-hued hair and a faint Dutch accent.

He was searching the liquor shelves for a bottle of Old Overholt when two men entered. Always alert, he slipped the hammer thong from his Colt from force of habit. Something about the two roused his danger sense. They were formless black silhouettes against the outside light.

He studied them from the corner of his eye. No badges on their vests. They wore Colts slung low on their right hips. Their faces were in shadow beneath their hats. Both wore their hair long, which put him on his guard. Long hair could be covering ears clipped while in territorial prison.

Both were young—in their twenties. They lounged, arrogant like most young men wearing iron, thumbs in gunbelts, while their gazes took in the clutter of store goods as if establishing their right to the place. He figured they were hunting someone. The taller of the two settled on the woman buying the doeskin dress and nudged his partner, who snickered.

The proprietress had wrapped the woman's purchases and was counting out the money, explaining, "The squaw brings us the items she makes on the reservation. We don't sell much, but the dresses are beautiful."

"They are also quite comfortable." The woman's sultry, throaty voice caught his interest. She was imposing-looking, about five-ten and full-bodied, her corset molding the hourglass figure—slim waist flaring out to full hips and bosom. She wore good but serviceable clothing, darkly subdued, with the hint of a bustle. A ridiculous flowered hat perched on her head. Her clothing, probably bought in St. Louis or Chicago, was fashionable but out of place in a rough mining town.

Closer inspection revealed a wide face dominated by a long, aquiline nose and firm chin. Thick braids wound about the head with its classical lines. Large, deep-set gray-green eyes looked out from beneath long, thick lashes. Her wide mouth curled in a jovial smile.

His taste ran to slim, petite women like Rose, but this female was decidedly a big, flowery rhododendron. Her educated manner of speech flew to the ear and sounded out of place, and her apparel was too good for that of the housewife of a miner or cowhand. Big diamonds on the third finger of her left hand marked her as being a married woman. He figured her for a mine owner's or rich cattleman's pampered wife.

"Do you live here, ma'am?" the proprietress ventured, somewhat in awe of the woman whose presence dominated the store. He reckoned the rhododendron would dominate any room she was in.

"No. Came in on the stage from California two days ago. On my way to Bridger's Rock." She gazed about her to take in the merchandise. "I would like to buy more from you. Not sure what Bridger's Rock has in its stores. Like your selection of clothing."

"If you'll leave your name, ma'am, I'll send you a flier by stagecoach. Do you know where you'll be?"

"Won't till I get there. Here!" She drew pen and notebook from her handbag. She scribbled on a leaf in the notebook, tore it out, and handed to the owner. "My name's Hildegard Hasso. Care of the Bridger's Rock School Board. Let me know what you have in stock in the way of clothing, list the prices, and I'll make my selection and send the money."

"I'm Mrs. Dow," the owner announced. "You're Missus—it is Missus, isn't it?"

The open, friendly smile widened as the big woman nodded. He noticed her skin was smooth and rosy, free of tanning caused by exposure to wind and sun. She carried a folded parasol.

"Husband's in Bridger's Rock, huh?" The proprietress smiled shyly, perhaps aware she was intruding but overcome with curiosity and the chance to talk to another female.

The woman pulled on her gloves and picked up her packages. The friendly smile stayed. "No. I'm a widow. I'm to teach school in Bridger's Rock."

The store owner stared. "Y-you're a *schoolteacher*?"

"You look surprised."

"You don't *look* like a schoolteacher."

"Well, I am." She laughed, showing white, even teeth. "Understand I have to be able to outwrestle the biggest boys in the class. Which, they tell me, is the chief criterion for qualifying as a teacher in a Montana mining camp. And after I break them, I must teach them." Here, she laughed softly. "With my heft, I'm sure to pass muster."

The two women relaxed and talked in the easy manner women used with each other.

Slocum, in the meantime, was keeping an eye on the two men who'd sidled up to the big woman. The shorter interrupted rudely with, "We're lookin' fer a man."

The big woman studied the two from her dominating height, brows arched in annoyance at their ill-mannered intrusion into her conversation. The shorter one had to look up at her. The big woman snapped irritably, "The streets outside are alive with men. I'm sure you can one find to suit you if you put your mind to it." She turned back to the store owner.

The taller man ignored the woman's dismissal. "We're lookin' fer a special man."

She rounded on him, angry now. "How would I know whom you're looking for?"

"Figgered he might've visited you. Big hombre. Black hair, green eyes. Mean-lookin'."

The woman reddened. "Why in the world would this man visit me?"

When he touched her clothing, she shook off his hand with a look of indignation.

He leered knowingly at his companion and said, "Only a ceilin' expert kin 'ford clothes like what she's wearin'. Whataya think, Sparky?" He elbowed his companion. "You buy thet schoolmarm bit?"

"Naw, Milge. Too fancy fer a schoolmarm. Kind of woman this here hombre we're lookin' fer would cotton to." Sparky's coarse lips split in a smile that showed tobacco-stained teeth. He nodded and leered. "She's a ceilin' expert—no doubt of thet."

She turned her imperious stare on him. "I beg your pardon?"

Slocum reckoned Sparky's tail would've been wagging if he'd had one. "You know! Ceilin' expert. Cyprian."

The woman stared in confusion. "*Ceiling* expert?"

Milge explained, "Figgered you might've entertained this man recent like."

Sparky snickered. "You know. On yer back. Studyin' the ceilin'. Figgered he'd build right up to the fanciest whore in town. Of all the wimmin we've seen since we been here, you look like you could be her." He grinned expectantly.

Milge explained, "What he means is—you're prob'ly a madam an' run a house. Figgered you'd know your customers. The man we're lookin' for is wanted. Big varmint. Meaner'n a skunk. Handle's Slocum. John Slocum."

8

Mrs. Hasso reacted by smashing Sparky on the head with her parasol. The blow drove his hat over his eyes. Milge grabbed her. She jabbed the end of the parasol into his midriff to drive him backwards. The blow doubled him up and knocked the wind from him.

Mrs. Dow screeched, "John! Trouble!"

John Dow surged from the back of the store. Milge straightened and tried to get his breath. He fingered the butt of his Colt. "Stay out of this—storekeeper! Spark! Grab her stuff!" Sparky grabbed the packages. Milge grabbed Mrs. Hasso's arm. His voice was an angry snarl when he said, "You'n me'll just mosey down the street to the hotel."

"Hotel? What hotel? What are you *talking* about! *Take* your filthy hands *off* me!"

"Where's your crib, whore?"

The woman's hand flashed out. The impact of her open palm across Milge's face cracked as loud as a pistol shot and jarred the grinning leer from his face. A grimace of fury replaced it. He slapped her back, hard enough to buckle her knees. She fell backwards against Mrs. Dow.

"Hit me, would you!" He reached out to grab her.

Slocum seized his arm and spun him about. Milge got out a surprised, "What the hell—!"

Slocum's right fist drove from the shoulder. The blow splattered Milge's nose like a ripe tomato, blood spraying everywhere. Holding the man's shirt, he jerked him back to throw a second punch that knocked Milge's head from under his hat. His Gatling-gun punches snapped Milge's head like a trip-hammer until he drove him out the door and into the street. Milge's face was a mass of blood as he lay his length in the road. When he feebly fumbled for his gun, Slocum kicked him in the side, jerked the weapon from his holster, and tossed it away.

Sparky, still holding Mrs. Hasso's packages, stumbled out the door. Slocum drew and put the muzzle of his Colt against his nose. Sparky gulped and dropped the packages. Slocum yanked him back, snatched the Remington from his belt, and tossed it aside.

Pulling the amazed man as close to him as possible without being overcome by his stench, he said, "Where'd you and this turd hear the name John Slocum?"

When Sparky stumbled over his words, Slocum jabbed him again with the muzzle. "Talk! Where?"

Sparky gulped. "Marshal Hank Yetty sent us after him."

"You two're *deputies*?" He pulled the man's hair aside. The exposed ear bore a crop mark. "He in prison with you?" He nodded toward Milge. Sparky nodded with a surly look. "What's his handle?"

"Milge Peters."

"What were you in for?"

"Beat up and robbed somebody." Sparky's voice was scared and sullen. He added, "Milge shot somebody."

"Who? A woman?" When he didn't answer, Slocum said, "Doubt if even Yetty would deputize two lowlifes like you. What orders did he give you?"

"We're bounty hunters."

Slocum slapped him across the head with his gun barrel. Sparky went to his knees. Slocum kicked him sprawling.

"He told you to kill me, didn't he! How much he paying you? Never mind! Get your cell mate and clear out of here! Catch you again—and I'll give you a shooting lesson neither of you will live to tell about."

He gathered up the packages and went back inside. Other than a fiery red cheek, Mrs. Hasso appeared none the worse for her scuffle. He bowed slightly, touched his hat brim, and murmured, "Sorry this happened. I'd be honored, ma'am, to carry these to your hotel."

Mrs. Hasso righted her ridiculous hat and gave him an interested look. "Where are those two animals?"

"Lying in the street, like the hogs they are. They won't bother you."

She studied him for a moment. "I'm just down the street. Your protection would be most appreciated, sir." She took his arm and permitted him to guide her out the store and around the inert forms of her assailants. She seemed to float along beside him, straight-backed, chin in the air, parasol on her shoulder like a rifle.

At the hotel, she took the packages from him. "Thank you, sir. I'm very grateful for your intervention."

He wondered if she was going to Bozeman in the Dougherty the following morning. Bozeman was on the way to Bridger's Rock. He decided to say nothing since he had no intention of going beyond Bozeman. Touching his hat, he again bowed, and murmured, "Ma'am."

He was in the Olive Branch Saloon later that afternoon, bellied up to the bar, savoring his third shot of Old Overholt when his danger sense prodded him again. He turned to see the bounty hunters enter and look about. He'd hoped the two would be on their way back to Idaho, but whatever Yetty was paying them for his scalp was probably too much to resist. Or maybe he had something on them and was using fear as a lever.

Milge's face was a mass of swollen, purple bruises from the beating he'd received. His vision, however, wasn't adversely effected. Spotting Slocum, he stopped dead. Sparky moved to Slocum's left. The others in the saloon, sensing trouble, crowded to the other side of the room.

"Owe you fer that rawhiding you give me." Milge said, his swollen lips slurring the words.

"Owe ya too," Sparky muttered.

"Yetty says you're good," Milge lisped through broken teeth.

Slocum relaxed against the bar. "You should've listened to him."

"Says you got a flier fer backshootin' a judge."

"At least, I don't have one for whipsawing women." He grinned his contempt. "You two the best Hank could do?"

When Milge reddened and took a stance, his right hand hovering over his gun butt, Slocum decided he was the dangerous one. Contempt was heavy in his voice when he drawled. "Bet you're a muzzle-loading daisy, Milge. A real snuffer." He glanced at Sparky, who was trying to look tough and dangerous but succeeding only in looking scared and stupid. "If you're counting on old Spark there, you're making a big mistake." He was aware that if Sparky was scared enough, he might fool him and draw first. Debating which to kill and hoping it was all bluff, he said, "Boys, take my advice. Go home and die of old age."

Milge was trying to smile, but it came off as a grimace. "Hank says you're past yer prime. You should be easy. I've kilt three men—"

"How? Backshoot 'em?"

Milge shot Sparky a look. He might as well have written a letter outlining his intention. Slocum waited. He'd done the routine enough to shut down everything but the telegraph line from eye to brain to hand. This wasn't the first flannelmouth to brace him. Usually, if he could, he let the loud-mouth live. Tension hung thick as smoke as he waited for them to act.

"Don't move!" came a female voice.

He stiffened, blood emptying from his heart at the voice in back of him, but he didn't take his eyes from the two gunslingers.

"Hand me your gun!"

"What the hell!" The second voice was that of an angry, surprised male. Slocum felt the blood flow back into him.

The female voice snapped, "Get over there! With your friends!"

Out of the corner of his eye, Slocum saw a man wearing a wolf-skin coat and a pulled-down campaign hat, hands raised shoulder-high, pass him and walk over to stand between Sparky and Milge. His animal stink filled Slocum's nostrils as he passed by. His pinched, mean-looking face reflected cold anger and mortification at having been outsmarted by a woman. He wore a double rig, the right holster empty.

Mrs. Hasso, holding the wolfer's Colt in one hand and her parasol in the other, came to stand by Slocum's side. "There are three of them," she announced.

He somehow found his voice. "How'd you know?"

"I've followed you all day. Didn't believe for a moment those scalawags would simply ride away. When I saw them waiting outside after you'd gone into the saloon, I knew they were up to no good. When the creature in the wolf coat joined them, then went in the back way, I followed him. When he sneaked up behind you, gun in hand, I stuck my trusty parasol in his back and told him to freeze."

"Ya lousy bitch!" The wolfer's teeth were a dirty yellow in his slack mouth. "A goddamn—*bumpershoot*? Ya got the drop on me with a—a—"

"Parasol? Yes."

"Ya rotten whore! I'll eat ya alive!"

"After I kill your man here," Milge said, grinding out the words and fixing his cold-eyed gaze on Slocum, "I'm gonna show you what real men is. And you, whore, are gonna pay fer the pleasure."

"Your auger's well-oiled," Slocum murmured. Then he addressed the woman. "Ma'am? Please get out the hell out of here."

"You'll need help, Mr. Slocum."

"Don't need you getting yourself killed." Slocum allowed nothing to distract his attention, which never wavered from the three.

Milge must've figured the woman was distracting him enough and that the moment to make his play had arrived. His right hand flashed to his gun.

Slocum dipped slightly to speed freeing his Colt. He drew, trigger finger holding back the trigger, thumb cocking the hammer. As the Colt streaked out across his body, he slip-fired the first round by lifting his thumb. The Colt roared, flame spat. Milge's gun had just cleared leather when the .36-caliber ball hit him in the heart. His eyes bulged, mouth flayed open, knees buckled. Slocum felt the Colt roll back in his palm as it recoiled.

He had the hammer back as he swiveled his body to Sparky. His thumb released the hammer. Sparky's Colt was still halfway in his holster when Slocum's bullet smashed his chest. Under the shock of the bullet, his thumb released the hammer too soon. The gun roared and flashed flame. Sparky's bullet took out the toe of his own boot. But he was slipping to the floor, dead. All the time this was happening, Slocum's mind raced ahead. The wolfer would have to cross-draw because his remaining Colt was on his left. If he wasn't left-handed. Slocum spun his body to his right to bring the Navy to center on the wolfer's chest. He was already releasing the hammer. A click. Nothing. The hammer fell on a bad cap.

In that split second, he saw the wolfer's right hand bringing up his gun across his belly. Slocum thumbed the hammer spur to cock the gun and rotate the cylinder to a good load, knowing he wasn't going to make it. He steeled himself for the wolfer's bullet.

The crack of a gun slammed his left ear. Flame streaked

by his cheek. A bullet doubled up the wolfer. His gun fired, the muzzle blast burning the sawdust on the floor, the bullet plowing up splinters. The man fell forward, dead, flames from burning sawdust edging out from under his skins. Standing beside Slocum, Mrs. Hasso lowered the smoking Colt.

It took him a full ten seconds to realize he was alive and unhurt. He waited for his breathing to catch up with his heart. It never ceased to amaze him how calm he was before and during a gunfight, and how shaky-scared inside when it was over. He managed to turn and stare at the woman.

"Thanks," he mumbled.

Ashen-faced, she nodded.

"You all right?"

"I just killed a man."

"You saved my life."

"Maybe that evens matters." Her mouth trembled at the corners, and he knew she was fighting to hold herself together. The last thing he needed at the moment was a weeping hysterical woman on his hands.

"They were bad men," was his only consolation for her.

Her only answer was to hand him the wolfer's gun. A commotion sounded outside, and a man wearing a star pushed through the doors and gazed about him. His eyes settled on the three dead men.

"It was a fair fight, Marshal." This from the barkeep, who had magically reappeared behind his bar.

"Them three on the floor drew on this gentleman and lady," another voice said. A churr of muttered exclamations in defense of Slocum and Mrs. Hasso rose and fell in the room.

The marshal, a middle-aged, spare man, faced Slocum. "I'm Marshal Kirby. What happened?"

Mrs. Hasso answered before Slocum could open his mouth. "These men accosted me in Mrs. Dow's store. This gentleman came to my defense. Later, when I saw them follow him into this place, I knew they were up to no good.

That one''—she pointed to the dead wolfer—''was going to backshoot him. I stopped him with my parasol.''

Kirby's eyes widened. ''Your—*parasol*, ma'am?''

''I suck it in his back. He thought it was a gun. I ordered him to give me the one he was going to shoot this gentleman with. Then, I shot him with it.'' When Kirby blinked in puzzlement, she explained, ''This gentleman's gun misfired. So I shot him. The horrid man in those stinking skins—not this gentleman.''

''I see,'' Kirby muttered, his look of confusion making it plain he didn't see. ''Your name?'' He looked at Slocum.

''John Slocum, Marshal.''

Kirby frowned as if trying to recall the name. ''Heard of you. Well—looks like self-defense.'' He fixed a stern eye on the woman. ''Ma'am, you coulda got yerself kilt. That one's Elisha Snaggs. Cold-blooded killer. You was plumb lucky.''

''Then you should rid the town of such riffraff, Marshal. Good day!'' With that, she raised her chin, opened her parasol with a flourish, and flounced out of the Olive Branch in an obvious huff.

Kirby studied Slocum with interest. ''You gonna be around long, Mr. Slocum?''

''Plan on leaving in the morning.'' He had the feeling the marshal wasn't fully satisfied with the reason for the shootout but wasn't going to push it.

He went out into the street, but his indomitable Valkyrie was already far ahead of him, her flowered hat bouncing on her dark, copper-red hair, bustle swaying, the parasol held over her head reminding him of a banner.

9

Slocum eased his butt off the hard leather seat of the Dougherty ambulance as it jounced along the road to Bozeman behind its four-up. His gray, strung out behind the wagon, trotted along. The wagon was made to carry sixteen passengers, but only seven filled the seats. Freight occupied the rest of the space.

Dust billowed in a steady cloud behind the horses. Slocum sneezed violently, then pulled his bandanna from his pocket and tied it over his mouth and nose. Mrs. Hasso, next to him, was getting an unwanted powdering that soon gave her a gray complexion. Despite the bone-jerking ride, she somehow managed to retain her composure and dignity, and held a lace handkerchief to her mouth and nose in a dainty, ladylike manner.

It was still a cold, cloudy, blustery day. Gramford had the seat behind Slocum. They'd left Virginia City early that morning and had headed east along a trail that wound around the treeless hills toward the Madison River.

Slocum studied his fellow passengers. Those whom he could see. Across from him sat a small, prissy, meek-looking man in his forties wearing a clerical collar and black suit. The short, skinny man next to the minister dozed, his loud yellow and black checkered suit and brown bowler hat resting on his long, thin nose spelling drummer. A large sample case sat next to him. The driver and shotgun guard showed only their backs. Slocum unbuttoned his duster to get at the flask in his coat pocket. He noticed the minister's eyes widen, then narrow when he saw the Colt nestled in the cross-draw holster.

Slocum took a pull on the flask, hesitated, then offered it to Mrs. Hasso. She stiffened, gave him an uncertain smile, and shook her head. Her murmured "I don't drink" made him feel as if he'd offered her a cut of chewing tobacco. He decided against offering the minister a drink. He tried to sleep, but the jolting ride over the cow track of a road, the clatter of wheels, and the interminable chitter of the wagon springs allowed him only fitful catnaps.

A shout, a shot, and the Dougherty braking to a stop threw him forward with a jarring thud. He blinked, recovered—and found himself staring into the muzzle of a Colt .45. The minister, a cold smile wreathing his thin, bony face, motioned with the pistol.

"Take your gun out with your left hand, friend."

Slocum hesitated as he weighed his options. When he decided there were none and that the deceptively mild-looking minister meant business, he used his thumb and forefinger to ease the Colt from the holster.

"On the floor," the minister ordered.

He laid the pistol between his feet.

"Push it over here."

He slid it to him with the toe of his boot.

Judging from the raised voices and stamping of horses outside, he guessed road agents already controlled the wagon. A rider pulled up at the window, peered in, and asked, his voice muffled by his mask, "Everything under control?"

The minister replied that it was, then ordered, "Everyone

out! And don't no one make a move. Hands over yer heads!''

The driver and the guard stood in the road, hands raised. Slocum counted six holdup men, masked and wearing dusters, all holding Colts. One masked outlaw dismounted and barked at the group of passengers standing in the road. ''Throw your purses into the wagon!'' The passengers tossed their purses and wallets into the Dougherty. The outlaw then peered at the woman.

''Who're you, ma'am? You aren't a soiled dove, are you?''

Mrs. Hasso drew herself up. ''How dare you suggest such a thing!''

''Then who are you?''

'' 'Tis none of your business, but if you must know— I'm Hildegard Hasso. I've been hired as a schoolteacher at Bridger's Rock.''

Something about the outlaw's laugh roped Slocum's attention. The man said, ''No need to toss your purse aboard, ma'am. Keep it. If you're going to wrangle those Bridger's Rock brats, you'll never get half of what you'll earn.'' He turned and addressed the guard and driver. ''Take the lady's bag and throw it down.'' The guard scrambled to obey, and the big carpetbag thumped on the road.

Slocum realized with a start that the generous outlaw's voice sounded very much like that of a woman trying to ape a man's gravelly tone. He couldn't tell much about the outlaw's figure because of the voluminous duster, but what he could see of the face above the mask indicated either a very feminine-looking man or a very pretty woman. The thin, arched brows and handsome, long-lashed eyes, coupled with the voice, made Slocum wonder.

The gnomelike robber dressed as a minister eyed the schoolteacher, his close-set eyes walking up and down her, his thick, wet lips drawn over large horsey teeth. He approached her, put out a hand, and ran it over her hip. She slapped it away. When the men moved to protect her, the robber leveled his Colt at them.

Face wreathed in malignant grin, the small man touched her again. This time, she slapped him hard enough to stagger him. The grin became a grimace, and the gun came up.

"Ya filthy bitch! Hit me, would ye! I'll—" He shoved the gun at her just as Slocum moved between her and her attacker.

"Joe! Stop it!" The leader's feminine-sounding voice rang with authority. "Take the reins of the wagon!"

"I want the woman!"

"I said—get on the driver's box!"

"Look! I ain't takin' orders from you—"

The leader drew a Colt. "One of these days I'm going to have to kill you."

The gnome licked his lips, his slightly mad gaze fixed on the man. "No ya won't. The boss wouldn't like thet. Worst he'd do is maroon me. Like he done Zeke an' Bead."

"Shut up, you fool!"

The gnome wavered, shrugged, and holstered his gun. When he climbed onto the driver's box to take up the reins, he reminded Slocum of an ape.

"Sorry, folks," said the false growling voice. "We need the wagon. You've a long walk ahead of you, but it can't be helped." The voice's owner motioned to the schoolmistress. "If you have more serviceable boots, ma'am, I advise you to change into them. Adios, gentlemen!"

With that, the leader pulled his or her horse about and galloped off. The outlaws followed, the Dougherty lumbering after them, its wheels rolling up dust that soon screened them from sight. Slocum got one last look at his horse as it disappeared from sight.

Slocum relaxed and looked about him. His seven companions in adversity were a roughly dressed laborer, the driver and guard, the drummer, the woman, and Gramford and Fotherby—who stood out like sore toes, feathered out as they were in beaver hats, long dress coats, and good boots.

Uneasiness washed over him. If the marshal in Bannack City had received word that he was wanted and decided to track him, he was dead. He couldn't be sure Milge and Sparky hadn't sought the law's help in locating him, though Marshal Kirby in Virginia City hadn't tried to arrest him.

The Army had closed the road to travel because of Indians, which didn't stop anyone willing to chance losing his hair. The trail was the only way to Bozeman other than straight across the mountains. He had no idea where they were except that they were in the middle of a rocky gorge covered with huge pines that towered on either side of them. Overhead, the afternoon sun gave them only a brief shot before the mountains edged in with their dark shadows.

The man in the checkered suit snatched his bowler from his head and hurled it to the ground, where it bounced and rolled away.

"Damnation! Them varmints got my sample cases—and all my money." He opened his mouth, probably to curse, saw the woman's look, and closed it again. He was a banty-rooster of a man with orange hair and blue eyes. Slocum judged him to be about fifty.

"What do you flog, my friend?" Mrs. Hasso asked.

"Ladies lingerie. Or—I did. Probably get set down 'cause of this." He relaxed, bowed, and spread his salesman's smile for her benefit. "Joe Jayko, at your service, ma'am. You in the market for fancy French lingerie? If you are, you're out of luck."

"Your company can hardly blame you for what's happened," Gramford observed. "We're all in the same boat."

Mrs. Hasso, shading her eyes with one hand, raised the other and pointed north, exclaiming. "*Look!* What's *that*?"

"What's what?" the startled driver demanded, and stared in the direction she was pointing.

"Looked like a big—big cloud. Moving east. There! See it? Right over that hill!"

Slocum stared, but saw nothing. Neither, apparently, did anyone else.

"I know I saw something," the schoolteacher maintained stoutly.

"What exactly did it look like, ma'am?" Fotherby asked.

"Big and round. Like a—like an upside-down chemical flask."

"What color was it?"

"Couldn't see it that clearly. Only caught a glimpse."

"It's what they calls mirages, ma'am. See 'em a lot out here," the driver said.

"Ye're a-seein' things, tha's all," Bill, the guard, assured her. "Happens to me whin I've drunk too much forty-rod."

She drew herself up like a ruffled hen. "I don't drink, sir! And I don't see things. I saw something big and round—and sailing through the air."

"Prob'ly a cloud," the driver mumbled, and impatiently dismissed whatever the woman thought she'd seen. The wind abruptly gusted to swirl up dust devils. He jabbed a dirty finger at the horizon. "See? There goes another one. A cloud. Wind out here whips 'em along like bullets."

"Anyone know where we are?" Fotherby asked.

The driver looked at the sun, then back at the wide river. "That there Madison River's thirty miles from Virginia City. It's another thirty to Bozeman."

A groan went up from the group. Mrs. Hasso asked, "Won't they come looking for us when the wagon doesn't show up?"

The driver spat a stream of tobacco juice and wiped his mouth with his sleeve. "We ain't due in till aroun' three, ma'am. They always allows at least an hour afore they commences wonderin' what's holding us up. Could be a broken wheel, loose tire, bad weather, hoss throwin' a shoe—whole passel of things." He shook his shaggy head glumly. "Doubt they'll take us not bein' there serious till five, six o'clock. And might not start lookin' for us till tomorrow mornin'."

"Then—what do we do?"

"Best get out your boots if you got any, ma'am, an' wear 'em. We got ourselves a long walk."

Slocum studied the men's footwear. Apart from Gramford and Fotherby and the laborer wearing moccasins, he and the others wore boots with underslung heels and pointed toes, boots made for riding—not walking. Mrs. Hasso had removed a pair of sturdy walking shoes from her bag and, seated on a log, was tugging them on, showing a profusion of frothy-white petticoats while doing so. Taking a large handkerchief from her purse, she wiped her face.

He noticed she was a handsome woman, her features too strong, the face too full of character to make for prettiness. He judged her to be in her late thirties or early forties. Standing, she shook out her skirts and picked up her bag.

"In light of circumstances, gentlemen. I believe we'd better set out. Mr. Driver—"

"Name's Luke, ma'm. Luke Hunnicutt."

"Well, Mr. Hunnicutt—"

"Jus' call me Luke, ma'am. Be easier. Hunnicutt don' slide too easy-like off the tongue—'specially if we meets up with a grizzly and you gotta get my attention quick-like."

She paled. "Grizzlies? Are there any, do you think?"

"Hope not, ma'am. Could be human grizzlies, though. Montana is awash with badmen. We'd best stay off the road. Anybody got a wippin?"

A grumble of "No, not me"—"Took mine"—"Mine was in my bag," and a shaking of heads.

"My Colt's in the wagon," Slocum said. He bent and drew the derringer from his boot. "Got twenty rounds for this peashooter. Won't be much good against grizzlies—animal or otherwise."

"Better'n nothing," Luke replied. "Well—guess the lady's right. Let's get walkin'."

Slocum fell in beside the woman, who surprised him by stepping out briskly. "Want me to carry that bag, ma'am?"

She surveyed him briefly, taking his measure, then let her features relax into a semblance of a smile. "You can, sir. I'm obliged. Have sandwiches in there that'll come in handy before long I'm sure. I'll spell you in a bit."

"By the way, my name's John. John Slocum."

"And mine's Hildegard. But like Luke says, if a grizzly charges us, or we're beset by Indians. Hildegard may be a bit much to get your tongue around if you're in a hurry. So—call me Hilda."

Her eyes crinkled in a friendly way, and she smiled to show white, even teeth behind a big, shapely mouth. She murmured in a demure voice, as if trying on the name for size, "John—John Slocum. Hmmm."

10

Slocum used his empty gunbelt to sling Hilda's carpetbag from his shoulder. She plodded steadily along by his side, her leggy gait matching him stride for stride, her open parasol resting on her shoulder.

Uneasiness hounded him as he surveyed the gorge that fenced them in and searched for movement among the rocks towering over them.

They could be in danger. Outlaws roamed Montana, preying mostly on prospectors. The marshal in Bannack might be mounting a posse to come after him. He wondered if the newfangled transcontinental telegraph connected remote towns. Probably not if Hank Yetty was forced to hire long riders to hunt him down and murder him. There wasn't much west of Bannack. The road they were on wasn't much more than a trail. It was obvious they weren't going to get far on foot.

"This road go in a straight line to Bozeman?" he asked Luke.

Luke shook his head. "Goes north for another ten miles, then east for another twenty."

"What if we cut across lots to Bozeman?"

Luke spat. "If you was a mountain man—or a bear—mebbe. Bodacious hills 'twixt us an' Bozeman. Niver make it. Best we keep to the trail."

Something about the holdup kept nagging him. He said, "Luke, that Dougherty . . . "

"Yeah?"

"Why do I have the impression that robbing us was an afterthought?"

Luke frowned. "Don't getcha."

"Seems to me the road agents were more interested in making off with your wagon than our pokes."

Luke rubbed his chin. "Well—the passengers we carry ain't gen'rly rich. Ain't niver been stopped before. An' we don't carry no gold." The driver looked over at him. "Why would they want a wagon what's made to haul passengers?"

"Don't know. But the answer might be interesting."

"When thim robbers ride into Bozeman big as you please with thet thir wagon, everyone's gonna know thir's a busted flush somewhirs. Ain't another wagon like it. Tracey Cartage Company's gonna be right on thim varmints with the marshal. Thir's no place they kin hide it."

Slocum remembered the vanished robbers and wondered.

Hilda, flushed with walking and breathing heavily, asked, "Where you from John?"

"All over."

"You talk like a Chiv."

"Chiv?"

"Southerner." She laughed. "Southern chivalry? It's what we Californians call Southerners." She studied him as if she might find his origins stamped on his features. Something in her voice, something about her manner, made him cotton to her despite her straitlaced schoolmistress demeanor.

He smiled. "I'm from Georgia. Guess that makes me a Chiv—though I'm not certain there's much chivalry in me.'' He told her about the war, but left out his service under Quantrill. He told about coming back to his farm, and then—throwing caution to the wind—about killing the Yankee judge. ''I'm a wanted man,'' he informed her.

''Is Slocum a summer name?''

''Nope. It's my handle. Trouble is, the marshal in Palouse Flats found me on a flier. One chance in a hundred of him having one, but there it was.''

''And he arrested you?''

He grinned. ''Made the mistake of hanging around too long in one place.''

''So, now you're on the dodge.''

''Yup.'' He looked over at her. ''If being in the company of an outlaw bothers you . . .''

''Wouldn't have anyone to tote my bag if it did.'' She hesitated, then asked. ''Do you have a wife?''

He grinned. ''Why? You looking for a husband?''

She laughed and shook her head. ''Had one once. Mine caved in on him. One man was enough trouble for me.''

''Well, I'm not married. Never came close.'' He stopped and turned his head at the muted sound of thundering in front of them. Horses.

She blinked in confusion and demanded. ''What's wrong?''

He seized her arm. ''Come on! Off the road!''

''Wh-what—?''

''Don't argue, woman! We got company.'' He dragged her into the cottonwoods bordering the river, the underbrush crackling beneath their feet. She hiked her skirts and plowed along behind him.

''What about the others?'' she demanded, panting heavily.

He dragged her behind a huge cottonwood. ''You're the one I'm worried about. Stay put! Whatever happens—don't move!''

''Who's coming? What're you going to do?''

He drew the derringer. ''Don't know who's coming.

That's why I want you here. May be help on the way—but I doubt it.''

If it was Indians, they would find her. If it was outlaws, she was probably safe. If it was help on the way, then it wouldn't matter. He wondered briefly why he was so concerned about the safety of a fortyish schoolmarm.

The riders, coming from the north, rounded the bend of the road in a swirl of dust. Five men dressed in wolf skins, as filthy and shaggy as their horses. Two ponies loaded with skins trailed them. The rearmost rider led a team of horses harnessed together. Another rider led Slocum's gray. He recognized the still-harnessed four-up from the Dougherty.

He surveyed the scene from his vantage point behind a tree. He hadn't had time to warn the others, the woman being his chief concern. Only the drummer, the laborer, Gramford, and Fotherby remained on the road, apparently too confused and startled to make a run for it. Luke, the guard, and the driver were nowhere to be seen. The riders reined in so abruptly they nearly ran down the men in the road.

The leader, clad in a dirty leather coat, muley hat, and leather leggings and wearing a Colt, approached the four at a slow trot. He carried a long Sharps Fifty across his saddle. Slocum, using trees for cover, worked his way silently to within thirty yards of the man, but saw nothing promising in the mean face covered with dirty gray stubble. The other four ranged behind him.

''Where's the wagon?'' the leader demanded, his voice harsh as a horseshoe rasp.

''Howdy, friend.'' The drummer, his patent smile frozen on his face, stepped forward. ''What wagon?''

The leader looked over his shoulder at his men and sneered.

'' 'What wagon?' he wants to know.'' The man leaned forward and peered between his horse's ears at Joe. ''The wagon haulin' passengers from Virginia City. The one you was on.'' He pointed to the team. ''The one thim hosses was a-pullin'?'' His laugh was a bark of disgust. "Or—are you out takin' the air?''

Gramford stepped forward. "If you mean the Dougherty ambulance—you're too late. Road agents held us up, took our money—and the wagon.''

"No more'n an hour past,'' the drummer added, then frowned. "You must've passed it if you was on the trail.''

The leader narrowed his eyes and studied the group.

"What kinda burro milk you givin' me? We saw no wagon!'' He studied the three from narrow, suspicious eyes. "Whir's the driver'n guard?''

The four looked about them, puzzled. "Gone.''

"Who else?''

The drummer blurted out, "The woman—'' but Fotherby instantly elbowed him to silence.

The riders stirred. "What woman?'' the leader demanded, purient interest lighting his bony, thin-mouthed face.

"Well—there was a woman—but she got off at the way station back yonder. . . .''

The drummer wilted under the five pairs of cold, cunning eyes staring down at him.

"What he means is—he's lyin'. What do we do to liars, boys?''

"Same what we did to thim Assiniboine bitches an' thir whelps up to Cypress Hills,'' a snaggle-toothed wolfer, his slack mouth stained with tobacco juice said, then cackled.

"Whir's the woman?'' the leader demanded.

"If I knew—I wouldn't tell you.'' Gramford replied.

The leader peered at the group through mean little eyes. "Fan out, boys! If she's here, we'll find her.'' The riders spurred their horses, two heading off the trail toward the west cliff of the canyon. "Can't go far this-a-way, Dick.'' Snaggle-tooth yelled over his shoulder, his horse high-stepping it through the underbrush.

"If you ketches her, you leave her be!'' Dick yelled in reply. "We'll toss fer her.''

He turned to group. "Which one of you's Gramford?"

Gramford hesitated, then said, "I am. Why?"

"Ye're the mine owner?"

"I operate a mine. Yes."

Dick's craggy face split in a maniacal grin. "Got orders to bring back yer scalp. With that head of white hair—can't miss."

He drew his skinning knife.

Gramford stood his ground. Slocum could see no fear in his face. "What's this all about? Who wants my scalp?"

"Git 'em, boys!"

Fear edging into him. Slocum cocked his derringer. The four on the road stumbled backwards before the relentless push by the men on horseback. Before Slocum could think, the man Dick drew his Colt.

"You!" He waved the gun at the drummer. "Whir's the woman?"

"There ain't no woman," the drummer yelled.

"Hey, boys! Thir ain't no woman! What ya say to thet?" Dick aimed and fired. The bullet slammed the drummer to the road, his checkered chest blossoming into an evil red rose. Two more shots. Fotherby slumped in death, as did the laborer.

Gramford, guessing what was going to happen, turned and ran. Dick let out a yowl and spurred his horse. Gramford crashed through the underbrush, his pursuer right behind him.

With the brush thick as it was, Gramford had the brief advantage of being on foot. Dick's horse kettled and nearly threw its rider. He steadied the animal and spurred it as he charged through the undergrowth. Gramford was almost to Slocum when Dick caught him. The Sharps came up in his hands.

Slocum stepped from behind his tree, aimed at the horseman—and pulled the trigger. The .32 made a popping noise. He fired again. Dick yelped and dropped his Sharps. Blood streamed down his face from a gaping wound under his left eye. His hands released the reins and flew to his face. He slid from his horse, limp as a sack of grain.

Slocum yanked Gramford backwards out of the way of the kettling horse. Grabbing the reins, he snubbed the terrified animal to a tree. He thrust the Sharps at Gramford and whipped the Colt from the dying wolfer's holster. A Winchester rested in a bead-decorated, doeskin scabbard. He pulled it out. Underbrush crackling behind him made him turn. Skirts hiked, flowered hat awry, a breathless Hilda joined him.

"Thought I told you to stay put."

"I can shoot!" She snatched the Winchester from him.

On the road, the remaining wolfers had dismounted and were squabbling over the contents of their victims' pockets. The two on the road fought over the dead Fotherby's gold turnip, one grabbing it only to have the other yank it from his hand. A meaty *splat* and one lay his length on the road, blood streaming down his face. The victor stood holding the watch before his face, mouth slack with greed, eyes glittering.

Hildegard calmly raised the rifle to her shoulder and fired. The wolfer staggered and went to one knee. Snaggle-Tooth and his companion reined in their horses at the firing and rode back.

She levered a round into the chamber, again raised the Winchester, and pulled the trigger. The .44-40 boomed, its 200-grain bullet smashing Snaggle-tooth backwards off his horse.

The Sharps cracked. The wolfer on the road was turning toward them in confusion at the shots when the .50-caliber bullet burst his head like a red melon. Slocum ran forward, firing the Colt. Shooting on the run, he snapped off shots at the remaining man trying frantically to swing his horse about and escape. The Sharps boomed again. The man tumbled out of the saddle, head drumming against the road in a wild tattoo as he died. Gramford, calmly fitting another round into the Sharps, peered at the bodies littering the trail.

"What do you think?" he murmured. "Any more?"

Slocum paused to let his heart catch up with his breathing. "Reckon we got 'em all. By the way—nice shooting."

"Speaking of shooting—you saved my life."

"Sorry I couldn't do the same for the others."

Slocum turned to Hilda, who stood, face grim, smoke curling from the Winchester's muzzle. "My congratulations, ma'am. Excellent work. We'd better get down there."

He asked Gramford, "Where'd you get the extra rounds for the buffalo gun?"

"Off our dirty friend here." Gramford prodded the dying wolfer with his toe.

"Take the lady down to the road, will you?"

Gramford hesitated. "What do you intend to do?"

"No need to upset her."

"Ah! I see. Yes. Come along, Mrs. Hasso."

Hilda, however, was not about to be led away. Bridling, she shook free of Gramford's hand and rounded on Slocum. "What do you intend to do to this man?" She nodded at the dying wolfer.

"Shoot him. Just don't want you to see me do it."

"He's not a horse!"

Gramford answered, "No. He's a man who would've vilely used you, let his men use you, then murdered you— if you were lucky. He's got two bullets in him. If we leave him, he'll die slowly. He mentioned the Assiniboine women and Cypress Hills. No doubt he was there with John Evans. He and his men raped and murdered thirty Assiniboine women, then killed the children. He should've hanged. And would've had it not been for our bigoted idiot of a state governor." He again took Hilda's arm. "Allow me, ma'am."

She managed one, quick anguished look at Slocum and a look of disgust at Dick, then let Gramford lead her down to the road.

Slocum knelt by the dying man. "Why did you want to kill Gramford?" he asked.

"Paid—me." The man gurgled bloody foam. Slocum saw his first round had hit his chest.

"Who paid you?" He pulled the filthy head up by the coat lapels.

"Ar—" He fainted. Slocum grimaced at the man's stink and went through his pockets, which yielded several gold and silver coins, Bull Durham, a pocket knife, and a bag of gold seeds. He unbuckled the fancy gunbelt and holster of tooled leather. Strapping it to his waist, he holstered the Colt.

There remained what he had to do to the dying man— "put him out of his misery," were the words usually used. He cocked the big .44. The man came to, his good eye focused on him, and the mouth, black with the vomit of blood, opened to say something. Then his head fell sideways in death.

Slocum breathed a prayer of relief that he hadn't been forced to give the man the coup de grace. He didn't like shooting a defenseless man, no matter how bad he was.

He examined the gun in his hand as if just then aware of it. It resembled his .36-caliber Navy cap-and-ball except that it was bigger, being a .44 with a seven-and-a-half-inch barrel. It had no strap over the cylinder, which had no rebating. When he hefted it, he noticed it wasn't as barrel-heavy as his cap-and-ball. He punched out a cartridge and examined it. It was a .44-40. He knew the 1871 model had originally been made for .44 rimfire cartridges, but a gunsmith had recently converted this one to .44-40 centerfire.

His own Navy Colt was God only knows where by now, so this one, he thought, would have to do. He found the feel of it much like his Navy other than its slightly bulkier weight. He would have to get used to the heft of it. One bandolier on the wolfer contained .50-110 cartridges for the Sharps, another, .44-40s. He took both. Untying the reins of the horse, he climbed into the kack and steered the animal down to the road.

Gramford's face reflected both sorrow and shock as he knelt by his dead companion, his hands fluttering uselessly over the man's wound. Hilda stood next to him and wrung her hands in obvious vexation.

"David Fotherby came out here to do a survey on some mining sites I own."

Slocum figured the mining business could account for the fancy clothes. "You mentioned you own a mine."

"Yes. Several." Gramford got slowly to his feet. "Own the Aces High Mining Combine in Nevada. We were on our way to my newest operation outside Bozeman. He was going to check it. We were also going to enlist the help of the Army at Fort Ellis concerning my stolen shipment."

"Does he have a family?" Hilda asked.

Gramford shook his head. "None that I know of."

Slocum looked about him. "Wonder where the driver and guard disappeared to."

"Here!" Bill, the guard, and Luke, the driver, stumbled through the underbrush to join them.

"Better gather up the horses," Slocum suggested. "They're our ticket to Bozeman."

Luke stopped and stared. Addressing the guard, he exclaimed, "Bill, I'll be damned if they ain't our team!" He gathered the reins and scratched the ears of the off-leader. The leaders and wheelers were still harnessed together. "Hey! Thet means the Dougherty must be ahead of us."

Slocum frowned. "The robbers would've been more'n a match for these boodoos. And why would they unharness the team?"

"Mebbe they jist wanted the hosses," Bill suggested.

"If thet thir wagon's up ahead, I needs to get it back. Can't be far." Luke swung himself into the saddle of a dead wolfer's horse and gathered up the reins of the team. "Gonna ride ahead a piece an' see if thet wagon's up thir. Bill, you stay here. Be back soon."

"Don't think you'll find it, Luke." Slocum called out.

"Whir would it be? Two-thousand-pound wagon like thet don't just vanish. Gotta be thir."

"Hope you're right."

Luke banged his hat against the horse's rump and galloped off.

Hilda and Bill gathered up the wolfers' four horses, the two packhorses, and the gray while Slocum and Gramford made a quick check of the corpses.

"What'll we do with bodies?" Bill asked.

"Take Fotherby, Joe, and the other fellow back to Virginia City," Gramford replied. "Leave the others for the buzzards."

Bill announced, "We've got a baker's dozen of horses, countin' the packhorses an' team."

"Strip the bodies of weapons," Slocum said, and dragged a dead wolfer off the road. He then parceled out the pistols and rifles to the group, hesitated, then handed Hilda a .44 Henry with a bandolier. "Reckon you know how to use this."

"I do."

She helped him load two of the bodies on the back of the packhorses and tie them down.

Bill said, "The little fella don't weigh much. Kin ride with me." He tied Joe's corpse behind the saddle of his mount, then climbed aboard. Slocum, keeping the Sharps and the Colt, took Dick's horse for Hilda. "Can you ride, Mrs. Hasso?" Gramford asked, his gaze taking in her voluminous traveling outfit. "We've no sidesaddle."

"If you gentlemen will excuse me." She took her carpetbag and strode off into the woods. Slocum and the others busied themselves cinching up and adjusting bridles. In a few minutes, she reappeared.

She'd changed into the doeskin dress, leggings, and moccasins she'd bought at Mrs Dow's. Her ridiculous hat was gone and in its place a narrow-brimmed muley sat on her head. Thick copper-red braids hung across her breasts. The loose dress hinted at the curves of her full figure and showed the smooth line of rounded thighs when she strode toward them. When the men cheered and clapped, she gave a quick little curtsy and laughed with them. Hanging her bandolier over the saddlehorn and shoving the Henry into the scabbard, she tied her carpetbag behind her and swung herself into the kack as easily as a man. She pulled the dress up to her knees so she could throw her legs over the barrel.

Gramford said, "Reckon we ought to head back to Virginia City."

Slocum shook his head. "I'm going on." The last thing he wanted was to ride back into the possible waiting arms of the law. Virginia City, left with only a fraction of its original population following the recent gold bust, was no place for a wanted man to hide.

"You sure you won't go back with us. Mr. Slocum?" Gramford asked.

"Got to get to Bozeman, Mr. Gramford."

"You understand, of course, that we've no choice but to return to Virginia City."

"Understand that, sir."

"We have to dispose of the bodies and notify the sheriff."

"Reckon so. I'll tell Luke you've gone back. By the way, Mr. Gramford. Dick's dying words were that someone wanted your scalp."

"Every banker and miner within a hundred miles wants my scalp."

"No. I believe he meant to take it. You got any enemies?"

Gramford's laugh was sardonic. "When you're a successful gold mine owner and operator, you have nothing but enemies."

Slocum leaned over his horse's ears, his tone hardening. "Any in particular, sir?"

"Can't think of any who'd deliberately hire someone to

kill me. Most who'd like me dead would do it face to face.''

''Well—watch your back—as well as your front. Good luck.'' He pulled the gray around.

Gramford hesitated, then announced, ''If you're going to be in Bozeman a spell, Mr. Slocum. I've a business proposition I would like to discuss with you.''

He wondered what that might be. Curiosity fired him. ''Ask at the first fleabag you hit on your way into town. I should be there for the next week.''

''Our thanks to you for saving our lives.''

''My pleasure, sir.''

''Mrs. Hasse? Are you ready?'' Gramford gave her a courtly bow at the waist.

''Sorry, Mr. Gramford—but I'm going with Mr. Slocum. I've a school waiting for me at Bridger's Rock.''

That startled everyone, including Slocum. Seeing his look, Hilda added, ''If he doesn't mind my company.''

''Don't mind at all, ma'am. Enjoy it.''

''Well—you'll be in safe company, Mrs. Hasso.'' The men touched their hats and swung their horses south.

''See you in a week, Mr. Slocum.'' Gramford waved.

When they had ridden away, Hilda looked over at him, the corners of her big mouth dimpling. ''Will I be in safe company, John?''

He grinned. ''You surely will, ma'am. Why?''

''Well, the school board sent me rules of behavior. Very explicit.'' Grinning, she ticked them off on her fingers. ''Wear at least two petticoats. The hem of my skirt can't be more than two inches above my ankles. Can't be seen with a man who's not my brother or father. No going to dances. Can't leave town without the school board's permission. Can't wear bright colors.'' Here, she chuckled. ''And I can't go riding with a man.''

He laughed and replied, ''Do believe those school twisters just met their match in their new schoolmistress, ma'am.''

11

As they rode boot to boot, Slocum looked over at his companion and said. ''You would've been smarter to've gone with Gramford and the others, Hilda.''

''Why? If it weren't for you, we'd probably all be dead.''

''Did the school twisters give you a place to stay in Bridger's Rock?''

''The school board promised me a room. I promised to be there by tomorrow.''

''If you're coming all the way from California, they could at least give you some spread in the time.''

''A promise is a promise, John.''

He had to smile at her rather prissy, prim bearing, which was oddly at odds with the big, almost blowsy woman she was. Curious, he studied her. Her profile showed features that added up to face of surprising strength—a face that stopped short of beauty because of the large nose and big, mobile mouth. But something else in it transcended mere good looks. He didn't associate prettiness with school-marms. She'd proved it would take a lot to spook her, and she clearly had a mind of her own. He hadn't figured on escorting her to Bozeman, but couldn't see where he had much choice.

She broke the silence. "How long do you think it'll take that marshal in Palouse Flats to figure where you're going? Now that you've killed his two hirelings."

He grinned and wondered what it took to shock her, and decided it might be interesting to find out. "He wouldn't have taken me but for the woman I was with. Dropped in most inconvenient-like."

Her expression remained wooden. "What was her name?"

"Rose. I was in bed with her when he broke in on us. Told her I was drifting to Oregon."

"Can she be trusted?"

"She broke me out of jail. Don't know if they're still interested in judge killers, but'll have to assume they are." He added wryly, "Add jail-braking and hoss thievery to the bill."

"Maybe your killing those two'll discourage him."

"Maybe. If he ever learns they're dead."

She studied him for a moment. "Are you a dangerous man, John Slocum?"

"No more'n a cougar or bear when they're threatened or cornered. You worried?"

"Not in the least."

He didn't share her confidence in him. They were following the Bozeman Trail, closed because of Indian troubles, and they were alone. And he wasn't that familiar with the area.

The sound of pounding hooves grew louder. He grabbed her reins and led her off the road, relieved when she drew the Henry from her scabbard and levered a round into the chamber. This woman, he thought, isn't down in her boots. A man could ride the river with her. They watched from cover as Luke rode into view. He would've ridden past them but for Slocum's shouted, "Hallo! Luke!"

The teamster reined in and stared about him in surprise.

"Mr. Slocum? Mrs. Hasso?"

"We left the others back on the road. They're returning to Virginia City. Mrs. Hasso and I are riding to Bozeman. Find the wagon?"

Clearly perplexed. Luke rubbed his chin. "Found where they unhitched the team. But the wagon? No sign of it. Gone! Plumb gone! Can't figger it."

"Didn't think you would find it."

"Trouble is—no one at Tracey Cartage is gonna believe any of this. Means my job fer sure." He rolled his eyes. "Gonna take some high explainin'—us losin' a whole wagon."

"Why don't you remind your boss of the bank robberies where the robbers simply vanished."

Luke barked bitter laughter. "A whole Dougherty vanishing? Who'd believe me?" He pointed his horse south. "Sorry you ain't a-goin' with us. Take care! This road ain't safe. Keep to the high ground whir you can." He waved and rode off.

Slocum and Hilda reached the end of the gorge where the road forded the river. The straight-up, rock-ribbed walls bristled with pines. The wind blew in coat-flapping gusts. She held her hat to her head and squinted against the dust. He led the way, the swift current shoving at his horse. They were belly-deep and wondering if they would have to swim for it when the water's depth decreased.

They rode north for what he reckoned was five miles to where the trail turned east and the land leveled out. The sun was about gone, and the cold was picking up.

"Reckon we ought to hole up soon, Hilda."

"The river's on our left. Grove of trees yonder." She pointed.

"Good a place as any."

He led her north along the east bank till they found a small meadow by the river. He helped her down and led the horses to the river to drink. When they had their fill, he hobbled them to let them graze. Then he set about erecting a lean-to. He used Dick's skinning knife to cut two thin lodgepole pines and trim them. Hilda buttoned two fish together to hang them over the poles for a covering.

"Hope to hell it don't rain." he muttered.

"Can we chance a fire, John?"

"Well, if Indians are our problem, not having a fire won't matter much. If it's anyone else, we're far enough off the trail. I'll dig a pit."

She said nothing and disappeared into a grove of trees nearby. He scooped out a hole in the turf, using his knife, lined it with rocks, and then filled it with tinder. He set the tinder ablaze, blew on it till there was a good flame, and fed in sticks, then a small, rotten log from a fallen tree nearby. When she returned, they had a warm blaze that gave off little light. They huddled about it to dispel the chill. The river gurgled and soughed, the ripples breaking up the moon's reflection into countless shards of sparkling light. She fished three sandwiches out of her voluminous bag.

"Roast beef with tomato and mayonnaise," she announced. "One for me, two for you. May be a bit wilted but they're edible."

"Wolf would be edible about now. I'll freshen our water."

He emptied the canteen and walked to the river to fill it. Returning, he grunted with pleasure as he sat by the crackling flame and munched on the thick, meaty bread and meat. He hadn't realized how hungry he was until his stomach reminded him with a painful lurch. Finished eating, she stood.

"Need a bath," she announced. "Get some of the dust off me." Like a magician pulling a rabbit from a hat, she dipped into her bag and came up with a big towel and a buffalo robe.

Alarmed, he murmured, "That water's freezing cold."

"Cleanliness, Mr. Slocum, is next to godliness." She

strode into the dark toward the river. He watched her tall figure move off.

He sat, ears strained for the sound of her, eyes staring into the embers of the fire. He threw on more wood and stood, muttering aloud, "She could be right."

He unshucked himself and put his boots back on to walk to the riverbank, Colt in one hand, Sharps in the other. Shivering in the moonlight, he heard her splashing about and caught glimpses of her as she glided through the water, sleek as a seal, moon glow waking small, iridescent fires on her smooth skin. Laying aside his weapons and pulling off his boots, he waded in up to his waist, the cold making him gasp. He then glided out to her like a gator sneaking up on unsuspecting prey. To his surprise, the water felt warmer than the air.

When he surfaced next to her, she gave a startled gasp and trod water furiously. "*John!* What're you *doing* here?"

He reached for her and pulled her into his embrace. She stiffened at his touch, pushed him away, then relaxed against him as they trod water together. Her full breasts, floating like halved melons, crushed delightfully against his chest. He reached down and cupped her round bottom in his hands and drew her to him. He half-expected her to fight him, and wasn't going to push it if she did.

To his surprise, strong arms encircled his neck, fingers tracing the muscles of his shoulders and back. She was warm and soft against him as his blood-gorged erection prodded her belly. She was a big, well-proportioned woman.

She dropped one hand to his groin, fingers working, exploring. "Good *heavens*!" she gasped. "Is that all *you*?"

"Hope so, ma'am." He laughed softly in her ear, then gently nibbled its lobe. She fingered his balls, then squeezed, causing him to grunt with pain and pleasure. Her breath was raucous as her mouth pressed against his throat. Aroused like a stallion with a mare in heat, he whispered hoarsely, "Don't know how long that ramrod of mine will last in this cold water. Better do something with it.''

"I agree." Laughing, she tried to insert it into her, but it was too difficult to tread water and handle him at the same time. He pulled her up higher to him, his mouth taking in a plump nipple that hardened like a juicy grape between his teeth as he gently nibbled on it, his tongue flicking against it. She gave a sharp little cry of agony and delight. Her fingernails raked his balls and penis, making him gasp at her touch.

One arm about her, he swam for shore. When his feet touched bottom, he picked her up and carried her to the bank. Panting heavily—she was, he figured, a good hundred fifty pounds of full-bodied female—he spread her robe and pulled her down on it. The bluish light glistened on her wet skin as she shivered, lay back, and pulled him down so that he lay on top of her.

Blood hammered in his ears as he coaxed her thighs apart and pulled her hips up to meet his. She felt deliciously warm against his shivering body. She reached down and inserted his erection into her, wriggled her hips to seat him deeper, then relaxed under him.

He withdrew his cock, sat back, and studied the form before him. She was big in the hips, full-breasted, her belly a smooth mound, glossy in the bluish light, her strong legs long and shapely.

He bent, took her nipples into his mouth one by one, then buried his face between her breasts, savoring their butter-like softness and breathing in her clean woman scent. He coursed his mouth down her belly, flicked his tongue at her navel, causing her to jump, then buried his face in the thick bush of dark curly hair at the yoke of her thighs. He breathed in the warm, salty taste of her cunt. She jumped and squirmed when he inserted his finger into her.

He pushed his face into the yielding softness of the silky skin of her inner thighs. He found her nubbin with his tongue and flicked it until her breathing became a ragged, breathless gasping. Her hips gyrated and her warm, wet, furry yoke ground into his face. Then, with a harsh, stifled cry, she thrashed wildly under him, nearly throwing him off, her hands painfully gripping his ears to pull his face deeper into her.

She gradually relaxed under him, her bosom heaving, the soft globes quivering delightfully, the nipples, round and stiff, centered on dark aureoles. He lay back down on her, took her in his arms, and murmured in a voice husky with passion. "Now!"

She reached down and again inserted the throbbing shaft of muscle into her and wriggled under him to draw in his full length. She arched her pelvis and worked her internal pincers, the muscles nipping at the head of his cock. It took an expert to do that, he thought, pleasure warming him like a furnace.

He moved, thrusting, halting, thrusting again. His lips found hers, and his tongue forced its way between them. Her teeth nipped at its tip. He increased his plunging rhythm to drive harder into her. She captured him with her legs, heels digging into the small of his back, hips thrusting up to meet his powerful lunges, her round, soft belly slapping against his hard, muscular one. Panting, grunting, he waited, trying to hold off the inevitable. She surged under him, fingernails digging into his back. She gasped, grunted, cried out, and bit his ear.

The pain goaded him like an aphrodisiac. His loins swelled to bursting as he emptied himself into her in a series of maddening thrusts that evoked little gasps of ecstasy from her passion-slack mouth.

Spent, exhausted, they relaxed in each other's arms. He eased himself off her and lay back, chest heaving, mouth gulping air. He looked over at the dim profile of the panting woman next to him. Laughing softly, he whispered, "If there is anyone out there looking for us—"

"They certainly must've heard us," she finished for him. A giggle escaped her. "Felt like we were going to knock the trees down."

"You're something, Mrs. Hasso."

"Good as Rose?" She turned on her side to look at him. He kissed her. "Now, don't get nosy. I'm not going to ask you how I stacked up with your late husband."

"He's dead and gone." She kissed him back.

"Mine caved in on him, you said."

"Four years ago. He was seventy when it happened."

"Miner?"

"No. Mine owner. Made a pile."

"Seventy, you say? An old buck for a young doe like you."

"I was the schoolteacher and the only unattached female around. He was the richest man in town. Love didn't mean much in the California gold camps. Security and protection did."

"How long were you married?"

"Fifteen years. He was fifty-five and rich. I was twenty-three and poor. Seemed like a good match."

"Were you a California widow?"

She laughed. "Hardly. He kept me with him always."

"Can't blame him. Reckon he got a good bargain."

"We got along well together. I miss him. In a way, I was more like a daughter to him." She traced a finger over his nose. "You're my first since him."

"I'm flattered. Truly am." He pulled her around so she straddled him. They savored each other's warmth then, hesitating, he asked, "He leave you with anything?"

Her laugh was a soft, sultry breath in his ear. "You trying to figure if I'm a rich widow?"

"Something like that."

"If I were, I wouldn't tell you."

"Any kids?"

"No."

"Ever want any?" He studied her face in the moonlight.

"The question's academic since I'm too old now. Not sure this is the country to bring children into anyway." She studied him in turn. "You ever married?"

"Not even close."

"Ever want to settle down?"

"Hopelessly fiddle-footed. A town looks best to me when I'm looking at it over my shoulder."

She was silent for a moment. "Want to stay with me until Gramford hires you?"

"What makes you think he's going to hire me? Or that I'll accept?"

She kissed him. "Guess it's up to me to make you want to stay."

His voice was sober when he told her, "I'm a drifter, Hilda. Not the kind of man you should depend on."

"I know that."

"Got fliers on me from every territory west of the Mississippi."

"Got no illusions where you're concerned. Don't expect anything from you. Just maybe a little time with me. With that thing of yours in me." She rotated her hips to grind them slowly against his.

Aroused, he pulled her face down to his. "Let's see what Gramford has on his mind."

"Meanwhile . . ." She laughed her throaty laugh, swung off him, and bent over his belly. She took his flaccid penis into her mouth and gently nipped its head. "Let's see if I can talk lazy old Sergeant Slocum down here into standing at attention again." Eventually, she did.

He woke with a start, the sun burning his eyes. Squinting, he looked over at where the woman should've been in his bedroll but wasn't. Alarmed, he sat up. The morning chill made gooseflesh on his naked skin. Where the hell was she, he wondered, panic building up in him. His hand fastened on his Colt. Standing, shivering in the morning cold, he looked toward the river.

Hilda, naked except for her moccasins, strode toward him hands busily fluffing her hair dry. A gold medallion glistened between her breasts, its chain circling her strong, shapely neck. She moved with sinuous grace, hips swaying seductively, long, rounded thighs and delicately muscled calves moving with purposeful strength, breasts jiggling with enticing earthiness.

"Morning, pardner." She raised her face to be kissed. "Take a dip while I rustle up some breakfast."

The medallion caught his eye. It was of intricate design and in the shape of a star of some kind. He pulled her to him, hands moving over her firm bottom, down the backs of the strong thighs, then up to her waist. He kissed her long and gently. Pulling away, he asked, "What've you got in that bag anyway? A kitchen?"

"Always go prepared. Go on! Get cleaned up."

She managed three hard-boiled eggs, jerky, and half a loaf of bread.

"No jam?" he asked, and grinned.

"Probably in there somewhere." She rummaged in the bag and brought out a small coffeepot, two tin cups, sugar and coffee. As she filled the pot at the river and prepared the coffee, he studied her. He hadn't expected anything more than polite conversation from his companion. She certainly belied the proper, ladylike schoolmarm she looked like. Underneath it all, she was hotter than a Spanish Gypsy.

He built up the fire while she combed out her thick mane of hair, then braided it. He watched, entranced, when she raised her arms behind her head and drew her full, rounded breasts up and out, knowing she was creating the spectacular display for his benefit. They dressed, then relaxed with deliciously hot coffee.

They packed, led the horses to the river to water them, then rode back to the trail. He wondered where she'd learned to handle herself in the easy, no-wasted-motion way she had. If the previous night was any sign, she was going to be a handful. He hadn't gotten two hours sleep. Neither had she, he reflected, but she wasn't showing it. Giving him a big, wicked smile, she winked seductively at him, and pulled her horse around.

He wondered if the school board at Bridger's Rock had any idea what they were getting in the way of a school-mistress.

12

Slocum and Hilda rode into Bozeman that afternoon. They had dinner at the California Restaurant—steak, potatoes, greens, and apple pie. He noticed she ate with demure, ladylike daintiness despite being as hungry as he. He swallowed a smile when the pictures of her shooting the wolfers and killing Elisha Snaggs popped into his mind. Hildegard Hasso, he decided, was a lady in her own right. Suddenly feeling the need to know her better, he suggested they get a room at the hotel, but she shook her head.

"Got to get to Bridger's Rock tonight, John. Said I'd be there by Saturday so I could start Monday."

"School doesn't open till May," he objected.

"The school board wishes to interview me." She took a notebook from her bag and consulted it. "Tomorrow's the twenty-sixth. Saturday."

"We could get a good night's sleep, and you could ride out early. You could be there by noon."

She considered the suggestion. "If last night's an example of a good night's sleep with you, sir, sharing my bed would be the last thing I would get." She was abruptly sober. "What happened between us was wonderful, John. But I don't want more of you. I would become too quickly addicted. Besides, why would you choose a widow older than you and a schoolmistress to boot?" She pulled on her gloves. "The local ladies of the night are what you're looking for. Not me."

"I'll get a room," he murmured. When she shot him a surprised look, he added, "And I'll ride out in the morning with you."

"You don't have to do that, John."

"You don't think I'm going to let you ride thirty miles in open country alone, do you." He took her hand and pulled it to his lips. "And I'll do my best to let you get plenty of sleep."

Her voice was a throaty growl. "Not if I've anything to say about it, you won't."

The next morning, he bought an extra horse with a pack-saddle to carry her purchases. She was apparently convinced Bridger's Rock would have few stores and that, by leaving Bozeman, she was leaving the last vestiges of civilization. They rode into Bridger's Rock late in the afternoon.

The town, what there was of it, bordered the river. Main Street was wide and dusty, lined with stores, saloons, two hotels, a jail, and a stockyard at its north end. Houses little more than cabins sat in rows along side streets. Alleys held abandoned mining machinery left over from the town's glory days when nearby rivers and streams yielded color.

An abandoned section beyond the stockyards bore the faded name of Mortification Gulch. Rotting store fronts with faded names on their facades—Smoky Joe's Eatery. Anabelle's Girls Fresh from Gay Paree, Smith's Gun Store and Miner's Equipment, Eagle Livery Stable—lined its single street. Loose shingles banging caused Slocum to shiver as the voices of a thousand ghosts sounded in the wind. Tailings lined the street, which petered out to the east where the mountain range loomed dark and ominous.

Despite the lateness of the day, Hilda inquired at the town hall about her job and where she was supposed to go. Slocum, drinking beer at a saloon across the street, listened to farmers complain about having no market for their crops, prospectors moan about gold-mining doldrums, and cattlemen agonize over the disappearing range. One old cowhand, slightly drunk, approached the wooden Indian standing silent guard at the door and saluted it with raised beer glass.

"Friend. I'm in sympathy with you. We run you off your land. Now, them goddamned nesters an' honyokers are running us cattlemen off ours."

Bridger's Rock stood in a valley formed by the Gallatin and Madison mountain ranges, and despite talk of depression hummed with activity. Wagons loaded with goods trundled and clattered in the street, people strode along the boardwalks, and the saloons were doing a thriving business. The lowing of cattle in the stockyards spoke of cattlemen chousing herds from as far away as Texas. A Texas cow grazing on rich Montana grass gained as much as three hundred pounds and brought a much higher price in Chicago.

He rose when he saw Hilda come out of the town hall. She held a key and written directions to the school outside town. He followed her to a log schoolhouse that stood in a grove of cottonwoods along the river. A log house with a stable in the back stood nearby.

"Don't know why a house goes with the job," she told him.

"Maybe because they figure you'll earn it."

"Start Monday. After being approved by the school board, of course." She dismounted before the cottage and led the horse to the stable.

He asked. "Am I going to be an embarrassment?"

She gazed at him with questioning eyes, a puzzled smile

on her lips. "Thought you were simply seeing me to my new job."

"Will the school twisters frown on you for having a man about the place?"

"If anyone says anything, you're my husband." She gave him a querying look. "That bother you?"

"No." He added with a grin. "Just so you don't try making it permanent."

"Then let's get settled. See what our house looks like."

It looked bigger inside. A bedroom, a dining room, and a kitchen with a newfangled hand pump for water, sink, and a big stone hearth with oven built in. The furniture was plain but functional. He eyed the big bed, the fanciest bit of furnishing in the place. She was already at work, dusting, sweeping.

"John! Take that feather tick and those pillows outside for airing while I ret up the place."

At her request, he built up the fire in the oven. That afternoon, she went shopping for sheets and pillowcases. While he accompanied her around the various stores and helped carry her purchases home, he felt stirrings of wanderlust warning him to ride out before the gate shut on him. Hilda's mouth-watering evening meal of steak, potatoes, greens, and apple pie washed down with delicious coffee fenced him in. That bothered him because he'd never let a woman pin anything on him since he was a baby.

The next day, he bought two boxes of .44-40s and rode out across the bridge spanning the creek toward the canyon. He set up bottles and examined his 1871 Colt. He missed his .36-caliber cap-and-ball, but had to admit newfangled cartridge pistols had their advantages. They were quicker and easier to load. He didn't have to mess with bear grease to seal the muzzles of the chambers before firing. He'd never gotten a sympathetic ignition of all six chambers at once, as happened too often with cap-and-ball pistols not sealed with grease, but had seen the results. Not pretty.

The pistol proved to be a good shooter. He stuck brass

casings in his ears to deaden the noise. The gunsmith told him that the 1871 model was the best gun Samuel Colt had manufactured to date. When Slocum splintered six bottles at forty yards with aimed fire, he knew he had a fine weapon. The pistol wasn't nearly as barrel-heavy as his Navy. Later, he practiced drawing, aiming, and firing. He then went through the motions by dropping the hammer on empty casings so as not to injure the firing pin and waste live rounds. After two days' practice, he had the feel of the gun.

Tuesday, he sat in front of the Laclede Hotel on the road into Bozeman so as not to miss Gramford. Down the street, two blacksmith shops rang with hammers on anvils. He studied the flow of people and wagons arriving and leaving, but saw no mine owner.

Week's a long time, he thought. Probably forgotten me— or got someone else for whatever the job was. He hadn't minded the wait. Hilda was even more satisfying with a bed around her, and her cooking got better with each meal.

He was sitting, musing about the hand fate had dealt him, when the rumbling made him sit up. Passing him were eleven wagons. A Studebaker, fourteen feet long, high, and fitted with wide iron tires, lumbered along, drawn by a four-span of mules. It carried what looked to be a huge folded tent. A sign on the side announced. ''Dr. Theodore Grace, Evangelist, and the Joy of Life Singers. Brothers and Sisters—Do Your Souls Need Saving? Then Grace Is with You. Rejoice!''

A well-dressed, florid-faced man stood on the driver's box and waved happily at the small crowd that had gathered. A tall, pretty woman walked along and passed out advertisements for a revival meeting to be held that night. The other wagons were Murphys and smaller prairie schooners loaded with tents and equipment, followed by five colorfully painted caravans such as Gypsies used. Slocum read his flier, then stuck it in his pocket. Spare paper always came in handy.

It was late in the afternoon when he spotted Gramford riding a sorrel.

He would've missed him if the mine owner hadn't hallooed him. He wore boots, canvas trousers, leather coat, and a black Montana hat that shadowed his lined face. He reined in and announced, "Mr. Slocum! Good to see you again. Hoped I'd find you."

"Curiosity's always been my weakness, Mr. Gramford." He unwound from the chair and stood.

"Let's find a saloon. Need a beer to wash the dust from my throat, then a second for pleasure."

Slocum led him inside the hotel to the bar. They found a table and settled back to take each other's measure.

"Get the schoolmarm settled?"

Slocum tried to hide his smile. "She's got a house in Bridger's Rock to go with her job. Given the rascals she must teach, reckon it was the least the school board could do for her."

Gramford got right to business. "Naturally, you're wondering what my proposition is."

Slocum waited while the boy placed beers in front of them. "Stayed around town to find out."

The mine owner hesitated, then asked, "Tell me. Is someone after you?"

He was instantly on guard. "Why?"

Gramford aimlessly turned his beer glass. "Two lawmen from Bannack City were snooping around looking for a John Slocum. Wanted for killing a federal judge in Georgia in '66."

"They ask you?"

"Well—the robbery and the stealing of the Dougherty piqued their curiosity. They talked to the survivors. Those they could find. Namely, me."

"What happened to Luke and Bill?"

"Working for the Aces High now. I told the lawmen that no one answering your description was in the Dougherty when the gang stole it. Apparently, the sheriff from Washington sent a couple of deputies to inquire about an escaped horse thief wanted for killing a federal judge.''

Apprehension flowed through Slocum. Just when I'm getting settled, he thought. Aloud, he asked. ''They coming after me?''

''Reckon they've given up. Finding a wanted man in this country is a hopeless venture. Especially, one wanted as far away as the Hoodoos.'' He added, ''Understand there was a shootout in the Olive Garden the day you arrived.''

''Yeah. Two bounty hunters drew on me.''

''Hmmm. Well, I told the Bannack boys no one fitting your description was in Virginia City. Don't reckon they'll push it.''

''Obliged to you for trashing my trail.'' Slocum folded his hands on the table. ''How can I repay you?''

''You owe me nothing. Mr. Slocum. Do you mind if I call you John?'' Slocum shook his head. ''If you killed that judge, you no doubt had good reason for doing so.''

''I did.''

''Too many judges as it is.. They need thinning out. What would you think about working for me?''

Slocum sat back. ''Doing what?''

Gramford hesitated as if unsure of his words. ''Want you to find that stolen gold shipment.''

A thrill surged through him. Gold! ''You mentioned you were in mining. Placer?''

Gramford shook his head. ''We've pretty well exhausted the source of free gold—nuggets and scads. We do hydraulic washing. Big overhead, but I have two mines that are producing. One's rich in quartz. Getting four ounces a ton.''

''Where?''

Gramford took a sip of beer. ''Afraid I can't divulge that. Near Alder Gulch and Nevada. I operate a smelter, stamp mills, and cast my own ingots for shipment. The Army escorts them to boats on the Yellowstone, which take them to Fort Abraham Lincoln. The government buys most of my take. Sixteen dollars an ounce.''

''Must take a lot of gold to make it worthwhile,'' Slocum murmured. ''How much are we talking about?''

''At the current price—approximately five hundred and fifty thousand dollars.''

''Right now, I've got eight double eagles, Mr. Gramford. Figure I'm rich.''

''Well—two thousand three hundred pounds is missing.'' Gramford finished his beer and motioned to the boy to bring two more. ''As I told you, half of it isn't mine. I'm an assayer. Purify and ingot gold for other people, mostly prospectors who bring me rough ore or free gold to be amalgamated to leach out the other metals—silver, copper, zinc, iron, and platinum. To make it pure enough to sell.''

''How do you do that?''

''Use mercury. Have to mine cinnabar to get it.''

''Cinnabar?''

''Mercuric sulfide. Mercury ore. Dangerous process, mercury being a deadly poison. Men who work with it and don't take precautions wind up mad as hatters. We also use acid. Gold's impervious to acid. Another expensive and dangerous process. I'm not the only one who processes ore, but I never cheat anyone. And I try to protect my workers. When the government pays me, I pay my suppliers after deducting my share.'' He paused while the boy set the beers and plates of free lunch on the table, then handed the boy a silver dollar. ''Keep the change.''

''You see, Mr. Slocum, I have a reputation for square dealing. Trouble is, with the depression, I'm operating hand to mouth. The long and short of it is—if I don't recover that gold, I can't pay those men who trusted me with their pokes—or my workers. And God knows they work hard enough for what little color they squeeze out of the ground.'' He studied his glass, his face suddenly old. ''Even if I liquidate my holdings. I can't begin to cover my loss. The men working for me will be out of jobs and money.''

Slocum made himself a sandwich in that slow, methodical way he did something when he was troubled. ''Seems odd a ton of color could just vanish.''

''You found the four cavalry troopers escorting the shipment bound and gagged. The outlaws simply rode off with the rig and the gold.'' Gramford absently slapped a sausage on a slice of bread. ''The leader talked like a woman, according to O'Reilly.'' He looked over at Slocum. ''Ring a bell?''

''Yeah. The leader of the gang that stole the Dougherty was either a woman—or a man who got kicked hard in the family jewels.''

''You noticed that too, eh? You're more observant than I hoped.''

''You think there's some connection with that Dougherty?''

''They want that wagon for something. And I don't believe it's for hauling passengers. Luke told us it simply vanished.''

''Hilda and I saw no sign of it on our ride here. Country's pretty open. But no tracks—no nothing.''

When Slocum pulled his Bull Durham from his vest pocket to roll a quirly. Gramford winced and presented his cigar case. ''Have a Havana.''

Slocum took one, bit off the end, spat it aside, and lit a lucifer. He held its light for Gramford, then lit his own, breathed in the rich taste, and closed his eyes to savor it. ''What's to stop the thieves from simply selling the gold?''

''No legitimate buyer is going to buy that much metal without becoming suspicious. Besides . . .'' Gramford flicked cigar ash onto the floor. ''I cast my ingots in the shapes of suit markers. Spades, diamonds, hearts, and clubs with an A stamped next to the mine's name and assayer's mark. It's my trademark. Hence, the name of my outfit— Aces High Mining Company.

"The thieves would have to melt it down and make it resemble scads and nuggets—and that would be next to impossible to do. Especially with gold already refined to ninety-five-percent purity. If they tried unloading that much legally, they'd have a big problem. The government's their most obvious customer, but the Treasury people would be instantly suspicious if they tried to market a huge quantity like that.'' He paused, then added, "No. They probably have another customer waiting. New York, New Orleans . . .''

"So—what does that mean?''

"Probably means they're going to try to take it to Fort Lincoln. The Bozeman Trail goes all the way.''

"Wouldn't be safe. It's closed on account of Indian troubles.''

"Well, they can't take it by river. No steamboat captain's going to take a ton of gold. Not with my chop on it. Not with Treasury agents watching them.'' He shook his head. "No. The only way they could do it would be to find a smelter big enough for the job and pay through the nose to melt it down. The smelter operator would know the gold was stolen and have the thieves between hay and grass. They'd be lucky to get a third of what it's worth. Their other alternatives would be to hide it till everything blows over and I'm out of business, or—''

Slocum finished for him. "Take it in the Dougherty ambulance cross-country to North Dakota.''

"Right. The Dougherty'll carry sixteen riflemen. That would tend to discourage renegade Indians—or other outlaws. They might make it.''

"They'd need fresh horses for that distance.'' Slocum added. "I doubt a Dougherty would carry that much weight.''

"They could take an extra wagon and string out a band of sixteen or so horses behind 'em. Change 'em back and forth on the way.''

"What happens in North Dakota?''

"It's the end of track for the Northern Pacific. They can ship it east by railroad disguised as freight. It would simply disappear. If that happens, I lose everything." He paused, then added, "My hands are tied. Can't report the shipment stolen because my creditors would eat me alive if they knew the hole I'm in."

"Yeah—you mentioned them."

"The banks would love getting my holdings. If they learned I couldn't meet my financial obligations, they wouldn't hesitate to foreclose on me." He grimaced as if in pain, shrugged, studied his Havana.

"Does anyone know?"

"The Army does. The United States Treasury Department does. They were expecting the shipment. I've managed so far to bluff it out. I've promised the men who entrusted me with their pokes they would get their money." He shifted on his chair and fixed Slocum with hard blue eyes. "Need someone to get the gold back for me on the quiet, John."

Slocum shifted in his chair. "Why me?"

"You impressed me the way you handled those wolfers. You saved my life. And the lives of the others. Liked the way you stepped in to protect Mrs. Hasso." He hesitated, then added, "I know something about you. That you rode with the Daltons and the Jameses. That you're supposed to've robbed trains. And, of course, I know about the judge in Georgia."

Slocum stomped on his uneasiness at this revelation. "Where'd you learn all this?"

"Make it a point to know about a man I hire."

"Didn't say I'd work for you."

"I know. But you'd be doing me a service—and a service to the several dozen men who do work for me."

"You'd hire a train robber?" Slocum couldn't help grinning.

"Maybe a man with the kind of gumption required to stop a train and relieve it of its money is the kind of man

I'm looking for. What I'm asking you to do won't be easy.''

Slocum pondered the offer. He had a balanced woman in Hilda. She was proving to be one of the best lays he'd ever had, she cooked better meals than any fancy hotel chef, she didn't nag, or try to throw her rope over him. He liked her—every part of her. He wasn't ready to ride out on her. Not yet. Aloud, he said, "If I go to work for you, what're my wages?''

"Eagle a day. Five-hundred-dollar bonus when you recover the gold.''

He tried not to show his elation. That was good money. Poker-faced, he rubbed his chin while he pretended to think it over.

"You got a deal. Need a list of the people working for you.''

"You think someone inside the company has a hand in this?''

"Good place as any to start. Somebody knew you were making that shipment. Somebody wanted you dead—with your scalp to prove you were. That's why they hired those wolfers.''

"You think there's a connection between them and the road agents?''

"Don't know. The gang, apart from the fake preacher, didn't appear bloodthirsty. The wolfers did. If the robbers wanted you dead, they had their chance. Maybe there's two factions involved. Need to talk to the commanding officer of the escort.''

"He's at Fort Ellis.''

Slocum pushed back his chair. "Where can I get in touch with you?''

"My office is in Virginia City. You might consider moving down there. Place is becoming a ghost town, so you wouldn't have trouble finding accommodations.''

Slocum shook his head. "That Dougherty headed north after cutting us loose. Chances are it's here in Bozeman.

Or close by. If I can find it, maybe it'll tell us something. I'll be in touch.''

As he walked toward the lobby, a tall, wide-shouldered man dressed in a black boilermaker suit, complete with gold watch fob and a pearl-handled .45 riding low on his hips, passed him.

Slocum got a brief glimpse of a hard face that looked chiseled out of granite. The way the man kept his coattails hooked back around the gun butt signaled gunfighter. Slocum nodded, but the *charro* ignored him. He watched while the man stopped by Gramford's table, pulled out a chair, and sat.

He didn't like the man's look, but couldn't throw a rope over what bothered him. Was he one of those who wanted Gramford dead? When he glanced at the table, the man and Gramford were deep in conversation.

Troubled and unsure how to begin, he rode back to Bridger's Rock and Hilda's.

13

Hilda had dinner on and bustled busily about the tiny kitchen, her starched white apron crackling. He pulled her to him and kissed her. She smelled delectably of yeast, lilac, and lavender.

"I'm not going to ask you where you were," she murmured, and kissed him back.

"I was down to Nelly's Pleasure Palace all afternoon."

"The girls nice?" She opened the oven. The delicious, steamy aroma of freshly baked bread, potatoes, and broiled catfish hit him.

"Tried 'em all. None compare with you."

"Hmmm. Well . . ." She sampled the gravy and made a face. "Here! Try!" She stuck the spoon in his mouth. He licked off the gravy and closed his eyes in ecstasy. She said, "If schoolteaching doesn't pan out, maybe you could get me a job there."

He put his arms about her and nuzzled her neck. "Naw. Think I'll keep you for myself. By the way, I've got a job."

She stopped to stare up at him. "Whom with?"

He opened his mouth to say, "Gramford," but changed his mind.

"Hired on as a wrangler. Spread north of here. They're short a man."

"Will I see much of you?" She didn't look at him, but busied herself laying the table.

"Much as I can manage." He pulled out a chair and sat. He wasn't certain how much to involve her, but she was all he had. "Hilda, if you spot that Dougherty anywhere in town . . ."

She paused in setting out the dishes and stared at him. "I tell you. Is that it?"

"Yes."

"Why's the Dougherty important?"

"Maybe my Colt is still under the seat. Like to get it back." He grinned and added. "Maybe I could rescue Joe's sample case of unmentionables for you."

Her reply was a sharp laugh and a muttered, "Oh."

The way she said "Oh," he knew she didn't believe him. She then asked, "Where will I find you?"

He reached over, pulled her down on his knee, took her chin in his hand, and drew her face to his to kiss her. "Under the covers next to you. Where I've been all week."

After supper, he sat at the kitchen table and listed the robberies, where they took place, when, and the people involved—the ones he knew about—and finished with the unusuals. The unusuals might be pretending to be the usual—and thus escape his attention entirely.

Hilda was at the church for organ practice. The week they arrived, the Reverend Mr. Brockwhite, the Episcopalian minister, had heard music coming from the church one evening and had gone to investigate. He'd found Hilda coaxing a Bach cantata from the ancient instrument. It happened the minister had had no organist at the time.

As schoolteacher, she was expected to attend church. The school board insisted on it. She now played the organ every Sunday and on special occasions such as weddings.

"If I didn't love Bach," she told Slocum, "I wouldn't be bothered. But it gives me use of the organ."

"The Reverend appears to be a decent man. What've you got against him?"

"It's Amanda Brockwhite I can't stand. I like Horace."

He looked up at her. "Horace?"

"The Reverend."

"Oh." A faint uneasiness hit him. "He must be fifty."

"Fifty-seven. That wife of his is only twenty-seven. Or, so she says. That spells trouble."

"Make sure you stay out of it."

She put her hands on her hips. "What're you suggesting?"

"I've seen the way he looks at you."

"Oh—*really*, John!"

He smiled. "Say hello to Johann Sebastian for me."

She left in a huff.

He frowned as he studied his list. "Somehow, all this fits together," he muttered as he sipped coffee. She had baked a pile of them for him that morning. "How, I don't know." He figured the Dougherty was the best place to start because if the road agents took the trouble to steal it, it must be important to them. He was assuming, of course, that the same gang was committing all the armed robberies.

He inspected every stable where a wagon as big as a Dougherty might be hidden, but had found nothing. He then rode rimrock and covered the area within a ten-mile radius of the town. Again, nothing. The few barns in which a Dougherty might be hidden yielded nothing. He rode to Bozeman and tried there with no success.

Fort Ellis, six miles southeast of Bozeman, sat on a narrow plain. A log stockade four hundred by five hundred feet enclosed the post. He rode through the gate and asked to talk to the adjutant. A sergeant took him to a Major Commerty.

The adjutant, forty or so, had the rugged, bored look of the frontier soldier. The early morning temperature was chilly enough to make the stove's warmth welcome in his small office. Hot coffee warmed Slocum and paved the way for business.

He displayed his badge appropriated from Marshal Yetty and a warrant he'd filled in, supposedly giving him. Deputy Sheriff William Bell, authority to pursue the gold thieves. Commerty, used to such documents, accepted its authenticity with only a cursory glance.

"Major, I'm looking into the disappearance of a gold shipment belonging to the Aces High Mining Company of Virginia City. I believe the escort came from Fort Ellis."

Commerty nodded. "I'm familiar with it. Got patrols out looking for it. So far, nothing."

Slocum chose his words carefully. "Is it possible someone on the post knew of the shipment beforehand?"

"And planned the holdup? It's possible." Commerty appeared unruffled by the suggestion of Army involvement. "We've probably got as many rogues and thieves as anybody else. Trouble is—I'd be your prime suspect if that were the case. I act on the requests for escorts." He leaned back and smiled. "And I'm not getting rich in this job. As for the men—no. Don't see them as having that much imagination. Besides, no one knows who's going to be on an escort detail or where they're going until we post the order."

"Got any ideas that could help me, Major?"

Commerty turned the question over in his mind. "We've had a slew of bank and gold robberies recently in Bannack, Virginia City, and now Bozeman. Whoever's behind them is clever. I would say they operate under some kind of legitimate cover. And they undoubtedly know about the gold shipments beforehand."

"Was there a very small man among the robbers?"

Commerty bellowed, "Sergeant! Get O'Reilly in here!"

Corporal O'Reilly shook hands with Slocum and beamed. "Good to see you again."

Commerty asked. "You two know each other?"

Heart in mouth. Slocum listened as the corporal related

the holdup and Slocum's part in freeing them. Relief flowed through him when it became obvious that O'Reilly had either forgotten his name or for some reason didn't mention it.

Slocum asked about the fake preacher.

The bandy-legged O'Reilly screwed up his leprechaun face in thought. Yes, there had been a wee man who'd shouted orders with a voice far too big for him. And yes, the leader did come off as a bit on the prissy side, come to think of it. Strange voice. Almost as if he were trying to disguise it.

Slocum told them about the Dougherty and the holdup, and his suspicion that a woman led the gang. When Commerty wondered where the Dougherty fitted in, he explained.

"Mr. Gramford figures they might use it to take the Bozeman Trail to North Dakota."

Commerty brightened with interest. "We'll keep an eye out for a Dougherty. You say the man in the carriage was disguised as a minister?"

"Yes. Meek-looking little guy. Sounds like the one Corporal O'Reilly saw."

The adjutant yelled. "Sergeant! Bring in those fliers we got the other day." The sergeant appeared and laid a file on the major's desk. To Slocum's relief, O'Reilly was dismissed.

"Take a look at these."

Commerty handed him three wanted posters. One had a drawing of a man described as Pilon Joe, five feet one inch tall, 120 pounds. He was wanted from Mexico to Montana. He had raped, then brutally carved up four women. He was also wanted for bank robbery, assault, and cattle rustling. He was mean, armed, and dangerous.

"He's the one," Slocum murmured.

Commerty grunted. "Reckon you can count yourself lucky he didn't kill you. For the fun of it."

Slocum's blood ran cold when he recalled the mean little eyes of the man on the wagon.

"Maybe a religious organization's what you're looking for, Deputy. Bible-thumpers. Got a slew of 'em out here. An easy way to separate yokels from their money. Glib tongues, promises of salvation, forgiveness of past sins." He chuckled and raised his hands. "Most everybody out here's got a passel of sins needing forgiving. And money to buy forgiveness with." He added, "Since this Pilon Joe was masquerading as a minister, thought it might tie in. Just a thought. How can I contact you if I hear anything?"

"I'll drop by. No telling where I'll be." He paused, then said, "Understand you're watching the river traffic."

"We're checking anything going east. They won't get by us. Not with that much gold."

"Couldn't the thieves simply melt it down and take it a bit at a time?"

"They could. But that would take too long. Don't believe they have that much time. The longer they hang about the area, the more chance they have of getting caught."

Slocum paused, then said, "These robberies. When did they begin?"

"Let's see." Commerty riffled through papers on his desk. "First was in Bannack two months ago, then in Alder Gulch, Nevada, Virginia City, and now Bozeman. If they're the same outlaws—and we believe they are—they appear to be moving generally from west to east. But, since there isn't much west of Bannack, we can't be sure there's a pattern. We do know there's a lot of wealth in the area between Bannack and Bozeman."

"Could they be working toward North Dakota?"

"That's a long way. The trail's closed. Nothing short of a company of cavalry would be safe covering the five hundred miles to Fort Lincoln." He shook his head. "No one in a wagon would stand much chance of making it. Outfits try shipping gold to Fort Lincoln, two or three men hauling it in a freighter. Maybe one out of three makes it. The Sioux and Cheyenne control the country.''

Commerty lowered his feet and sat up. ''Let me see that warrant again.''

Slocum put a foot on his uneasiness and presented the paper. Commerty studied it briefly, then said. ''You're a long way from home. Why're you interested in this area?''

''Because we had the same kind of robberies in the Hoodoos. Banks and gold shipments. We'd pursue the outlaws, run 'em into a box canyon, and—when we figured we had 'em cold—they'd vanished. Always left their horses as if they'd gone somewhere on foot. The horses, it turned out, were always stolen.'' He hesitated, uncertain how much he should tell Commerty. But, he figured, if he couldn't trust the Army . . .

''Something else. Don't know if it means anything, but we killed two lobos on the Palouse who'd murdered a couple of grubstakers and took their pokes. Before they died, they babbled about having belonged to a gang that flew. They must've done something to make the gang cut 'em loose because they said the gang deserted them. They kept talking about flying away after each robbery. And they mentioned a preacher. The preacher was apparently the leader. They said he'd marooned them.''

Commerty listened, but without conviction if his look of skepticism and disbelief was any sign.

''Those boys must've been drinking trade whiskey cured with locoweed.'' The major chuckled softly and shook his head. ''Don't figure this Pilon Joe's your man. He's too stupid to ramrod a bunch of road agents. And with his size, he'd stand out like a sore toe.''

Slocum thanked him and left. He figured it wouldn't be safe to use the badge and warrant at the Bridger's Rock town hall, which should know of any revival meetings going on nearby. The town was supposed to give permits, but given the looseness of local law and order, maybe not. However, he doubted if any local official would pass up the chance for a bribe. Against his better advice, he enlisted Hilda. He met her when school let out.

Waiting until the flood of screaming, shouting children abated, he took her books and gave her his arm.

She laughed. "The brats'll think I've got a beau."

He kissed her, which flustered her. "You do."

She scolded, "John! Don't do that in public! Someone might be watching."

"That's right. The school board won't let you have a beau either, will they. Do you have to get permission to visit the outhouse?"

"Oh, *really,* John!" She gave an exaggerated shudder. "If the school board discovers I'm a desperado's mistress, they'll tar and feather me. Like Caesar's wife, I'm supposed to be above reproach."

"Need you to help me."

"Might've known you wanted something—you carrying my books and all."

"Can you find out at the town hall if there's any revival meetings going on?"

She stopped cold and turned to him, suspicion clouding her face. "Why? You hankering to be saved?"

"Something like that."

Her eyes narrowed. "John. What's going on? And don't give me that pap about wrangling horses. I know wrangling. If you were breaking horses, I'd see the bruises on you— and you don't have any."

"Knew I should've kept my nightshirt on in bed."

"Why? You won't let me keep mine on." A blush diffused her cheeks and throat. "Fair's fair." She sobered a little. "Saw your scars, though. That one on your belly—"

"Breed tried to gut me once. In Soccorro."

"He still alive?"

"Nope."

"And that wound on your chest?" Her hand came up in the gentle way she had to touch him there.

"Yankee pistol ball. Spring of '65, it was. Lawrence, Kansas. Collapsed a lung. Damn wound took a long time healing."

"You've been around," she murmured, her voice holding a faint tremor.

"Yup. Lots of miles on me." He hesitated. He didn't want to put her in danger, and the more people who knew about the missing gold and that he was hunting for it, the more desperate the thieves were likely to become. But he needed her help. As schoolmistress, she was in a position to corral information. Taking a deep breath, he told her everything.

"Makes sense," she murmured when he finished. "Especially, the part about a woman being the leader. Noticed that myself. Not the voice, but her solicitude for my being a woman."

"Can you help me?"

She frowned in thought. "Could ask for my students. Claim they wanted a little religion in their lives. Horace would probably know." She nodded and gave his arm an affectionate squeeze. "See what I can find out."

"Tonight clear?"

"Suzie Stevens is coming for tutoring from seven till eight-thirty. Be at the back door at nine." She grinned. "I'll have the crib ready." She held out her palm. "Five dollars gold in advance. Pony up!"

"You got a deal." He fished a gold piece out of his vest and laid it in her hand. "You better be worth it."

"Satisfaction guaranteed. See you tonight."

Shortly after nine, he lay with her in her big bed. She straddled his hips, bending forward and swaying her torso to let him try to catch her nipples with his lips.

She said. "There's four groups of revivalists working the area. Two have permits. *Ouch! That hurt!* You've got lips that would do a woodpecker credit, John Slocum! Where was I? Two religious outfits apparently paid off the town council."

"Where're they located?"

"One's at a settlement ten miles north of here called Penntown. Another's south, ten miles. Small settlement there. Those two would appear to be on the up-and-up. Not enough money among the small crowds the revivalists are drawing to be worth a fleecing operation.

There's two big evangelist outfits in town. One belongs to the Reverend Mr. George Sharker—tents, lots of help. Better than any gold mine, according to the clerk I talked to. Holds torchlight revivals every night with lots of bible-thumping, brimstone and hellfire, and hat-passing."

"And the other one?"

"More like a traveling sideshow from what I'm told. The holy man's Theodore Grace. Has a female assistant named Mary. Poses as Grace's wife but don't think she is." She pulled her head up and grinned. "How's that for detective work?"

"Sounds promising."

"If you go snooping around, they might recognize you. John."

"I'll be careful."

The next morning at breakfast he found three silver dollars by his plate with a note that read. "Charge my friends only two dollars. Your food is warming in the oven." He grinned, pocketed the money, and settled back with a cup of coffee.

That afternoon, he rode to Penntown where the minister, Brother George Strumpf, held his revival meeting at the end of the town's short street. On it Slocum counted five buildings, all run-down as if they'd seen better days—a saloon, a restaurant, a fleabag, a stable, and a warehouse. What the warehouse held was a guess. Its double doors stood open. He rode up and peered inside at its empty vastness. Sunlight peeped through holes in the roof. The interior's musty smell of manure, rotted flesh, and mice hit him.

He decided it must've been used to store buffalo hides at one time, but now served no purpose. No Dougherty stood there.

He stayed for the preacher's sermon. The man's interest seemed focused on saving souls and not filling his pockets with money. A gentle, quiet man, he looked poor and shabby enough himself. Slocum left five dollars in the hat and left.

The next day, he visited Brother Sharker's huge tent, which a work gang was striking and loading onto wagons. He wandered about, but saw no one who looked suspicious. A roustabout informed him they were heading for Bannack.

A stab of irrational disappointment hit him. Sharker's move west could destroy his theory that the robbers were moving east as they cleaned out every bank and gold outfit before heading for North Dakota. Of course he could be wrong.

Sharker was big, magnificently mustachioed, and resembled a Mexican bandit more than an evangelist. His laugh was the booming, hearty laugh of the humorless man. He and his group, he said, were saving souls in the Bannack, Virginia City, Bozeman, and Bridger's Rock area, and hoped to return to St. Louis via steamboat when the tares had been gathered and burned and the wheat ready for the harvest. Slocum was welcome to attend the next meeting.

As he followed the wagon train to Bozeman to make sure they were heading for Virginia City, he felt someone was watching him. Twice, he hung back, hoping to surprise anyone tailing him. But he saw no one.

14

Main Street in Bozeman boasted a new, two-story brick building with an arched facade below and semi-arched windows with fancy stone lintels above. It held a number of businesses, including a barbershop, where Slocum got a shave and haircut. Later, he sipped a beer in the Prosperous Dollar Saloon.

Cowhands, miners, and farm laborers crowded the place. Three tables accommodated faro games in noisy progress. He was sipping his beer and idly studying the customers, when the doors swung open and two men stood silhouetted against the afternoon light.

He was instantly alert when the two surveyed the crowded saloon as if looking for someone. The noise died. The doors closed, and the men approached the bar. The only sound was the ominous clink of their spurs. The way they elbowed their way up to the brass rail spelled trouble. The barkeep, a fat man wearing a white shirt and red galouses, wiped a beer glass clean and asked warily, "What'll it be, gents?"

"Whiskey. An' don' make it the house slop."

Both were rough cobs. The only clean parts of them were their Colts slung low on their hips. Their gunbelts were fancy tooled leather bossed with Mexican silver. One was tall and bearded: the other, short and thin, wore stubble. Both had long hair. That alerted him. He doubted the inside of a territorial prison was a mystery to them. The crowd at the bar, smelling calamity, drifted away. Even the faro games came to a halt. The newcomers had gunslick written on them in big letters. Sullen and mean-looking, they toyed with their whiskey. Slocum eased the hammer thong from his .44.

The tall man spoke, his voice a gravelly growl. "You the fella what's bin askin' questions 'roun'?" He didn't look at Slocum.

"You talking to me?" Slocum stomped down his apprehension.

"Don't see nobody else standin' here. Do you, Barro?" Barro shook his head and put his glass down.

"Hear tell ye're a backshootin' judge-killer. Thet right?" The bearded man put both hands on the bar and peered over at Slocum.

"Reckon you got me mixed up with somebody else, friend." Now where in the hell did he hear that, he wondered.

"You ain't a white-livered Rebel dog then?" The saloon was suddenly silent as a tomb.

Slocum picked up his glass of whiskey with his left hand, his right thumb hooked in his gunbelt. "Tell me. Who hired you to brace me?"

The flicker in the men's eyes told him he'd struck paydirt. The barkeep came alive. "Don't want no trouble in here. You got a quarrel—take it outside."

The shorter man flared, "Hobble yer mouth, sonny—"

The two stared into the barrel of a cut-down Greener tengauge that appeared from under the bar. The barkeep cocked the twin hammers. "Like I said—this is a peaceable establishment. Hang your honk outside. Will?" He nodded to the boy serving drinks. "Get the marshal!" Will ske-daddled out the door.

The gunmen glowered, threw their drinks back into their throats, slapped a half dollar on the polished wood, and sauntered out. A sigh of relief went up from the few customers, and the noise soon returned to normal.

"Who were they?" the barkeep asked as he refilled Slocum's glass.

"Dunno," he replied, tossing down the whiskey. He laid a dollar on the bar. "Reckon I'll find out soon, wouldn't you bet?" He managed a grin he didn't feel and left.

He thought about the two. They'd appeared to be down on their luck. Maybe the depression, maybe because a man on the right side of the law thought twice before hiring ex-convicts. On the dodge and desperate, they'd been willing bait for someone wanting him dead and willing to hire killers to do it.

Who'd want him out of the way? Bannack's marshal? No. He'd want the reward. Sharker? Sharker's outfit was pulling out. The Reverend Mr. Grace?

He half expected to be backshot when he hit the sunlight. He took the gunman's sidewalk—the middle of the street—and watched for anything unusual from the corners of his eyes.

People, horses, and wagons crowded the dusty thoroughfare, making it easy for an assassin to lose himself. Slocum made a show of climbing into the kack and riding in the center of the street. He wanted whoever might be watching him to see him riding north out of town. As he rode through the street, he saw the tall figure of the man in black who'd been with Gramford in the hotel. He lounged against the side of the Special Saloon, a cheroot clamped between his teeth, and watched Slocum, his face twisted in a grin that never got to his eyes.

Slocum dismissed the man and concentrated on the situation at hand. If the gunslingers were after him, they would no doubt follow him. He would make it easy for them. It was getting dark, and he was still a long way from home.

On the ride north, the wind picked up. To his left, the Gallatin glittered under the dingy moon. When it became so dark he couldn't see his hand in front of him, it was time to camp and wait for light. It wasn't safe to keep moving. The river had left him to flow west. He was now riding a creek. He found a small clearing, hobbled his horse to let it graze, and made a fire. Getting water from the stream, he fixed coffee, all the while sensing something was wrong. He could smell it.

He sat by the flames, tensed, every muscle waiting for the slam of a bullet in the back. It took all his nerve to sit quietly, knowing death stalked his fire like a cougar on the prod. His Winchester lay by his side.

When the fire had burned itself into embers, he arranged his bedroll and put his hat where his head would be. Taking his rifle, he edged quietly into the brush under a stand of cottonwoods and alders—and waited. He got between the road and his campfire, which threw out a faint glow. His horse's nervous nickering and the shouting silence confirmed his fears. Someone was out there. He waited, every nerve, every muscle tense.

The sound of heavy footsteps trying to pick their way in silence through the underbrush pumped fire into his veins. He held his Winchester's action under his coat to deaden the sound as he eased back the hammer. Judging from the sound, two men were walking and being clumsy as hell about it in the dark.

A muffled curse. "Goddamn—"

"Hobble yer mouth!"

He waited for their shouted "Hallo, the fire!" but the greeting didn't come. Instead, he heard muted voices no more than ten feet from him.

"Red?" A harsh whisper.

"Yeah."

"There he be. Asleep."

"Yeah. Like a baby." The metallic click of a hammer being drawn.

"Let's get him!"

"Move in closer. Don't wanta miss. Can't see shit in this black."

"We're gonna have to take back proof we got him."

"Whatcha figger on doin'? Takin' back the body? Hell! Take his wippin'."

"An' his badge. They won't pay us if we can't prove it's him."

"His scalp'll do it. He ain't stirred. Close enough. Let him have it!"

Forty-fives flared the night in orange flame. Shots cracked. Slocum watched his hat whisked away from the bedroll. Others tore the bedding to shreds. Then silence. The acrid stench of gunsmoke burned his nostrils. He was behind the two. He stood.

"Evening, boys!"

A startled hiss of surprise. The two whirled and fired, but he had them silhouetted between him and the glow of the embers. His Winchester bucked in his hands as he levered with maddening speed. Forty-fours knocked the two sprawling in bloody heaps. A yelp of pain, the dying echoes of the five shots, a groan—then silence. He drew his Colt, waited, then edged toward the two bodies. He kicked their pistols away, then moved back into the darkness to wait. He assumed there were only two—but he could be wrong. Dead wrong. Trouble was, the darkness made it impossible to move. He'd have to wait till morning.

He sat, stiff and cold, his back to a tree, and fought to stay awake. He reloaded the Winchester from his belt. Temptation to approach his plunder bag and take out the bottle of whiskey almost made him break from cover.

He recalled the times in the war when he'd lain wounded on the battlefield and faked death so the Yankee looters wouldn't finish him off. He wondered how many dead

Yanks he'd looted who were only playing dead. The memories made him shiver.

He thought of springtime, a good horse under him, another packing his plunder, new boots, food—and good whiskey. He licked his lips, stilled his fears—and felt his scars. It was odd how they ached at times like these. He hungered for Hilda's warmth and her unbridled, eager desire for him.

She was a good woman. A born teacher, the kind kids never forgot. He still had trouble matching the prim, proper, no-nonsense schoolmarm who made her students toe the line, with the woman whose gluttonous passion drained everything from him in wild abandon. She was damn good. Someone he could depend on. And she was just as good out of bed as in, a happy, jolly, loving woman, interesting to talk to and a fountain of information. Guilt stabbed him as he realized she deserved a heap more than the little he could give her.

He recalled how she'd coaxed him to Sunday services. He had to admit she could make the ancient organ sit up and sing. When she introduced him to Amanda Brockwhite, the woman stared icily at him, then at Hilda. He could almost hear her thinking, "You Mrs. Hasso, are not supposed to know any man well enough to introduce him to anyone." Hilda had explained, "Mrs. Brockwhite is on the school board." That might be so, but he hadn't cottoned to the woman despite her being an attractive female. There was something about her. . . .

Dawn at last burned the horizon, the hills slowly flaming. The cold had him numb and stiff. If someone else was backing the two lying dead by the smoking remains of his fire, he would have trouble handling his Winchester. He didn't dare check to see how many rounds he had left in his yellowbelly. The noise might alert whoever was out there. Its magazine held eight rounds. He'd fired five. He couldn't remember if he'd loaded it fully. He should've known. He remembered then that he'd reloaded after firing.

His life could well depend on it. The dingy light showed his horse grazing. He waited, motionless. The slightest movement, and whoever might be out there would have him cold.

But the more he thought about it, the more he doubted the two had had backup. The awkward way they'd stumbled noisily into his bivouac had said they were gunslicks. But then, it amazed him they'd managed to track him in the inky blackness of the night as quietly as they had. He wondered who was paying the two to drygulch him. The man in black? He'd watched Slocum ride out.

Slocum moved with stealth toward the road, keeping to the trees. Nothing. Then he saw the two horses, hobbled. His danger sense no longer prodding him, he partially relaxed.

He went back, smothered his fire, and examined the dead men. Their pockets contained makings and a few coins, but nothing that tied them to being hired killers. Pulling back their hair, he found—as he expected—cropped ears. The two had served time in prison. He took their rigs—a .45 Colt and a .44 Remington, two Henry rifles—and left them for the coyotes. He picked up the two horses and rode out.

He halted by the river to water the horses and survey the surrounding area. He didn't look straight at an object; he looked from the periphery of his vision. That was when objects that shouldn't be there popped out. Again, nothing unusual.

It was noon when he rode into Bridger's Rock, cobwebs in his brain from no sleep, feet hanging loose from the stirrups, riding with the knees. The two horses of the dead men were strung out behind him. He decided not to tell Hilda about the attempt on his life. She had enough on her mind running her school.

Distant gunfire, shots popping like firecrackers, shattered the morning quiet and snapped him out of his languor. He pulled back on the reins when six masked riders thundered down Main Street and hurtled by him, guns blazing at the sky. People on the street scurried to get out of the way.

He necked up his horses and yanked the gray aside to keep from being run down. A teamster with a wagon load of hay tried to steer his terrified team off the road, only to have the wagon hit a watering trough and tip over. Bales of hay broke and scattered, yellow dust making a smoke screen.

Slocum hesitated, exhaustion momentarily braking his reaction, then quickly recovered. He tied the reins of the two horses around a hitching post and pulled his horse about. Digging in the spurs, he galloped after the fleeing outlaws. For six miles, he followed them north through a narrow valley with a creek running along its west side. Looking over his shoulder, he thought he saw dust, but it was a long way behind him. A posse in pursuit probably. He hung back. He didn't want to get close enough for the outlaws to spot him.

The valley east of the Gallatin River gradually broadened into a rolling plain before butting up against the hills forming Bridger Range that humped dark and massive to the east.

When they approached the mountains, the outlaws slowed to a trot. Slocum kept off the trail and stayed a quarter of a mile behind them. Two riders dropped off and stood just off the trail at the entrance to a canyon, rifles ready to stop pursuers.

Puzzled, Slocum worked his way toward the high ground to his left. When it was obvious he couldn't maneuver his horse onto the steep, heavily treed hill without being seen, he dismounted and tethered the animal. He kept the two outlaws in sight as he climbed and worked his way north up the slope until he reached the peak. Panting from the exertion, he stopped and peered.

Across a narrow, steep valley stood a needlelike pinnacle and a higher hill. In the valley, or gully, between them was another peak. Except that this peak was round—spherical— and moved—or rather, wavered. He rubbed his eyes and peered again, unable to fully take in what he was seeing.

15

The sphere was a huge ball more than 120 feet high, its sides and top painted a crazy quiltwork pattern of greens, blacks, blues, and yellows, which made it difficult at first glance to establish its exact shape. The underside was painted blue-green. Looking closer, he saw a maze of netting covering the top and sides, and tapering to a point below the ball to support a huge round basket.

"My God!" he muttered aloud. "It's a balloon!"

The shape resembled a huge turnip, the underside tapering down to an opening. With a start, he recalled Hilda's insistence she'd seen something resembling an upside-down chemical flask. Zeke's and Bead's puzzling reference to flying now made sense.

The outlaws had ridden into the narrow clearing and dismounted. They threw the four bags they carried into the basket and climbed in. A gunshot, and the men guarding the road left their posts and galloped up. Sliding out of the saddle, they went to where several ropes anchored the contraption to the ground. He heard voices, but since the men were probably three hundred yards away, he couldn't make out words. The crew untied the ropes, then scrambled into the huge basket. Two people—probably the crew—were shouting orders. Using his glasses, Slocum studied the contraption more closely.

A metal column whose base rested on a tripod four feet off the basket's deck rose inside the balloon's mouth. He was too far away to make out the faces of the outlaws. When they removed their dusters, he thought one of them was too slim and shapely to be a man, but he couldn't be sure.

A faint red glow inside the column turned a bright blue when two men spun wheels on opposite sides of the column. The balloon lifted slowly, ropes trailing, the bluish fire roaring. As the huge sphere rose eye level with him, he saw that the basket was probably twelve feet in diameter, made of metal, and contained a furnace that forced hot air up and into the giant mouth at the balloon's bottom. The gang—he counted eight—stood around the rail, laughing, joking, and watching the ground below them. The contraption rose, cleared the ridge, and floated north in eerie silence through the north-south Blackfoot Pass to become lost among rows of peaks.

Slocum sat back to let his amazement subside. Below him to his right, a posse thundered into the canyon. He watched as they rode by the trail leading to where the balloon had been tethered two minutes earlier. It amazed him that no one in the posse had seen it, but like hounds with their noses to the ground, they were too busy studying the ground for tracks.

The posse was soon back. The marshal hollered to the others to join him. They swung their horses about and thundered into the clearing where the balloon had been tethered to find six saddled horses grazing in placid unconcern. He watched the posse's perplexed search, their confusion when they found no robbers, then the ride back, the six riderless horses strung out behind them. He saw their defeat and perplexity in the disheartened, angry way they rode, digging in their spurs, faces grim, shoulders slumped.

He thought of joining them, but instantly discarded the idea. In their frustration, they were likely to arrest him— even hang him on the spot, a favorite pastime in Montana's vigilante approach to the law.

"A balloon," he muttered again. "I'll be damned! That explains how the robberies were done. All the way from California. Probably the answer to the disappearance of Gramford's gold."

Could a balloon, he wondered, lift an object as heavy as a Dougherty ambulance that weighed nearly a ton? It had presumably lifted Gramford's 2,300-pound shipment. The robbers had to have a camp somewhere, he reasoned.

He recalled how the Union Army had used balloons filled with hydrogen to spot troop movements and observe artillery fire during the war. He also remembered they'd had to anchor them to the ground because there was no way to control their flight. Wondering how these balloonists controlled theirs, he stared north, hoping to see the sphere, but it was gone. Its piebald colors would make it hard to spot against foliage. And who would ever think of searching the clouds to find bank robbers?

He waited until the posse was out of sight, then retrieved his horse and rode into the opening. Dismounting, he searched it for some clue to the balloonists' identity. At the edge of the clearing, he found two large casks. Sniffing them, he smelled coal oil. He found no markings that might give a clue to where the balloonists had bought the fuel. Kerosene, then, fired the furnace used to heat the air. He rode back to Bridger's Rock, satisfied he had at least part of the answer to the puzzle.

When he stopped at Kate's Cafe to get breakfast, the room buzzed with talk of the robbery.

"Ya hear? Hayes Shipping Office was robbed this morning."

"How much they git this time?"

"Nigh unto two thousand dollars, hear tell."

"That's the second holdup this last month."

"Catch 'em?"

"Naw. Ned says they got clean away. Like last time. Disappeared into thin air."

"Gotta git the vigilantes back. They'd kitch 'em."

"An' string 'em up good!"

"Now ye're a-talkin'!"

That night, he and Hilda went to the river to bathe. After cavorting about in the water, they lay in each other's arms on a blanket and talked.

"You were right," he murmured, his chest rising and falling.

"Right about what?" She yawned and traced her fingers over his chest.

"That you saw something that day on the trail. When you saw something big and round."

"No, darling—it's *long*—and big and round." Her fingers scoured his limp erection.

"Be serious! You won't believe what I saw."

She sat up and looked down at him. "What?"

"If you'll stop snickering, I'll tell you."

"All right! I've stopped. What did you see?"

He told her his adventure that afternoon.

She gasped, "A—a *balloon*!"

"A balloon. Bigger than a tall building. Bigger than *two* tall buildings! These robberies are starting to make sense, Hilda. The only mystery is how they steer the damn thing."

"They can't, John. There's no way they could counteract the wind. Not with something that size. It's a huge sail."

It all came to him in a flash. He gave a bark of laughter.

"Sweetheart, what direction does the wind usually blow here?"

It was her turn to laugh. "You mean all the time you've been leaning against it, you don't know?"

"West to east?"

"Yes. The wind almost always blows from west to east."

He lay back with a thump. "Hilda—the robberies occurred first in California, then in the Hoodoos. A couple of months ago, they occurred in Bannack, Alder Gulch, then in Virginia City. Then Bozeman. Now here. Same pattern. A bank holdup, a gold shipment stolen, the robbers always fleeing east. They abandon their horses—and simply disappear. When the posse arrives, they find only the horses. But no robbers. The robbers are in that big basket."

"Gondola. It's called a gondola."

"Okay, Miss Schoolmarm—gondola." He turned on his side and kissed her. "Now I know how they do it. A balloon. You're right about the wind. That's why the robberies are done west to east. So they can use the balloon and the main air current. They rob a bank or a gold shipment and ride to a secluded canyon. The balloon's waiting for them. They get in, fly away, and come down miles from the posse. They deflate the balloon, load it on wagons—and no one's the wiser."

She said, "Then they hit the next town east. John, if they've stolen that much, they must have it hidden somewhere."

"Yeah. Probably figure to pick the area dry. They could do it in a balloon."

She ran her fingers absently over his belly, tugging the mat of hair, entwining her fingers in it. "You know, John, if they plan to go east with their loot, they could be planning to fly. Makes sense. They could ship the gold east by rail, no questions asked."

"Hilda. It's over five hundred miles to Fort Lincoln. Through hostile Indian territory. Could they fly that far?"

"They'd need to refuel along the way." She was silent for a moment. "You know—maybe that's why they stole the Dougherty. It could carry enough riflemen to fight off Indians and enough supplies to keep the balloon aloft."

"That's it! You know, sweetheart, you are one very smart lady."

"I'm also one helluva good lay. Or so you keep telling me."

He gathered her to him. "You're that too. But you're smart, which may be even better."

The next day, he visited Grace's outfit, which had come from Bozeman to Bridger's Rock. Two big tents stood just outside town in a field. Wagons were lined up neatly, the animals grazing in the nearby field. Seeing nobody about, he entered one of the tents. The canvas swayed slightly in the breeze, the four big poles moving like masts of a ship under the pull of the canvas, the tent rigging creaking. Wood planks set on boxes made up rows of seats. There was plenty of standing room on the sides and in the rear. A garish altar stood in front flanked by two tall brass columns that supported lanterns. No bibles or hymnals were laid out on the benches.

"Can I help you?"

He spun about at the sound of the female voice. A tall woman wearing a long orange robe stood at the entrance. She approached him.

"Heard about your meetings. Wanted to see what you've got." He made a show of gazing around him. "Doesn't look like any bible-thumping bunch I'm used to."

"That's probably because we don't thump bibles." The woman's cool voice held a note of refinement that most women on the frontier didn't have. He tried to determine if it sounded familiar.

"What kind of religion you flog here?"

"The Truth of the Lotus."

He grinned. "Opium, eh? You run an opium den? In the open?"

She ignored his attempt at humor. "Our lotus represents the truth within that flowers when it's properly nurtured."

"I see. Can I attend one of your meetings?"

She bowed slightly. "If you wish. This evening at seven."

"I'll be there." He hesitated, then asked, "Are you Brother Grace's assistant?"

"No." She studied him with interest, a faint annoyance clouding her face. "I'm his wife."

"I'm John Slocum. You are . . . ?" He waited expectantly.

She hesitated, then replied, "Mary Grace."

"Pleased to make your acquaintance, ma'am. Try to make it tonight."

"We'll look for you, Mr. Slocum."

When she walked away from him, he studied her. She was slim and regal and her hair, what he could see of it peeking under the hood, was dark. Her eyes were also dark. He remembered then that she had been the woman handing out the fliers the day Grace's outfit came to Bozeman. She could be the woman leading the road agents, he thought as he walked outside and eyed the other tent. It was plenty big enough to hide a Dougherty, but it was more likely the living quarters for the outfit.

As he rode back to town, his danger sense hammered slowly at the base of his skull. Convinced someone was trailing him, he pulled his horse off the road and waited. When no one appeared he rode on, uneasiness making his back an itching target.

He decided to ride to Virginia City to inform Gramford what he'd learned. Knowing he'd be away from Hilda for a week, he took her long and hard in bed that night, bringing her to orgasm six times with tongue and cock.

"Got to tell Gramford. He's gone back to Virginia City to check his operation there."

"I know." She kissed him with a sigh. "I'll keep the bed warm for you. And be careful!"

He knew by her tone she expected him to ride out of her life. He had no intention of doing so—not yet, anyway. But neither could he let her believe she'd succeeded in throwing her rope over him.

He left early the next morning and three days later sat

in Gramford's office. The mine owner, mouth wrapped around a Havana, eyes fixed on his desk top, listened to his story.

"So *that's* it. Since they tried to kill you, they must think you're closer to the truth than they're comfortable with. What do we do, John?"

"They have to deflate that balloon to haul it around. They can't steer the damn thing. Not for any great distance."

"So, they depend on wind currents."

"Yes. And a lot of big wagons to haul the contraption. They inflate it when they plan a robbery, use the wind current, pick up the robbers east of the holdup, then float off."

"They wouldn't have horses waiting when they descend. And they'd need horses."

"Imagine you can bring a balloon down anywhere you want to. Just stop feeding it hot air. They could land where their hideout is. Figure they keep a band of horses with 'em. Hilda thinks they figure to float their loot all the way to North Dakota."

"If we telegraph the Army at Fort Lincoln . . ."

Slocum shook his head. "Finding a balloon on that prairie would be like finding a rowboat on the Atlantic Ocean. Yours isn't the only gold they've stolen. If they've been hitting gold camps from California to Idaho to Montana, then they have a bodacious amount of loot. If they plan to carry it, they'll have to keep the weight down, which means a small crew—maybe two—with the rest of the gang in the Dougherty and wagons carrying supplies. They can't land near Fort Lincoln—the Army would be looking for them. I figure they'll rendezvous with a boat on the Missouri and head for an outpost near Fort Lincoln. Place the soldiers call The Point. Saloons, whore houses, the like. The Northern Pacific's end of track is there to take them and their loot east."

"What do you know about balloons, John?"

"Not much."

"The gang would need wagons—big ones—to haul the balloon and gondola. A traveling circus would be the perfect cover."

"Or a traveling revivalist outfit. I killed two men in Idaho when they tried to drygulch me. The talked about flying—and about 'the preacher' and how he'd marooned them there. Didn't make sense at the time. But it does now."

Gramford replied, "They must have someone who knows balloons. And meteorology. The science of weather. Someone who could forecast weather and plot winds and their direction."

"There are such people?"

"The science of synoptic meteorology is well advanced—yes. Networks of weather-observing stations exist over much of the world. They're used in preparing daily weather maps. Just last year, an international conference on meteorology was held in Vienna to promote the exchange of weather information via telegraph. A great boon to shipping."

"Or to a balloonist turned outlaw."

"John, you're on to something."

"Got to find their hideout first."

"Don't want you getting yourself killed, boy."

"You're paying me to find your gold. That's what I aim to do."

"What do you want *me* to do?"

"Move to Bridger's Rock for a spell. That appears to be their center of operations for the moment."

"Good! I'll ride back with you. Must tell my foreman I'll be gone. Be ready to ride at noon."

They had ridden only a short distance out of town when they met a caravan of wagons. Slocum recognized the Reverend Mr. Sharker at the head. The heavyset Sharker, clad in black riding clothes, waved and approached them. As his caravan rumbled by, he reined in his horse.

"Howdy, Reverend," Slocum said.

Sharker peered at him over his horse's head. "Ah! Mr.—ah, Slocum, I believe. Yes. We met in Bridger's Rock."

"This here's Mr. William Gramford of Virginia City."

Sharker reached his hand to shake the mine owner's. "My pleasure, sir."

Slocum said, "Heard tell you were moving out, Reverend."

"Yes. To Bannack City. A Sodom and Gomorrah." Sharker gave his leonine head a dismal shake and clucked his tongue. "The Lord has called us to go there." His face brightened as he produced two fliers from his coat pocket. "If the harvest demands workers and the Lord gives us the word, we may stop over in this fair city. You're invited to attend our revival if we decide to hold one here." He touched his hat and said, "Good day, gentlemen. Godspeed!" He rode off to join his troupe.

Slocum watched the big Studebakers with their four-span of mules clatter down the trail. "Takes a big wagon to haul one of their tents."

"If they are tents."

He stared at his companion. "A balloon?"

"A balloon is made of a fabric lighter and less coarse than canvas. When I was in the Union Army, I saw one. Felt the material. A light silk covered with varnish of some sort. Colonel—then General—Custer rode in one. Quite an experience. But—yes! I imagine a wagon large enough to haul a big tent could haul a balloon." He turned in the saddle and stared at the retreating wagons. "We must determine if that evangelist outfit is carrying one."

"Maybe there's a quicker way, Bill. You got any influence in Washington?"

"A little. Why?"

"Since both Sharker and Grace have the wherewithal to haul big tents, and since both are preachers, maybe we should check them. If you could get information about them, it might help."

"Got contacts in the Treasury Department's Bureau of the Mint. Used their services before. Give me the details, and I'll telegraph them."

When they rode into Bozeman the next day, Slocum took Gramford to the telegraph office, where he sent his inquiries to Washington. They then rode to Bridger's Rock and arrived that evening.

16

Hilda wasn't expecting company. When Slocum entered the house with Gramford, she was momentarily too flustered to say or do anything. She shot him a look of pure venom, then quickly composed herself to graciously welcome the mine owner into her home. If the obvious relationship between him and the schoolmistress shocked Gramford, he kept it hidden. She prepared a delicious meal as if atoning for living in sin with a man.

While they ate and talked, Slocum had to smile. Gramford apparently found nothing unusual in Slocum taking his pleasure where he found it. His look, however, said that he hadn't expected the schoolmistress to provide that pleasure. With no condemnation and censure evident in his expression and tone of voice, he studied her with more than ordinary interest.

He's wondering what the school twisters would do if they learned the truth, Slocum thought. If they discovered the woman they entrusted their offspring to wasn't the respectable woman they thought she was. If they learned the woman preparing their children to meet the evils of the world and setting an example of proper behavior for them slept each night in the arms of a man not her husband, they would run her out of town. Or stone her in the public square. Judging from Gramford's look, her guest found the situation both amusing and fascinating.

Apparently, he also found Mrs. Hasso fascinating in her own right. She was by nature a happy, friendly woman, witty and fun to be with, but she was also well educated. Slocum realized they had squeezed him out of their conversation, not intentionally, but because they discussed subjects beyond his limited education. They were deep into something called *The Critique of Pure Reason*, by someone named Immanuel Kant, which made little sense to him. He knew that Gramford, a mining engineer, was an educated man, but he hadn't thought of Hilda as an educated woman. He realized with a jolt how little he really knew about her. She was easy to get along with, and that belied her sharp, incisive intelligence. He wondered if she deliberately played down that aspect of herself because of his lack of book-learning. If she did, he thought with anger, it would be the same as her faking it with him in bed. And he couldn't believe her response to him wasn't genuine.

Before Gramford left the house, he told him, "Hildegard agrees with me. We need to know as much about ballooning as we can. I telegraphed a friend of mine in Washington. Professor Thaddeus Lowe, an expert in the field, and asked him to send me any information he has."

"Will it get here in time?"

"He'll get it out on the next train. The information will go via Army Headquarters in Chicago to the Army commander at Fort Lincoln, Colonel George Armstrong Custer. Knew him during the war. He'll forward the information by boat to Fort Benton. Can depend on him. I'll have my man Angus MacTaggert waiting for it there. If everything goes as planned, we should have the information by July."

"That's a month away."

"Best we can do."

When he lay beside Hilda that night, jealousy hit him with surprising force, which surprised and troubled him. He'd always taken women as they came, enjoyed their sexual favors, then moved on. No strings attached. No remorse. Was he jealous of Gramford's attention? He frowned into the darkness.

Was the woman whose broad, shapely bottom was snuggled tight against his belly trying to fence him in? He'd warned her he was a drifter, but had she listened? He ran his hand over the swell of her hip down to the valley of her waist, then gently kneaded the satiny skin of her belly. He let his hand stray to the thick, silky bush at the yoke of her thighs.

She groaned and raised her thigh to let his fingers explore the warm wetness of her slit. His fingers found the nubbin cradled between her lips, and he gently worked it between thumb and forefinger.

She moved under his caress, gasping, hips slowly undulating, belly pushing out and in, pelvis grinding, the twin mounds of her big, firm rump shoving into him, then retreating. He worked his other hand under her and took a full, round breast in it, fingers working the nipple into a mound firm as a ripe grape.

Her body heaved and spasmed under his fondling, the bed creaking. Then, giving a low, gurgling cry, she orgasmed, her cunt pumping against the finger inserted in it, gripping, pulling, sucking.

He was sorry he had nothing left to respond with, but she had already drained him. Heaving a shuddering sigh, she turned her face over her shoulder to kiss him and murmur in a gentle scold, "John, go to sleep. Morning will be here before I know it, and I've a busy day ahead of me."

He had to laugh. She had been all over him the moment he'd climbed into bed, her sexual desire insatiable. He wondered. Was her cooking, her performance in bed, her making a home for him merely an attempt to drop her rope over him? He wasn't complaining, but he had to be careful before he became too deeply involved.

A week later, he met Gramford for lunch. "Got news," the mine owner muttered, excitement coloring his face. The cafe was crowded with miners, lumberjacks, and drovers, all eating, some with their fingers, others with some semblance of manners apparently carried over from better times. Gramford held up two papers.

"Replies from Washington. The Treasury people contacted the War Department. Get this." He put on his spectacles and read: "Grace, Theodore B., Captain, Balloon Corps, United States Army. Cashiered 1865 for bad debts. Speciality: aeronautics."

"What's that?"

"Aeronautics? Ballooning. His specialty was observation balloons. There's more. He wasn't cashiered because of debts. That was the official excuse used to obscure what really happened. Grace served under a general of artillery, a Bartell Lipton, who had a young wife. Got involved with her when he served under McClellan as a balloonist. They worked with Thaddeus Lowe, who organized the Union Army Balloon Corps. The woman was a trained—get this!—meteorologist and served in the Army as a civilian specialist. She and Grace worked together. She was the reason he left the Army. The general, her husband, caught them *in flagrante delicto*."

"Whoa!" Slocum laughed. "In English—please!"

"He was hiving her behind her husband's back."

"So they kicked him out?"

Gramford grinned and shook his head. "Not exactly. The general wanted a duel. He was deadly with either sword or pistol. Had Grace jailed to await either being hacked to pieces with a saber or shot at twenty paces. The general's honor was at stake and nothing would do but that he kill the man cuckolding him. The wife somehow freed her lover. They fled in an Army balloon. That was the last anyone ever saw of them."

"Did Washington know the name of the woman?"

"Mary Lipton."

"Grace has a female assistant. Tall and slender. Calls herself Sister Mary Grace. Figure she's his wife."

Gramford shook his head. "According to my contact, Mary Lipton never divorced her husband."

"Could be our man—and woman. If Sharker's on his way west, that takes him out of the picture."

"John, where's this gang's hideout?"

"Probably move it regularly. If they're moving east, then they must keep shifting it east. Easy to do in these mountains. Especially if they use the balloon to move their plunder. If they've been hitting mining camps, banks, and gold shipments all the way from California, then they must have a pile of loot. They've got to keep it somewhere."

Gramford murmured. "Wonder what the capacity of their balloon is"

"Hope your friend Lowe has the answer." He gave a dry chuckle. "Who'd expect an evangelist to be a bank robber?"

Gramford put a hand on his arm. "Be careful, John."

"Don't worry. I'll find 'em."

"I'll be staying at the Guy Hotel in Bozeman for a week. They've got a telegraph office there," he added by way of explanation. "If you need help, holler."

"Bill, I'd go easy on using that telegraph. If these people are as well organized as they appear to be, then they could have the telegrapher in their pocket."

The next day, Slocum reined in at the Bale of Hay Saloon and dismounted. The wind gusted with coat-flapping force to swirl dust devils in the road. His mouth felt brick-dry. He smelled the mouth-watering aroma of freshly baked bread coming from the Mechanical Bakery next door as he entered the saloon. In the cool, cavelike saloon, he threw back the first drink to clear his throat and carried a second to a table to enjoy. He pretended not to notice the man who'd been dogging him since he'd left Gramford the day before and who had followed him in.

When the tall, hard-eyed *charro* broke away from the bar and approached his table, Slocum eased the hammer thong from his Colt. The man was the same one he'd seen with Gramford in Bozeman, and later when he rode into the ambush the men he'd only known as Red and Barro had set up. He was feathered out in a black suit, boiled shirt, string tie, and good black boots. A fancy gold watch fob bisected the black vest. His Montana hat hid his face in shadow so that all Slocum got was a pattern of harsh, clean-shaven planes. The pearl grips of a .45 in a black, fancy-tooled rig emblazoned with silver hung stark against the black coat. Polished spurs chinked loudly.

Slocum watched the reactions of the rough cobs in the saloon to the stranger's entrance. If a man wanted a fight on his hands with no delay, all he had to do to was to show up dressed as this one was. The depression had everyone on the prod. Disgruntled miners, cowhands ready to sell their saddles, and hard-up honyokers, who hated anyone richer than they were, grumbled in threatening tones. A boiled shirt alone could get a man fitted for store-bought teeth. Add a fancy string tie and a suit of clothes with a good hand, and you could figure on being fitted for a pine box pronto if you ventured into a hellhole.

The high-loper looked about him, his coattail drawn back to free his gun. Eyes flat as a snake's challenged the crowd. Luckily, no one was stupid enough or drunk enough to put his bellicosity into his fists and cut up ugly. The man's arrogant grin remained on his heavy lips and never got to the cold eyes. His catlike movements with no wasted motion, the Colt, and the flint-hard eyes made him an undertaker's dream. Those glowering at him quickly hauled in their horns. Slocum figured death had a right to wear anything he wanted. The man approached Slocum's table in a loose, spur-chinking stride, wearing arrogance like a good suit of clothes.

"Mind if I set?" He stood legs apart, thumbs in his gun-belt. He had gunfighter written on him, but in different letters than the two who'd tried to bushwhack Slocum. Slocum wondered if the man had known Barro and Red. If he had hired them.

This one wouldn't be easy, he thought, and murmured, "Set! Don't own the place."

The stranger deftly pulled the chair out with his toe and sat. Glancing over his shoulder at the bar, he ordered. "Old Overholt. Bring the bottle." When the saloonist set it down with a glass, the stranger tossed three dollars on the table so that they rang. The man picked one up and examined it.

"What's wrong?" The stranger grinned. "Think it's one of those platinum counterfeits?"

The barkeep grunted, rang it against the table, and swept the rest of the coins into his palm.

"Keep the change, friend."

The man nodded and ambled back to the bar. The *charro* pushed back his hat to reveal a strong, coarsely handsome face. Slocum put his age at forty or so. His voice rumbled, "Name's Argus. James Argus. Pinkertons."

"Name's Slocum. John Slocum." He watched for the man's reaction. If he were a Pinkerton, he would know the name. Slocum figured he was right up there at the top of the Pinkertons' wanted list. To his surprise, Argus didn't respond, which put him on his guard.

"Hear tell you're a deputy out of Palouse Flats, Mr. Slocum." He frowned, then said, "By the way. Slipped my mind. Who's the lawman there?"

"Deputy Sheriff Hank Yetty." Slocum had the feeling he could've answered, "Andrew Jackson," and satisfied him. Argus, he figured, didn't know who Palouse Flats' lawman was and was testing him. "Where'd you hear I was a lawman?"

"Talked to the Army at Ellis. They mentioned you were hunting a missing gold shipment. Only, they said your han-dle was Bell." He poured from the bottle, raised it, and motioned toward Slocum's glass. Slocum nodded: Argus poured.

"That's right. Bell's the name I go by."

"Gramford's hoard, isn't it?" Argus raised his brow slightly, a curious smile touching his hard lips.

Slocum swallowed his annoyance at this inquisition. Better play along, play dumb, and maybe learn something, he thought. He sipped the whiskey and savored it. "Yeah. He's missing a shipment. Trying to locate it."

Argus toyed with his glass. "Aren't you out of your territory?"

"Gramford claims I saved him from being killed in a holdup outside Virginia City. He asked me to try to find his shipment."

"You saved his life?" Argus looked interested. "He's never mentioned it."

Slocum related the incident, finishing with; "That's how he came to hire me. I'm in no hurry to get back to Washington."

A slow, knowing smile creased Argus's face. "Can't blame you. Seen the schoolmistress. Good-looking woman."

Argus might as well have thrown the contents of a spittoon on him. Anger flooded him. So did his fear for Hilda. Blood drained from his face as he half-rose from his seat, his hand reaching for his gun butt. His voice was steel-spring tight when he said, "Now wait just a damn minute!"

Argus pulled a Havana from his coat pocket and lit it with a lucifer, his hard smile never leaving his face. "You rile easy."

"You're treading on my toes, friend."

"Maybe you're treading on mine." He studied the rich blue smoke.

Interested. Slocum asked. "How's that?"

"Bill Gramford's a friend of mine."

"He's also a friend of mine."

Argus puffed, then flicked ash onto the table. "Don't

want to see my friend hornswoggled by a confidence man.''

"Reckon you better talk a sight clearer.''

"You getting frothy?'' Argus calmly puffed his Havana. "I know all about you. Slocum. Got your dossier.''

"My what?''

"Your criminal history. Makes interesting reading.''

Slocum considered that for a moment. Something didn't ring true about the man. If he knew who John Slocum was, he would know he'd helped the Jameses rob a train. He would know about his killing of the carpetbagger judge. He would know about the fliers on him from a half-dozen territories. If he was a Pinkerton, he wouldn't waste time on auguring. He'd be trying to take him.

"Since you don't know the lawman in Palouse Flats, how do I know you're a Pinkerton?''

"Doesn't matter if you know or not. You're drifting. Back to Washington. Or wherever. Want you gone by tomorrow.''

Slocum threw his drink back in his throat and poured another. "Sounds like a threat.''

"Call it an ultimatum. The school twisters won't be happy to learn the schoolmistress is living with you.'' He looked up from puffing his Havana's tip into a glowing ember. His cold grin never wavered as he added. "Or—some other rather unpleasant facts about her.''

Uneasiness edged into him. "What other facts?''

"Some aspects of her life she's apparently never told you. Or the school board.''

Was there something she hadn't revealed to him? Probably plenty. Hell! He didn't know her that well. Aloud, he replied. "Whatever it is, it's her business. Not mine.''

"Let's hope the school board feels the same way.''

Slocum drew a tight rein on his anger. He needed to know what Argus was getting at. "What're you getting at?''

"No reason not to tell you. I'm under contract for the Department of the Treasury to find that stolen gold.''

"Does Gramford know this?"

Argus took his Havana from his mouth. "No. It's none of his concern. The government wants the gold."

"So—why are you threatening the schoolmarm? What's she got to do with this?"

Argus's icy control filled Slocum with foreboding when he replied. "She's your woman. I want you out of the picture. She's my way of controlling you."

"I don't understand."

"I want the reward. Don't want to share it."

That announcement surprised him. As far as he knew, there was no reward. Was Gramford dealing in secret with the Pinkertons? Unless the Pinkertons had some other reason, such as getting back the money stolen from the banks, why would they be operating without Gramford's knowledge? And how had Argus learned about him and Hilda? Slocum decided to play his hand close to the vest until he had all the facts.

"And if I don't disappear?"

"Then your woman'll be looking for new work." The *charro* sipped his whiskey, flicked the ash from his Havana, and grinned like a cardsharp holding a full house and with an extra ace up his sleeve as he added. "If the school twisters and the town don't tar'n feather her first. And maybe you along with her." He studied his cigar, his self-assured smile never faltering.

"Hear you're fast, Slocum."

"Didn't hear it from anyone who ever tried me."

"Too bad you're leaving town. I'd enjoy killing you."

Slocum had to forcibly keep his hands in his lap. He wanted to yank Argus across the table and whipsaw the truth out of him, but he couldn't afford to endanger Hilda. He rifled through his mind for alternatives but found none—unless he killed the man.

But that posed a problem. If he killed a Pinkerton operative, he would have the entire agency hounding him forever. And they would know he shot Argus. He would have to play along. It occurred to him to bow to Argus's threat, but if he did, Argus might wonder why he'd caved in so easily. If he knew Slocum's reputation, he would know better. Besides, Slocum had to protect Hilda.

He pushed back his chair and stood. Looking down at Argus, he ground out his words in a low, steady voice. "I sure as hell don't take to you threatening the woman. She has nothing to do with any of this. Any harm comes to her—and you'll more'n get that chance to try to kill me." With that, he turned and walked out.

17

The next morning, Gramford looked up from his desk in surprise to find Slocum standing before him. The mine owner now had a temporary office over the bank in Bridger's Rock. Sinking into a chair, Slocum demanded, "Know a Jim Argus?"

Gramford nodded. "Yes. He's a Pinkerton operative. Wanted me to hire him on the side to be in charge of my security. When I insisted on telegraphing the Pinkerton office in Chicago to verify him, he left. Didn't trust him. Why?"

"Had a talk with him yesterday. Claims he's working for the government to recover your shipment."

Gramford snorted his disbelief. "News to me. What did he say?"

"Warned me to get out of town. Says it won't be good for Hildegard if I don't."

Gramford leaned forward, his body tense, his expression registering bewilderment. "He threatened Hildegard? Why?"

"He wants the reward he claims the government's paying for the gold. Doesn't want me interfering.''

''You figure he's mixed up in this? The marshal at Bannack said something about him shooting a miner over a card game. A bad hombre.''

''If he is in on the robbery that could account for his threat. I must be getting too close to something.''

''Anyone else know about the balloon?''

''Hildegard.''

Gramford set a bottle on the desk and poured two glasses. Slocum nodded and took one. Gramford said, ''We can find out about this Argus quickly enough. I'll send a telegram—''

''Don't know if that would be wise, Bill. If their operation's as big as I think it is, we can't trust anyone. Not even a Pinkerton operative.''

Gramford gulped down the whiskey. ''What do you want to do, John?''

''Let's wait and see what happens. Now that we know how they're pulling off the robberies, we know what to look for.'' He stood. ''By the way. Any gold shipments going out?''

''No. A cattle drive's coming in from Texas in a week. A Chicago meatpacker's buying the herd here and letting them summer in eastern Montana before shipping them east. Could be a sizable amount of money involved. It would be at the bank.''

''I'll keep in touch.'' Slocum left the office and strode along the boardwalk, his gaze searching for anything suspicious. The crowds on the street could hide anyone spying on him. He headed back to Hilda's.

That Sunday, Hilda persuaded him to attend church with her. He knew she wanted to show off her musical skill to him. She received plenty of praise from Horace Brockwhite, the minister, and from the congregation, but he knew she wanted to hear her play. And to hear him praise her. She did wonders with the ancient instrument, booming out "Old Hundreth," the congregation's voices hard put to rise above its soaring notes. The hymn brought him back to Georgia and his boyhood. He remembered standing wedged between his mother and father, feeling the vibration of their voices in the old country church as they sang, "Be Thou, O God, exalted high. And as Thy glory fills the sky . . ." He'd felt protected, loved, and wanted then. Tears started in his eyes at the memories the hymn invoked. At the end of the service came the doxology—"Holy, Holy, Holy . . . Lord God Almighty . . ." the congregation singing all out to rise above her playing.

She lingered after church to discuss music with the minister. Slocum stood aside, his limited knowledge on the subject preventing him from participating. Nevertheless, he felt warm pride for her. She was playing a particular movement on the organ—something she called a Schuebler chorale from a Bach cantata—and making the windows rattle, when Amanda Brockwhite appeared.

She shot Slocum a look seething with contempt, then another look filled with hate at Hilda. The music stopped. Horace Brockwhite turned his gentle, beatific gaze to his wife. She, however, snapped, "Come along, Horace! You have some decent *Christians* waiting to pay their respects outside!" She took her husband's arm and dragged him off.

Hilda turned deathly white. Slocum murmured, "Did you get the impression that she doesn't like either of us?"

"Oh, my God! John—you don't suppose she knows—"

"She knows something."

Outside, he recognized Jim Argus, who was talking to a man and woman. The woman was Mary Grace. He assumed the man with her was her husband, the Reverend Mr. Theodore Grace. He was of medium height, probably in his forties, and dressed in black with a clerical collar. Horace Brockwhite, his wife clinging to his arm, was led to the group. The five were soon in an animated discussion. What stood out to Slocum was the difference in ages between

Horace and Amanda. He wondered what the young, good-looking woman saw in the older, faded minister.

"Wonder what they're talking about," Hilda whispered.

"Not what. Who. Let's hope it isn't us."

As he escorted her to her buckboard, he thought. So, they all know one another. At least, Amanda Brockwhite knows the Graces. And they know Argus. Don't get the impression Argus is real at home in a church. Maybe there's some other attraction. Such as Mrs. Brockwhite herself.

He wondered if the others caught the looks between the two. Or Mary Grace's odd expression, something between jealousy and censure. He wondered why he got the impression Amanda and Mary knew each other.

He helped Hilda into the gig but didn't go with her. He was only supposed to be a casual acquaintance, a subterfuge both were having increasing difficulty carrying off in public.

As he was walking away, he heard loud voices, Hilda's among them. He turned to see two men accosting her, their voices raised in anger. He'd seen them in the saloon. Hoodoo Smith and Willy Borscht, drunks and ornerier than cat piss.

Hoodoo, tall and mean-looking, had hold of her mare's bridle. He shouted, "Ya better git outa town, woman!"

"Yeah! Better git out now!" Willy repeated. He was squat and pathetic-looking.

"We knows all 'bout ya! Don't think we don'!"

"Don' wan' yer kind a-teachin' school! Ye're nothin' but a whore!"

Before he could reach the two, a furious Hilda stood and laid about them with her whip. The spooked mare kicked at the traces and nearly threw Hilda from the buckboard. Hoodoo and Willy covered their heads and tried to ride out the furious woman's blows, then ran.

"Are you all right," Slocum demanded as he watched the two slink off.

She was visibly shaken. "I-I don't know!" She sat heavily, tears of fury wetting her eyes. The ruckus had gathered a small crowd.

"Move over!" He climbed up and sat next to her. Taking the reins, he urged the mare into a trot. She gave him a look of relief and gratitude. He said, "Don't know what this is all about, but I'm sticking close to you till I find out."

It was Wednesday, and she'd had an appointment with Dr. Zimmermann. When he'd asked her why, she'd been vague. When he'd pushed her for an answer, she'd become angry.

Now he sat in the buckboard and impatiently drummed his fingers on the driver's box, waiting for her to come out. He knew he shouldn't be seen in public with her, but worry gnawed at him. He'd wanted to accompany her into the office, but she wouldn't let him.

"Don't want you in there with me, John."

"Look! If there's something wrong with you . . ."

Her mouth tightened, and her eyes flashed. "I said I don't want you in there! You stay here. Keep the horse company. It's mortifying enough that I have to go."

If something ailed her, he wanted to know. He didn't believe her talk of "female troubles."

He caught himself dozing off. The sun was warm and lulled him to sleep. He yearned for a beer, but it wouldn't be right for him to be drinking in a saloon while she was being examined for God only knows what kind of ailment.

"Draw! Ya sonuva bitch!"

The yell jerked him awake.

"Ya miser'ble varmint! Draw!"

Across the street, a small crowd had gathered. Hoodoo Smith and Willy Borstch stood, legs spread, facing Bill Gerber, the owner of the hardware store and the president of the school board. In stark contrast to the filthy two, he was neatly turned out in a boiler-maker suit, bald-faced shirt, and bowler hat.

Smith put his face, gray with stubble and dirt, an inch

from Gerber's clean one. Gerber wrinkled his nose and re-coiled from the man's obvious stink.

Smith yelled, "Don' care if thet heathen schoolmarm has got cri-dentials—whatever they is. You run her off! Hear?" Smith's hand strayed to the ebony butt of his .45.

Gerber somehow managed to maintain his composure. "Who put you up to this? What business is it of yours what the school board does? You and this ruffian have no chil-dren. Doubt if either of you can read or write. Doubt if you've ever been inside a school. What does it matter to you who teaches?"

Hoodoo stuck his nose an inch from Gerber's. "Ya don' listen good, do ya, school twister. Ah'm a-tellin ya to git thet thir heathen woman outa town afore sundown—"

"Or you'll what?" Gerber stood his ground. He had craw, Slocum had to admit as he jumped to the ground. There was going to be trouble.

"Draw! Ya miserable sidewinder!" Hoodoo's hand poised above his gun butt. Willy planted his feet and struck a pose of ornery meanness. He then blinked in obvious confusion. Slocum figured Willy had only a slight edge over a cow for brains.

"I'm not heeled." Gerber said. "Don't hold with guns—"

He got no further. Hoodoo flailed a fist at him. A meaty splat, and Gerber sprawled in the dust. A surr of voices rose in protest. Smith bent, grabbed the stunned man's la-pels, and yanked him to his feet as if he'd been no more than a sack of grain. He shook him like a rat, his coarse face livid with fury, spittle streaming from his thick lips.

"Ah tol, ya, school twister—thir's folks what don' want thet Christ-killin' female a-larnin' our kids! Don' cotton to her livin' in sin with a hombre who ain't her lawful, mar-ried husban', neither! Now—ya git her outa town pronto or . . ." He measured Gerber and drove his fist into the man's face. Gerber lay on his back and didn't move, dust settling around him.

The crowd stared but did nothing. Smith brushed off his hands, spat, then motioned for Borscht to follow him into the saloon. Slocum ran to where Gerber lay, a hysterically crying woman cradling his head on her lap. Others gathered around and oohed and aahed like sheep.

"Out of my way!" Dr. Zimmermann, Hilda right behind him, elbowed the crowd aside. He knelt beside the dazed man and examined him. Gerber groaned and opened his eyes to stare dazedly about him. Blood poured from his nose and reddened his shirt. Blinking, he looked up at the doctor. Zimmermann demanded, "Can you see me, Bill?"

Gerber managed a nod.

"Let's get you over to the office. You!" Zimmermann pointed at Sam Nunner, the blacksmith. "Get a door!" Nunner returned with his helper and a board. Slocum and Hilda helped the doctor put Gerber on it.

"I can walk," he objected, and tried to sit up.

Zimmermann gently pushed him back down. "Stay put! Want to look you over. You're no young buck to be raw-hided like that." They carried him across the street, the crowd mumbling and staring. Zimmermann yelled over his shoulder, "Get the marshal!"

"Who did this?" Hilda demanded of the crowd.

Slocum slipped the thong from his Colt's hammer and stared at the saloon. "Our old friends. Willy and Hoodoo."

"Why?"

"Seems they don't want you teaching *their* kids."

"They haven't *got* any kids. Leastwise, none that're human."

"Reckon, somebody put 'em up to it. Whipsaw the president of the school board. Make him run you out of town. All because I didn't leave when Argus warned me."

Before Slocum could stop her, Hilda kilted her skirts and stormed into the saloon. The breeze from the swinging door stirred the sawdust on the floor with the force of her entry. Alarmed, he pushed in after her.

The Golden Goose was no place for a woman. It was no

place for anyone under six feet, three hundred pounds—
and lugging a Gatling gun.

Hoodoo and Willy were bellied up to the bar, the crowd
of dirty, smelly customers milling around them, crowing
their admiration of them, and slapping Hoodoo on the
shoulder.

"Oughta make you marshal," one weasel-like toad-eater
crowed.

"You sure as hell tol' him," a big fat man wheezed.

"Don' need thet kind a-larnin' our young 'uns," a drifter
echoed.

"Oughta tar'n feather her," suggested a beanpole who
could've doubled for a scarecrow. Slocum couldn't push
his way through the crowd to grab Hilda before she elbowed her way to the bar, her parasol sweeping the riffraff
aside like a scythe cutting wheat. She planted her feet before Hoodoo. Slocum swore under his breath and tried to
get to her before she got hurt, but the crowd hemmed him
in. Her mouth was a hard thin line of anger and disgust.
Talk had died to a murmur at her entrance. No respectable
woman would be caught dead in a saloon.

Hoodoo lounged on the bar with one elbow and surveyed
her with contemptuous amusement. "Wal—whataya know!
Here she be. The Christ-killer in person. Missus Adult'tris
herself."

She flared, "You miserable curs! You talk about children. Not one of you has a child you know of. If you did,
it would be covered with hair. Who are you to tell the
school board—"

Hoodoo straightened, his coarse face wreathed in a demonic grin that never got beyond his coarse lips. "Reckon
we got us some fun here, boys." He laid his hat, brim up,
on the bar. "Throw in yer money. Then we'll toss for her.
After I've had her first." He added, running his tongue over
his lips. "Always wondered what it'd feel like stickin' it
to a schoolmarm. Two dollars apiece, boys. We'll use the
bar." Hoodoo made a lewd gesture of unbuttoning his fly.

Slocum drew his .44. Those beside him shied away at the sight of the gun and the sound of it being cocked. He wanted to yell, "Hilda, get the hell outa there!" but didn't want to distract her. Hoodoo and Willy were unpredictable as rattlers.

She drew herself up and demanded. "Barkeep. What's your most explosive drink?"

"Huh?"

"Which has the greatest percentage of alcohol?"

The barkeep blinked.

"You *dolt*! Which liquor burns best?"

"Why—uh, white lightnin—I reckon." The room fell silent. Even Hoodoo and Willy watched her, puzzled, curiosity temporarily shoving aside the promise of rape. Seeing Hilda's bemused look, he explained, "Corn-squeezin's, ma'am. Pure alky-hol. We calls it everclear. The only reason we keeps it on hand is in case the undertaker runs out of embalmin' fluid. The men roared their laughter.

"Then pour me a large tumbler of—whatever it was you said."

Hoodoo leaned forward and leered in her face. "Naw! Don' give her none! Want ya fully awake whin I sinks my ramrod into ya, woman. Want ya to in-joy it!"

The barkeep leaned on the bar with his fat hands. "He's right, ma'am. Thet thir likker would burn right through the glass." Then, he smirked. "Besides, we don' serve female wimmin in here. You'd best skedaddle."

Hoodoo roared, "She ain't goin' nowhirs!"

More laughter and jeers. She looked calmly about her, then yanked the schooner of beer from a small cowhand leering up at her.

"That's a nice big mirror behind you, barkeep."

Talk ceased. Slocum readied himself to shoot both Hoodoo and Willy. The barkeep straightened and gave a nervous glance over his shoulder. "Yeah, it is."

"If you don't come up with that glass of everclear-stuff in the next two seconds, you're going to have glass all over the place." She drew back to hurl the mug. Those nearest the bar scrambled to get out of the way.

The barkeep, pale now, stammered. "O-okay, lady! Don' do n-nothin' rash! Thet mirror come all the way from Saint Louis. By boat. One everclear comin' up!" He poured clear liquid into a tumbler with shaking hands that held a stone demijohn. "Say whin!"

When the tumbler brimmed to overflowing, she picked it up. The men watched her, fascinated. Slocum steeled himself. He'd never seen that look on her before. The men gasped in surprise when she reached down to a small man, pulled a quirly from his vest pocket, and stuck it in her mouth.

"Give me a light!"

The small man blinked like a gopher staring at a rattler. Without taking his eyes from her, he lit a lucifer and held it up. She took it from him.

In a motion too swift for him to follow, she dashed the tumbler's contents on both Hoodoo and Willy. They stood paralyzed, blinking, dripping. Then, she threw the lucifer.

The two exploded in flame. Screams of rage and surprise came from the blaze engulfing them. Customers fell over one other to escape through the swinging doors. Hoodoo and Willy danced, hopped, yelped in pain, and slapped themselves wildly. Willy's hat blazed like a bonfire on his head. He yanked it off and hurled it away. Flames seared Hoodoo's stubble to make a sickening stink. His gunbelt blazed, the leather curled in the heat. A looped .45 round cooked off. The explosion and fragments of brass emptied the saloon.

The barkeep leaped over the bar, a superb feat for a man as fat as he was, and doused Hoodoo with bucket of water. Slocum yanked Hilda back from the burning men. He picked up the spittoon and hurled the contents on Willy. The two smoldering men threw themselves on the floor and rolled to smother the remaining flames. Sawdust on the floor blazed up. The air reeked with alcohol, singed skin, burning pine, and the sweet cloying stench of tobacco.

The barkeep did a one-legged dance as he stamped out flames. Hoodoo, black as a crow, got to his feet and stood unsteadily as he blinked and gulped air. A second round exploded in his smoldering pistol belt to blow it in half. His belt and gun fell to his feet. He yelped and slapped at his hip. Willy, the color of burnt toast, his hair smoldering, sucked in air like a bellows.

Slocum stuck the muzzle of his .44 against Hoodoo's scorched nose.

"Both of you better be ten miles from town by the time I get this lady home and come looking for you. But first— who hired you to whipsaw Gerber and threaten Mrs. Hasso?"

Hoodoo swallowed and tried to salvage something of his pride, but since that commodity in him was almost non-existent even under normal circumstances, he failed. "The preacher's wife," he mumbled in defeat.

Slocum stared at Hilda. "Mrs. *Brockwhite*?"

He wiped his mouth. "Yeah. Tha's her." Men crowding back into the saloon murmured in hushed voices.

"You mean the minister's *wife* put you up to this?"

He nodded.

"What did she tell you to do?"

"To rough up thet thir Gerber feller. Said he was the school board's big augur. We was to make him fire the schoolmarm."

"How much did she pay you?"

He licked charred lips. "Said she'd give us the school-marm's salary fer the month whin she was gone."

Slocum was having a hard time believing what he was hearing. It irrationally disappointed him that Argus wasn't behind forcing Hilda out of her job. He could deal with Argus. But—the *minister's wife*? Even he didn't think she would go that far.

Choking with anger, he ground out the words, "Punch the breeze out of town. Now!" He prodded Hoodoo with his gun. "If I see you within a hundred miles of here, I'll kill you. That goes for you, too, Borscht. Now—*git*!" He turned to the crowd. "If anyone else threatens Mrs. Hasso, they'd better be heeled because they'll answer to me."

He heard a murmur of voices in the crowd and caught mutterings of: "Hey! Didn't thet Slocum pal around with Cole Younger?" "My uncle claims he saw him face down three gunslingers in Denver. Made 'em eat thir cart'ridges, he did." "Mean with a gun, I hear."

By the time the marshal got to the saloon, he saw Slocum standing in the street, Hilda by his side, her hand in his, both watching an ever-diminishing cloud of dust made by two riders moving rapidly south.

When the mine owner showed up at the house that evening, Slocum related the encounter with Argus and the scrape with Hoodoo and Willy.

"Looks like you're in danger, Mrs. Hasso."

"Wish you'd call me Hilda, Mr. Gramford."

"I will. If you call me Bill." He chuckled. "It appears we're all in this together."

"What do you want me to do?" Slocum asked.

"Well, this Argus has laid it on the line." Gramford paused, clearly embarrassed for Hilda. "He learned about you, my dear, and passed it on to Mrs. Brockwhite. You're the lever Argus intends to use to get John out of the way."

"I'll quit my job!"

Gramford held up his hand. "No! No! That won't do! They'll merely find another method. This way, we have some idea what to expect. We must have them worried if they're going to all this trouble."

Slocum said, "What if I agree to Argus's demand and leave?"

They stared at him.

"Or—pretend to leave."

"Where would you go?"

"Hide out somewhere. Continue looking, but on the

sly." Slocum sipped his coffee. "If they think I'm gone, they'll let Hilda be."

"Hope you're right," Gramford murmured. He thought for a moment, then said, "Let's give it a try and see what happens. We'll set up a way to exchange information. I'll have my man MacTaggert deliver wood to the school, Hilda. Any messages from either John or me will be in the wood box."

Slocum said, "I'll see Argus tomorrow and tell him I'm leaving."

Gramford rubbed his chin. "Wonder what connection Amanda Brockwhite has with this Argus." Putting his hands on his knees, he gave them a pat and stood. "We'll see what we can find out."

18

It was nearly midnight when he and Hilda lay back and fought to catch their breath. When he moved off her to lie panting, she waited, then slid herself onto him, straddling his hips, teasing him by leaning forward to let his mouth try to capture her swaying breasts. When she sat up on his hips, he filled his hands with the full, butter-soft globes, his thumbs working the nipples into stiffness. The gold medallion winked yellow fires from her deep cleavage. Curious, he took it and, pulling her down, examined it in the light of the guttering candle on the nightstand.

It was a circle of fine gold wire intricately woven into a braid and superimposed by a series of tiny rosettes. The circle held a six-pointed star. The medallion was at the end of a fine gold chain.

He frowned as he studied it, knowing that the symbol held answers to certain questions about its owner that had bothered him.

"This a Star of David?" he murmured.

"Yes."

"Where did you get it?"

"My grandmother gave it to me."

"Your grandmother?"

"My paternal grandmother. When we lived in Pomerania."

He tried to fix the geography in his mind. "Where's that?"

"By the sea. That's what it means in Slavic. *Po* is a preposition meaning *by*. *Mer* is *sea*. By the sea. Part of East Prussia." She added, "My father was a professor of mathematics at Greifswald University."

"You're—you're *Jewish*?"

"Yes." When he was silent, her voice became defensive and defiant when she demanded, "That bother you?"

"Should it?"

"It does some."

"Is that what Hoodoo and Willy meant when—"

"When they called me a Christ-killer? Very crude. But yes. Though, how they found out I'm Jewish, I don't know. Maybe, my German accent . . ."

He stirred and took her face in his hands. "You're—*ashamed* of being Jewish?"

"Of *course* not. But I live in a largely Christian community, and you Christians are notorious for ignoring your prophet's origins. I have less trouble if my being a Jewess stays my secret."

"Does anyone else know?"

"You mean the school board?" A bitter laugh escaped her. "No. If they did, I'd be out of a job. As far as they know, I'm the nice, comfortable Christian widow-lady who plays the organ every Sunday at the Episcopalian church."

He chuckled softly. "You're nice and comfortable—but you're no lady."

Her voice was stiff with anger when she said, "You, on the other hand, are a good old bible-thumping Georgia redneck Christian who believes niggers look best when they're strung up by the neck."

"Hey! Don't go getting frothy! I didn't do anything."

"I suppose you're going to tell me that you never owned slaves when you lived in Georgia."

"That's precisely what I'm going to tell you! My family never owned slaves."

"I'm sorry. It's just that I—I've lived with injustice. . . ."

He pulled her reluctant form down to him and wrapped her in his arms. "You were born in this—Pomerania?"

"Yes. Thirty-nine years ago." She lay stiff and tense in his arms as if waiting for the combined revelations of her religion and her age to have their effect on him.

"When did you come to this country?"

"When I was twenty. The year I graduated from my father's university."

"Your English is almost perfect."

"My English *is* perfect!"

"I meant—you have virtually no accent."

"I worked hard at losing it."

He held her angry, unyielding form for a moment. "Did Bill Hasso know you're Jewish?"

"Of course! He would've been quite happy to get me even if I'd been a Turkish harem girl."

A low chuckle escaped him. "Hell! You're *better* than any Turkish harem girl. The sultan would be glad to have you." He kissed her with loving gentleness. "You have parents?"

"Yes. In Chicago. I was born Hildegard Rebecca Bruckmann. My father thought Hildegard might make people think I was German and make it easier for me. It did while I was in Prussia." She added, "My father worried about me."

"What do they think about their daughter living on the frontier?"

When she didn't answer, he traced his finger over her wet face and realized with a start she was crying. "What is it?" he murmured.

"I'm dead and buried where they're concerned."

He raised her face in his hands to stare at her. "What do you mean?"

"When I married Bill Hasso, they had a funeral for me. They're very religious. As far as they're concerned, I'm dead." She was quiet for a moment. "You don't care?"

"That you're a Jewess? Hell, no! How could I? I don't put much stock in anything I can't load and shoot."

"Must be lonely for you. Not being able to believe in anything."

"It was. It isn't now." He traced his finger over the fine, delicate scimitar of her nose, then kissed her. "Bill must've been quite a man."

"He was a *goy*. A very kind, intelligent, and loving man—but a *goy*. A Gentile. A squarehead Lutheran."

He floundered for words but found none. Instead, he held her close. The school board would hear about her. He wondered what their reaction would be. Christian values were never very much in evidence in mining camps, though Bridger's Rock did have churches. He stirred with uneasiness.

"I'm not helping your situation much, am I."

"You want to leave?" The voice was coldly querulous.

"No. Why would I? God and I have never exactly been on speaking terms. We occasionally nod to each other, but that's about it. What you are doesn't matter to me a bit."

"Just as long as I'm the perfect mistress, huh? Good lay, good cook, and I don't nag." The voice was bitter.

"That's not fair, Hilda." He kissed her with all the gentleness he could muster. "You're also my very dear and loving friend."

She abruptly buried her face in his shoulder and wept, her body convulsed with sobs. He knew words weren't what she needed—and like Job's friends, he had none for her—but instead, he held her close to let her cry herself out. Most people, he thought had some dark corners in their past, but Slocum had come to believe the big, good-natured, apparently unshakable woman in his arms was the exception. But even she had dark memories to weep over. Later, cried out and exhausted, she fell asleep in his arms.

The following evening he hesitated going to Hilda's. If Argus were watching and saw him with her, he could make good his threat against her. He might even have people with him to act as witnesses to the schoolmistress's wanton behavior. Slocum waited until after dark to knock on her back door.

To his surprise, Andria, the black woman who acted as janitor and general factotum for the school, answered his knock. She stared at Slocum, gave him a fleeting smile of recognition, then looked troubled.

"Andria. Tell Mrs. Hasso I'm here."

"She's over to the meetin' house, Mr. Slocum."

"Meeting house?"

"Yes, sir. School board meeting. Oh, Mr. Slocum! They's fixin' to set her down." Andria wrung her hands with anguish. "They's fixin' to fire her. The terrible things they're sayin' 'bout her."

Anger and disbelief surged in him. Had Argus made good on his threat to tell the board about him and his relationship to the schoolmistress? Andria's frightened, angry voice jarred his musings. "An' if she hasta go, who'll larn my young'uns? She's a good woman. Mrs. Hasso is! They got no right to set her down like that."

"I'll be back, Andria. Stay here!" The delicious aroma of freshly baked pies and bread hitting him made him think of home. He rode for the meeting house.

When he strode through the door, a dozen lamps had the starkly plain, whitewashed interior gleaming. Six school board members—five men and one woman—sat at a table in front and faced the crowd of parents. Bill Gerber held the gavel. Despite a black eye and a bruised cheek, he looked surprisingly chipper considering what he'd been through. The woman school twister he recognized as Amanda Brockwhite. The minister sat in the front row.

Amanda's eyes blazed with the righteous conviction of a religious zealot. She was loudly berating someone in her high-pitched, scolding voice. That someone was Hilda, who sat alone.

"And we'll not have a jezebel teaching our children. A hussy living in unspeakable sin with a man not her husband! A Messalina, a Joan of Naples! In our school, no less! Dirtying the minds of our babies! I need not remind you"—she fixed her pinched, hard look on the group of parents—"that our vines have tender grapes!" Seeing that she had their full attention, she screeched, "Worse! This woman's a Jew! How can we expect a heathen to impart Christian values to our children? I ask you!" The crowd mumbled and stirred uneasily.

The Reverend Mr. Brockwhite, clearly uncomfortable with what was going on, admonished her in a gentle voice, "Amanda, my dear, I believe—"

"Don't interrupt me, Horace!" She glared at him, then turned her venom back to Hilda, who sat in impassive silence. Stabbing her finger at her as if it were a lance, she stormed. "You—you charlatan! Attending our church, pretending you're a Christian. Playing the organ."

"She plays a very good organ, my dear. Her Bach cantatas—"

"I told you to shut up, Horace!" She turned back to her victim. "We want you out by tomorrow! If you're not, I'll have the marshal evict you!"

An uneasy murmuring rose from the crowd. The five male members of the board looked uncomfortably at one another.

Hilda stood, and the room fell silent. Standing tall and straight, her face full of fierce pride, she dominated the gathering as she announced, "You need have no concern over my willingness to leave. I have no desire to sully myself in the company of a woman—I'm sorry, Reverend— to sully myself by having to answer to a bigoted hypocrite who clearly decides for the rest of you how your school will be run. As for attending your church, I wasn't aware our mutual God confined himself to a building built with hands. I'm a member of this community. I and the few other Jews in it meet to find our way in this life as do all of you. I never lied to you about whom I am. But then, you never asked me, did you. Until now.'' She turned her gaze on Mrs. Brockwhite. ''You and I both know why you're doing this, Amanda. You talk about me living in sin! You should be ashamed of yourself! You're the one who hired those two despicable men to attack Mr. Gerber and me. Go on! Admit it!''

Horace Brockwhite paled, put his hand on his wife's arm, and whispered hoarsely. ''Amanda! What's she mean?''

His wife turned ashen and was momentarily speechless. Then, spluttering like a fuse, she managed to look outraged. ''Why—of all the—I *never*—''

''Both Willy and Hoodoo admitted you did!''

Horace turned pale as he stammered, ''I wondered what you were doing talking to those two.''

''I-I was merely trying to get them to attend church,'' Amanda declared. She looked with righteous indignation at the crowd. ''How you could *ever* believe that I would—''

''You're lying, my dear. I believe we'd better go.''

She angrily shook off his hand and snapped. ''Hobble your mouth, you fool!''

The crowd chittered its disapproval. Horace blinked, opened his mouth, then closed it. The difference in age between the minister and his wife struck Slocum anew even though he'd seen them together before. They looked more like father and spoiled daughter.

Hilda hiked her skirts slightly as she prepared to leave and shot the male school board members a look of withering scorn.

''What a lily-livered bunch you are! I'm well rid of you! You have my resignation!''

''Hold on there!'' All eyes turned to Slocum standing in the back. Hilda jumped with surprise and watched him with an expression wavering between relief and anguish as he marched to the table, spurs chinking. Looking at the minister, he said, "Hope you don't take this wrong, Reverend, but I can't figure how a good, decent man like you ever teamed up with a female like your wife. If ever a woman needed to have her skirt dusted, she's it."

Amanda gasped in horror. "Why—of all the—"

"Shut up—and sit, my dear." The Reverend put a hand on his wife's arm.

She shook it off in stunned disbelief. "Have you lost your mind?" she demanded, eyes blazing.

"Mrs. Hasso's quite right, my dear. You are a bigot and hypocrite. Now, be still!"

"How—how *dare* you!"

Slocum looked out over the crowd. "Reckon I'm what this is all about. Trouble is, you don't know the full particulars. I was with Mrs. Hasso when we were held up by road agents on the way from Virginia City. In the scuffle, I was shot." He saw Hilda stiffen at this lie. "This good woman took me home with her and nursed me back to health. When I recovered, we found we could just about make ends meet on what money I had combined with those Boston dollars you pay her."

He looked out into the group, searching. "You! George Harper! Didn't you tell me just the other day your son can read, write, and cipher well enough to help you in the store? That he couldn't read worth a hoot before Mrs. Hasso gave him after-school learning?"

"Yup! That's right." Harper looked about him and nodded.

"And, you, Mrs. Stevens. Your Suzie's at the schoolmarm's house three nights a week for extra work." He added, "For which she gets paid nothing."

Mrs. Stevens's blond curls shook vigorously as she agreed.

"And let's not forget all those mincemeat pies she bakes

and brings to school. If she didn't, there's some children who'd get little to eat otherwise.

"And, you, Sol. And Ester. You gonna just sit there and take Mrs. Brockwhite's guff about your people?" He glared at the owners of the haberdashery, who squirmed uncomfortably.

"Go ahead! You let this bunch of school twisters let Mrs. Hasso go. You sure don't want a heathen filling your kids' heads full of reading, writing, arithmetic, history, and spelling. Even if she has a university education and more booklearning than all of you put together. Why—you can do all that teaching at home yourselves. Between chores." An angry hum rose from the parents. "Because you sure aren't going to get another fool to come here and work her head off stuffing learning into all those mule heads she's got for students. Not for fifty dollars a month. But you're right! Keep 'em home—where they'll drive you loco!"

He took Hilda's arm. "Come on! Let's get outa here!"

Harper was on his feet shouting, "Wait a dang minute! We ain't had *our* say! Me and my wife want the schoolmarm to stay on!"

"So do I!" Hands went up, and people stood and yelled at the school board. Bill Gerber banged the gavel to establish order, then said, "Let's take a vote!"

Amanda Brockwhite shot to her feet in a rage. "I won't tolerate this! If you reinstate this—this *jezebel*—then you'll no longer have my services! Nor those of my husband!"

Gerber, his face set, like stone, shouted, "All those in favor of accepting Mrs. Brockwhite's resignation?" Nearly every hand in the room shot up. "Carried." Gerber stood, bowed stiffly, and said, "Mrs. Hasso, forgive us. We hope you'll stay."

"A raise in salary might help," Slocum suggested.

A hasty putting together of heads, then: "Ten dollars a month, Mrs. Hasso?" The school board watched her intensely.

Chin in the air, Hilda nodded. "I'll consider your proposal.'' She turned and sailed regally from the meeting. Slocum hesitated, then followed her out. Behind him, the hall exploded with arguing, yelling voices.

Outside, she threw her arms about him. He locked his fingers under her bottom, lifted her, and held her, his face buried in her neck. They held each other in silence.

''Are you all right?''

She nodded fiercely. ''Yes! Oh, yes! I am now! Let's go home, John.''

''You're not afraid to be seen with me?''

She whispered, her lips against his ear, ''Baked two pies, apple and mincemeat. Your favorites.'' Her teeth nipped his earlobe. Pulling her face from his, she grinned wickedly at him.

''Better get you home,'' he murmured. ''No telling what an evil, heathen female like you could do to an upright town like this if you were let loose on the streets.'' He took her arm and led her to her buckboard.

He stayed that night. When both were content to lie side by side and talk, she murmured in the dark. ''Thanks for coming to my defense.''

''Not sure my showing up helped you any.''

''No one was going to argue with a man who ran with the Daltons. Or who wears a cross-draw Colt .44.''

''Hate to think that was what changed their minds. You gonna go on teaching?''

''Yes.''

''Why? You don't need the money.''

''Who says so?''

''Figure your late husband left you well heeled.''

''You're only guessing. But—yes—he did. But that has nothing to do with it. I like children. I *like* teaching.''

''Is that all?''

She said nothing for a moment, then murmured in a slightly tremorous voice. ''I've always wanted children. A child of my own. Maybe my students fill a need in me.''

Something was wrong. He didn't know what it was, but

she was somehow different. But it wasn't a difference he could throw a rope over. He turned on his side and gathered her into his arms. Pushing his face between the warm, yielding softness of her breasts and breathing in the woman scent of her, he fell asleep.

19

The next day, Slocum waited in the hotel lobby until Argus showed up. He had trouble corralling his fury when he confronted him.

"You and Amanda Brockwhite could've got Hildegard Hasso hurt with that stupid play."

Argus looked puzzled, then grinned. "You talking about that fracas with those two sticky lopers in the Golden Goose? From what I hear, the formidable Hildegard nearly did for them both."

"Those two could've killed her. They threatened to rape her in the saloon."

Argus chuckled. "What in the world was she doing in there in the first place? What did she expect?" He lit his Havana and drew on it. "And you think Mrs. Brockwhite and I were behind it?"

"You threatened Hildegard if I didn't get out of town. Last night. Amanda Brockwhite called a special meeting of the school board and the parents and set her down."

"I hear she said nothing that wasn't true."

Slocum ignored him and continued. "Fortunately, the

parents and the rest of the school board didn't agree. They refused to accept her resignation and set down Amanda Brockwhite.''

Argus shook his head in mock sadness. ''Tragic! How will she ever busy herself now that she can no longer lord it—or should I say—lady it over the clods of parents of those little beasts your woman teaches.''

''You'd probably know that better than I. The lady's considerably younger than her husband. In the right light, she's not bad looking. You apparently know her well. Wouldn't have something going behind the good Reverend's back, would you?''

Argus blew smoke at him, his arrogant smile never deserting his face. ''If I did, it would be none of your damn business.''

''If it threatens Hildegard Hasso, it's my business.''

''Neither I or nor Mrs. Brockwhite can be responsible for the way the townspeople behave when they learn how the schoolmistress carries on.''

''The way you and Amanda are apparently carrying on?'' It was getting to him that he couldn't pierce Argus's cast-iron shell.

''I'm sure, Slocum, that Mrs. Brockwhite's perfectly willing to stop the persecution of the schoolmistress if you leave town.'' He drew on his cigar. ''By now I imagine everyone knows about you and her.'' He pulled out his pocket watch.''I'm late for breakfast.'' When he strode into the dining room. Slocum followed him.

He waited until Argus ordered, then said, ''I don't want Hildegard hurt.''

Argus smiled. ''That's up to you.''

''If I leave town, what's in it for me?''

''If you need jawbone—''

''I'm not broke.''

Argus was silent for a moment, then asked, ''What's Gramford paying you to find his missing shipment?''

''Five hundred. When it's returned.''

He hesitated, then pulled a small leather bag from his pocket and tossed it on the table between them. Slocum watched him pour out its contents. Five-dollar gold pieces chinked richly as they clattered and rolled on the table.

"Thirty pieces of gold, Slocum." He laughed softly. "Sorry it's not thirty pieces of silver, but deputies living off poorly paid schoolmarms can't be particular."

"One of these days you'll push your luck farther than it'll stretch, Argus."

He ignored him. "Hundred and fifty in gold dollars. Take it! And ride back to Palouse Flats. Just so you're gone from here."

"And the schoolmistress?"

"If you're out of it, she keeps entertaining the town brats at the slate board. And drawing her fifty dollars a month."

"You're in with bank robbers, aren't you." It wasn't a question.

"All I'm interested in is recovering the money they've stolen to collect the rewards."

"And you don't care whom you hurt doing it."

"No. Now. If that's all . . ."

Slocum pretended to slump in defeat. "Okay. You got a deal."

"Good! Square it with Gramford and move on." He chuckled and pushed the pile of coins toward Slocum. "See? Easy, isn't it. Don't have to tear yourself up hunting that gold."

"Going take me a bit to get my plunder together."

"You got till tomorrow. Time for one last dip into the schoolmarm."

Slocum stilled the fury in him and warned, "You may've just branded me, but watch your mouth where the lady's concerned."

"Too bad you're leaving. Like I said, I'd enjoy killing you, Slocum."

"Keep auguring, and you'll get the chance."

He rode back to Hilda's, knowing that his continued

presence threatened her. That much, he was sure of.

Ordinarily, the situation would be the ideal excuse to ride out of her life. The trouble was—he didn't want to leave her. Not yet. He was gathering up his gear when she walked in.

"Leaving," he told her.

She stood by the table, her hands still on the books she'd set there. "Figured you would. Sooner or later."

He went to her. "Hilda—we've talked about this. I can't stay here. It isn't as if I want to go."

She searched his face. "What is it, John?"

"I'm getting too close to whoever's committing these robberies. Argus made it plain that you could be in danger if I stay here."

She paled. "Who is he, John?"

"Not sure. But none of this is worth your getting hurt over."

"It is to me, John. You're worth it."

He pulled her to him. "You stay put."

"Where will you go?"

"Into hiding. See if I can't flush them out. I'll be back."

"Can I help?" Her worried face searched his.

"You can. By staying in one piece. By the way. I want you to have this." He put the bag of coins Argus had given him on the table.

"What is it, John?"

"The money Argus gave me to disappear. Keep it and use it."

She kissed him hard and rough, and whispered, "To-night?"

"We'll see." He carried his bedroll out to the stable and tied it on his packhorse with the rest of his plunder.

Moses, the big shaggy dog that had wandered into the yard and adopted Hilda the month before, sniffed his hand and licked it.

"Keep an eye on her, boy!" He climbed into the kack and rode out.

20

The sun was a glow in the east, fire touching the ridge of the Bridger Range. Slocum rode for about eight miles until he hit Middle Cottonwood Creek. Tethering the packhorse, he doubled back to see if he could spot anyone following him. The valley was flat and unbroken except for a few rolling hills. When he used his glasses to survey the terrain, he saw them.

Two men. One was of medium height, the other unusually short, almost squat. He reckoned they were about a mile behind him. He muttered to himself, "Could the short one be the fake minister in the Dougherty?"

He rode back to his packhorse, making sure he kept to the gullies so not to raise dust. He continued north, edging over into the shadows of the mountains east of him. Every half hour he would stop and search the area behind him for the two. They stayed with him until almost noon, then rode back. No doubt to report to . . . somebody. Watching them go, he tried to make sense out of the recent events.

If the squat man was the fake minister, he was part of the gang. Either Argus would have his own tracker to make sure Slocum rode out, or he would do it himself. But Slocum saw no one else. He rode east into the foothills to find a place to hole up.

He found a shallow cave no animal was occupying in the foot of the mountain and hobbled his horses in a small, enclosed meadow. As he built a fire, he wondered how long he could stay under cover.

The Grace Church of the Lotus of Truth was holding nightly revival meetings just north of the town limits. He waited until dusk, then rode back to town. He pushed the gray because he wanted to get there before it was too late so he could examine the wagons and equipment.

A huge tent held the crowd. Wagons, surreys, gigs, and horses belonging to the people inside being saved crowded the area. Slocum dismounted, tied his horse in the shadow of a huge cottonwood, and moved in the darkness to where the wagons were lined up behind the tent. The distant sound of singing reached him.

He moved quietly to each wagon. Most were empty. Five were caravans, colorful houses on wheels, living quarters for Grace and his assistants. Four smaller tents apparently housed the roustabouts and other workers. A chuck wagon was next to several tables, the tantalizing smell of food and coffee reminding him he hadn't eaten all day. The five big Studebakers were empty. Tarpaulins covered the loads of the three Murphys. Mules grazed in the field nearby, their occasional raucous braying causing him to jump in alarm. The operation required a lot animals. Had to, he figured, to haul the tentage and equipment required to run an outfit as big as the Grace bunch. He found nothing that felt like a balloon. He was moving down the line of wagons when he heard faint voices coming from a caravan.

A woman's voice said, "Ted thinks we've squeezed this town dry."

A male voice replied, "Mary, we've got to get out of here."

"I know. The marshal's becoming suspicious after what

happened with Hoodoo and Willy. What about that lobo Gramford hired to snoop around?''

A low laugh. "Slocum? He's gone. Your sister and I got rid of him. He caved in when I threatened his woman.''

Slocum recognized the voice as belonging to Jim Argus.

"He was getting too close for comfort.'' The woman's hard tone held a cold, sinister note. "Told Ted that hiring those two drifters to bushwhack him was a mistake.''

"Amanda's hiring Hoodoo and Willy to rawhide the head of the school board was a good idea. It worked.''

"Amanda figured threatening Slocum's woman would be enough to spook him. She didn't plan on those two going as far as they did, though. Now the marshal's suspicious. And Horace is furious.''

Argus chuckled. "When you hire idiots to do a job, you get what you pay for. You got to admit the Hasso woman's a snuffer. Damn near burned down the saloon.''

"We don't need that kind of publicity, darling.''

"All the more reason to get out of here.''

"Jim, where did Amanda learn about the Hasso woman being Jewish? That was a stroke of genius.''

"Still have my Pinkerton connections. Easy enough to find out. Her folks live in Chicago. Told Amanda, and she spread the rumor. As a member of the school board, it would be a simple matter for her to persuade all those sanctimonious parents to fire her.'' He laughed. "After all, the woman's masqueraded as a Christian, teaching Christian values to all those little bastards.''

"Horace is quite upset with Amanda over this.''

"That sanctimonious bastard would be. But it got rid of Slocum. What's it matter? She's leaving the good Reverend anyway. When I think of that ass in bed with her . . .'' A muffled laugh sounded. "Within the week, the three of us will be in North Dakota. A week after that, we'll be in New York. Richer than we could possibly imagine.''

"Look, Jim! I don't want you getting any closer to Amanda.''

"What's wrong? You jealous?"

"Yes."

"She's your sister, for Christ's sake. She's kept us informed of all the grubstakes in the area, the shipments, bank transactions. She found out about Gramford's gold shipment and the route the Army would take. Horace's circuit covering all four towns has proved a godsend. No pun intended." Another chuckle. "Wonder how many bedroom ceilings she had to look at to get all that information?"

"She's not finicky when it comes to selling herself. I'm sure she made a lot of bank presidents, clerks, and grubstakers happy."

"Wonder if she seduced Gramford."

"She didn't say so. She wouldn't if she had. Jim! I don't want you in her bed anymore!"

"It's strictly business."

"Don't give me that! Any woman is strictly business where you're concerned. Business between the sheets." In a rueful voice, she added, "I ought to know."

"Can't help it if I find both Geisher sisters irresistible. Guess what? A cattle outfit from Texas is bringing in a big herd. Amanda learned from Horace the deal's going through next week. Around fifteen dollars a head. The money's going to be in the Cattlemen's Bank." Argus added with a low chuckle, "Your brother-in-law learned that at prayer meeting the other night when Joe Biggs, the clerk at the bank, told him. They're putting on extra guards until the deal is done." Another sinister laugh. "Wonder what your sister has to do to get your brother-in-law to reveal spiritual confidences to her."

"Amanda would suck a horse if it put money in her purse. Horace doesn't know about me, or that she's leaving him when we fly out of here for North Dakota."

The word *fly* caught Slocum's attention.

"Can't blame her. Life with that lily-livered bible-thumper must really cramp her style. If she's anything like you."

"She is. Too much so."

"With her share, she'll be able to live the life she only dreams about now."

"Just as long as she's not living it in your bed."

"One more job, my sweet, and we're on our way."

"You sure we can haul all that booty across Montana?"

"You're the wind expert. And Ted's sure."

Slocum waited during the long silence that followed, still unable to believe his ears. The minister's wife was in with the gang?

Argus murmured, "So far, we've been lucky."

"With this Slocum gone, we'll get even luckier. How much do you suppose the schoolmarm knows?"

"Nothing she can use now that's she's wearing a big red A on her bosom."

"I'd feel easier if she were out of the way. Are we going to hit the bank, my darling?"

"Have to set it up first. Talk to Theodore. He's getting nervous."

"He's not up to this, Jim."

"Known that all along. He's afraid somebody'll get hurt. Hell! Remember—what were their names? The two who killed the bank clerk in Oregon?"

"You mean Zeke and Bead?"

"We should've killed them. But no! Old Sanctimonious wouldn't have it. Set 'em down in the wilds of Idaho, he said." Argus laughed. "It's a good thing he doesn't know about the two we sicced on Slocum."

"We've done well so far, Jim. Without killing anyone."

"Only because you and Ted let me plan the jobs and you lead them."

"Did this Slocum know you're not a Pinkerton man?"

"Doesn't matter. He's gone. Joe and Moss followed him. Just sorry I couldn't have killed him. Would've liked to see if he's as fast as they say he is."

"Got to admit you're a real snuffer, darling. You handle

both your guns well—the one you wear and the one I've got my hand on.''

A soft laugh. ''Watch it! It's fully loaded. Might go off. How soon will Ted finish plucking those pigeons?''

''Don't worry. Hear that yelling? He's got a ripe bunch tonight. We've plenty of time, sweetheart.''

''Mary—this'll be our last job. We've got to get the gold to North Dakota. I've people waiting in New York to buy it. We can be in South America free and clear in a month.''

''I know, Jim! But we still need Ted to work the balloon. I've plotted the prevailing wind currents, but I'm not an aeronaut. And neither are you. Are you sure that boat'll be there on the Missouri waiting for us?''

''Yes. I'm sure.''

''Then, be patient, my darling.''

''How can I be when you're doing what you're doing to me?''

''Then I'll stop.''

''No! No—for Christ's sake—no!''

A giggle. ''You're taking the Lord's name in vain, sweetheart. And in Ted's very own bed. Shame on you!''

''Looking forward to the day I kill that son of a bitch.''

''You sound like my former husband. He couldn't wait to kill Ted either.''

''The hell with your husband—and Ted! Keep doing what you're doing!''

Slocum listened to the creaking of the wagon and the muted groans of pleasure. Ted, he thought. Theodore Grace. He hadn't seen the man up close, except for that time after church. Slocum wondered with a surge of alarm if Argus had plans for Hilda. He had to protect her.

He edged quietly away from the wagon. He needed time to sort it all out. One aspect he was sure about: Argus was a cool killer who wasn't going to share with anyone.

He wrote out what he'd learned about Argus and the Geisher sisters, Mary and Amanda. And the possibility that the gang would hit the bank. When he deposited the letter in the wood box behind the school, he found no instructions for him. He rode back to his hideout and arrived in time for three hours' sleep before dawn.

The next day, he hunted. No one could bring him food since no one knew where he was, so he would have to live off the land. He bagged two deer watering at the creek, dressed them out, and cut the meat into strips to make jerky. He dug a hole lined it with rocks, and built a fire. He then cut green willow branches to make a foot-high platform over the coals. When the fire was hot embers, he laid out the lengths of venison on the platform to dry them.

On the third day, the distant sound of cows lowing and bellowing brought him to the mouth of the canyon. Dust clouds swirled up by hundreds of cows told him the Texas outfit had arrived with their herd and was pasturing it in the Gallatin Valley between the river and the Bridger Range, an eleven-mile-wide rolling plain with plenty of water. He spotted drovers moving the herd in a circle. Its arrival meant the Chicago buyer would be arriving soon with the money, which would be secured in the Cattlemen's Bank. He wondered how the gang would do it.

They would first steal horses. That much he knew. The next day, they would hit the bank. The balloon would be waiting for them in some box canyon. The robbers would ride into it, leave the horses, climb into the gondola—and disappear, the prevailing west wind taking them east over the mountains to where they would set down, probably close to their hideout. They would then deflate the balloon, hide it, and later load it onto wagons to be hauled to a new area. At least, that was what he figured they would do. The question was—when would they rob the bank.

He rode out that night to the school to check the wood box and leave a request for any maps of the area. He also wrote, "Ask the marshal to tell you if there are any horses reported stolen. The gang usually robs the day after. I'll check for a reply in two days."

He added, "Don't contact the Pinkertons. We can't trust anyone."

He found a note from Hilda telling him she missed him and to be careful—and that the Grace Church of the Lotus was holding revival meetings all that week. He stood in the shadows and stared at her house. Lamplight glowing inside filled him with hunger for her. He wondered if she was in bed, the thought of her causing an erection. The temptation to visit her hit him hard, but somebody might be watching.

On the impulse, he rode over to the Lotus revival meeting, but stayed within the line of trees. To his surprise, roustabouts were taking down tents and loading them on wagons. He noticed a big Studebaker with a big tent on it loaded and tied down, an eight-up of mules already harnessed to it. Two smaller wagons each drawn by four mules were strung out behind it. He tethered his horse and moved stealthily toward the wagons. He saw no one about. Standing in the shadow of the Studebaker, he reached up and felt the canvas of the tent. A thrill surged through him.

It wasn't canvas; it was a heavy silk-like material impregnated with a varnish that had an oily feel to it. The balloon. Because its material was thinner and lighter than canvas, it would have more volume than a tent of similar weight.

He worked his way back to his horse, the sound of singing coming from the revival tent. He counted roughly fifteen men striking and packing the other tents. He stayed and watched as the Gypsy caravans were brought into line. Grace was moving out. That meant the robbers would hit the bank soon.

It was an hour before dawn when the procession rumbled east through rocky canyon on a trail that had been opened only a year before. Slocum followed at a safe distance and wondered where they were heading. No town he knew of was anywhere near. The only way through the mountains was Sixteen Mile Creek, and he wasn't sure wagons could get through that. Twenty miles on the other side, the land leveled out. He continued to follow the trail of dust in the distance.

21

The wagon train traveled along Blacktail Creek and into a divide hemmed in by rolling hills. To Slocum's immediate south, Blacktail Mountain loomed, dark and massive. Another mountain lay north, the hollow between the two forming the divide. He saw black storm clouds roiling and churning west of him, a huge black brush of rain sweeping the land like a giant broom. The procession rolled deeper into the divide, the hooves of the draft animals and the heavy wheels of the vehicles throwing up clouds of dust. He rode south of them, kept off the skyline, and watched their progress through his glasses.

"Where in the hell're they going?" he muttered aloud. "They can't get over those hills ahead of them."

He saw Grace ride down the line of wagons, waving his arms to direct the wagoneers to pull into a circle. They cracked their whips and guided their teams into position with skill born of long practice.

Dismounting and hobbling his horse, Slocum sat out of sight among the boulders on the north side of the eight-thousand-foot mass of rock behind him and watched the activity below.

Workmen pulled off what looked like a huge tent and laid it flat, a four span of mules drawing it to its full length. It would cover a large parade ground, he thought. He recognized it as the balloon. It lay in a hodgepodge of colors against the yellow ochre of the grass. He blinked in surprise when he recognized Amanda Brockwhite walking over the field of silk in her bare feet as she checked the canopy, probably for tears and holes. She carried a basket with her and halted periodically to kneel and sew up rips in the silk.

"My God!" he murmured, "she *is* part of the gang."

The crew placed six long stilt-like poles into holes in the metal load ring below the balloon's seven-foot-wide mouth. Ropes ran from the ends of the poles to mules, which pulled them upright so the mouth, supported by the poles, hovered fifteen feet above the ground and was level with it. Workers hauled part of the balloon to allow the hole to rise freely. Two Murphys rolled up and braked, and the teamsters stripped off their canvas coverings. Each wagon carried a half of the basket. Planks were laid on the tailgates, and mules pulled the halves off the wagon beds and onto waiting dollies. The crew pushed the halves under the balloon's mouth, then bolted them together and secured the maze of load ropes.

A third Murphy, carrying the furnace and blower, rumbled into place to be unloaded. The crew carried the furnace to the basket, placed it aboard, and assembled it. A fourth wagon contained containers of kerosene. Slocum timed all this activity with his watch. It took the gang less than twenty minutes to assemble the flying contraption.

When Grace didn't order the balloon to be inflated, Slocum inferred from this that he wasn't ready yet for the bank robbery. The presence of Amanda Brockwhite was something he hadn't counted on. He recalled Mary Grace telling Argus that her sister was leaving her husband, and this could only mean she had left Horace and was going with them. He figured he still had time to get back to Bridger's Rock and contact Gramford and the law.

A faint cloud of dust rose to the west. Partially blinded by the late afternoon sun, he watched two riders approach the divide. Sentries stationed on both sides raised their rifles. The riders reined in, then were waved ahead. He recognized Jim Argus and Mary Grace. They rode into the wagon circle and dismounted.

Grace embraced the woman, who then entered the colorful Gypsy caravan where she'd lain with Argus the night Slocum had heard them together. He wondered if Grace had any idea what was going on behind his back. Argus and Grace talked for a moment, then walked together toward the gulch that lay directly below Slocum. He ducked behind a rock and watched.

At the head of the gulch and to its right was a black hole half covered by underbrush. He wondered why he hadn't noticed it earlier. An abandoned mine running back into the mountain, he thought. Rusted mining machinery and the ruins of a sluice lay scattered about the entrance thick with nettles and Scotch broom. The two vanished into the hole.

Urgency and curiosity prodded him to go down and follow them inside, but caution won out. There could be sentries hidden. If the mine was the hideout, then Grace would hardly leave it unguarded. When a man came out of the mine, propped his rifle against a sluice box, and urinated on the rusted tracks, Slocum knew the mine was being guarded. He could only wait.

Ten minutes later, Grace and Argus came out, talked briefly, then headed back down to the wagons. The man with the rifle followed them. At the bottom of the hill, Slocum spotted what he assumed was the guard's relief climbing the steep, rocky rise to meet them. He figured he had three minutes to get in, see what was inside, and get back out. Keeping to the rocks, he moved quickly to the entrance.

It took a bit for his eyes to adjust to the dark. A faint light showed at a junction of the main tunnel with one that intersected further in. He drew his Colt and edged his way into the hole. Damp and cold chilled his skin. Water coursing down the rocky walls and falling from the low ceiling made hollow dripping sounds. Puddles of greasy stagnant puddles under his feet stank. Bat guano covered the floor for the first fifteen feet. Bats hung from cross-timbers and squeaked their annoyance when his hat brushed against them. The rank sweet stench of guano, rotting wood, and mildew filled his nostrils.

An intricate pattern of supporting timbers shored up the shaft, which narrowed to four feet. A narrow track for hopper cars ran back to vanish in the dark. He turned right at the intersection.

This tunnel narrowed to three feet, and he had to stoop. He walked toward the light, where the tunnel abruptly widened into a room some twelve feet wide and twenty feet deep. Its door stood open. A lantern on the table lit the place.

A pile of canvas and leather bags with the names of banks stenciled on them lay against one wall. Stacks of ingots and pokes presumably filled with dust, scads, and nuggets, all stolen from grubstakers, lay beyond. A table, lamp, chair, and cot made up the furnishings. Shelves filled with airtights and cooking utensils stood at the back of the room. Boxes of .44-40s lay on the table with the parts of a Colt pistol scattered on it. The lamp's flame guttered in the close, damp air.

He read the names on a few of the bags: California Merchants Bank, Lockwell Mining Company, Hayes Transfer Company, Wells-Fargo, San Francisco, Agricultural Bank of Palouse Flats. There were others whose names were obscured by the dark. He counted money sacks from California, Oregon, Washington, Idaho, and Montana.

What brought him up short, however, were the four piles of ingots that gleamed dully in the meager light. Each pile consisted of ingots cast in the shape of card suits—spades, diamonds, hearts, and clubs. Unable to believe he'd run the stolen hoard to ground, he picked one up—a spade—and marveled at its weight. Holding it to the lamp, he saw the assay stamp on it and the words "Aces High Mining Company, Nevada Montana, William Gramford, Mar. 1873." According to Gramford, there should be 128 ingots. The scrape of a boot somewhere in the tunnel alerted him.

He edged down the cavelike passageway to the intersection and peered around the corner. The dazzling light of the entrance silhouetted an approaching figure stumbling over the rubble. Slocum moved to his right and worked his way back into the main tunnel until darkness swallowed him. He watched the relief guard turn and disappear. He waited tense and ready, the feel of the gun in his hand reassuring, then picked his way between the tracks to the intersection and again peered around the corner. Twenty feet from him, the guard was seated at the table, his back to him. Slocum continued on down the tunnel, setting his feet carefully so not to trip over some object.

Outside, he blinked in the bright sunlight, and was moving quickly to his horse when he saw a Gypsy caravan near the mine entrance. He hadn't noticed it before because of its dirty brown color that blended with the foliage. It had windows, a door in its end, flower boxes under the windows, and was about fifteen feet long, five feet wide, ten feet high, and sat on small, spoked wheels.

Puzzled, he moved into its shadow and carefully surveyed the area, but saw no one. With a start, he realized the caravan's side was canvas. Closer inspection revealed the door, windows, and wheels were painted on the canvas. And very cleverly and realistically too.

At a distance, it resembled the real object. Picking up a side of the canvas covering, he peered inside. Darkness obscured his vision, but not enough that he couldn't see a large wagon wheel. He pulled the canvas higher. A black, varnished side and two gold letters, "TR" stared at him. He pulled the cloth higher. There, in gold emblazoned letters, he read "TRACEY CARTAGE COMPANY—BANNACK CITY." He quickly dropped the canvas. So, he thought, the Dougherty had been with Grace all along. A deep satisfaction flowed through him that his efforts had paid off. He again took up his vigil.

Late that evening, eight riders, Jim Argus and Mary Grace leading them, mounted and rode west. Watching them go, he thought, That's it! They're heading for Bridger's Rock. He wondered why eight riders instead of six. Argus was apparently going to lead the bank holdup. Slocum mounted and rode south to pick up their trail.

The eight gang members reined in outside town and gathered around Argus. Then, they split up. Three rode west, three east, and Argus and the woman proceeded down the trail that led to the north end of Main Street. Slocum rode east to make a wide circle before working his way in the darkness through alleys and side streets to the schoolhouse. He dismounted in its shadow and listened. The moon bathed the landscape in a ghostly bluish white glow. Hilda's house had a light in the window. He carefully reconnoitered the area before knocking on her door.

She gasped in surprise, then pulled him inside. Throwing her arms about his neck, she kissed him soundly. "Are you all right?" Excitement made her breathless.

"I'm fine. I need you to—"

She held his face in her hands and studied him with her intense gaze. "You look tired and hungry! Are you? Hungry, I mean?"

"Hungry as a wolf in a die-up. But—"

"I'll fix you something."

He impatiently pulled free and said, "Hilda. Get Gramford!"

She arched her brow in surprise. "Why?"

"Need to talk to him."

"I saw him yesterday. Said he was expecting news of some sort. We could go to his room at the hotel."

"Don't think that's a good idea. They may be watching him. Has anyone been around here?"

"No. Sit. I'll rustle up—"

"No! Go now! And be careful. I'll fix myself something."

She grabbed him, kissed him hard, and was out the door. A few minutes later, he heard her horse and buckboard clatter as she drove from the stable past the kitchen.

When she returned, she had both Gramford and his foreman, Angus MacTaggert. Gramford took papers from his portfolio.

"Angus here returned this morning with Professor Lowe's papers. Colonel Custer was gracious enough to rush their delivery by boat to Fort Benton."

He spread the papers and charts on the kitchen table as Hilda poured coffee for the three men. "Bear signs, gentleman. Baked 'em last night." She set the platter on the table.

Gramford munched one and closed his eyes in ecstasy. Angus MacTaggert followed his boss's example. Gramford murmured, "You are, my dear, the best cook in Montana. If John continues to partake of your culinary delights, we'll have to roll him about like a barrel."

Slocum asked, "Did the marshal get any reports of stolen horses in the last day or so?"

"Said he would tell me if he did. So far, he's said nothing."

Gramford donned his spectacles and peered at the papers. One had a drawing of a balloon with written information on it.

"Let's see. The gas bag's called an envelope. That's easy enough. Has a network of ropes covering it. They hold the basket—or gondola. Load ropes lines run from the net to hold the basket."

"Gondola," Hilda corrected him.

"Gondola. Hmm. That panel running from the apex to the, uh, equator's a—a rip-panel. Tug on that line running from the rip-panel to the basket and you open the panel to allow hot air to escape. It's called a maneuvering vent. Interesting.''

Hilda murmured. ''That part that falls from the envelope like a skirt is called . . .'' She laughed. ''The skirt. Simple enough. The gondola has a furnace in it. Wonder if the skirt is fireproof.''

Gramford frowned. ''Probably. The hot air the furnace generates goes up into the mouth at the bottom of the balloon and forces the whole contraption to rise.''

''Why?'' Angus asked.

''Where's the hottest part of a room on a hot day?''

''The ceiling.''

''Right. Hot air takes the envelope straight up.''

She pointed to the drawing.''Here's what's called a deflation line. We wondered how they could instantly deflate the envelope. See?'' She laid her finger on it. ''The cap on the envelope is like a hat. It has a round deflation port that's held shut by a—a hook-and-loop closure. Whatever *that* is. The rip-line descends to the gondola and is pulled by the pilot upon landing to effect an almost instantaneous deflation of the envelope. A tug on the line and the closure comes open to let the hot air rush out.''

''Ingenious!'' Gramford murmured.

''Play hell getting me in one of them things,'' MacTaggert muttered.

''Must be a big bag to carry all those men,'' she murmured, munching on a bear sign.

''Says here that this gas balloon''—Gramford pointed to a print—''has a-one-hundred-thousand cubic-foot capacity and can take up thirty passengers. It's a hydrogen balloon.'' He made a rapid computation on a piece of paper. ''If we give an average weight of, say, a hundred and fifty pounds for each passenger, then we have . . .'' Another scribbling with his pencil. ''A weight of four thousand five hundred pounds.''

''Enough to lift your gold shipment and two crewmen,'' Slocum observed, and added, ''Our balloon is *big*.''

"Look here!" Hilda held up another print. "This balloon could take up to fifty-two passengers. How much weight is that?"

"Close to eight thousand pounds," Gramford replied. "Here's another that could lift fourteen thousand pounds."

"Then it wouldn't have been impossible to lift the Dougherty," Slocum murmured.

"How high can this contraption go?" Angus asked.

"Well, it says here trial flights have gone as high as three miles. A balloon filled with hydrogen, of course. The danger is cold and lack of oxygen. Since we're nearly six thousand feet up already, two or three miles could present problems for an aeronaut."

Hilda observed. "A hot-air balloon wouldn't function well at high altitudes where the freezing temperature would rapidly cool the hot air."

"All they have to do is go high enough to climb over the mountains," Slocum said.

"Apparently, they must go with the air current," Gramford added. "John had it right. Since the wind blows from west to east, that's how they plan their robberies."

She pointed to a line of text. "Says here there are different layers of wind. A thousand feet up, the next layer might have wind blowing the opposite direction."

Gramford studied the page. "Well, it's clear that this is a realm none of us knows much about. The balloon robbers must have a trained aeronaut and perhaps a meteorologist helping them."

"And we know who they are," Hilda murmured.

Slocum said, "I followed Grace's wagons into a divide north of here. Runs into the Bridger Mountains. Blacktail Mountain's on one side to the south, Table Mountain to the north. Their wagons are in there. Three miles, I figure. Their hideout is an abandoned mine. They've got loot from banks all the way to California. And a pile of ingots—yours included, Bill."

Gramford's relief lit his face as Slocum continued. "Counted fifteen people. Amanda Brockwhite's with them. That must mean she's left her husband. Has Horace said anything?" He looked at Hilda.

She shook her head. "He probably hasn't missed her yet."

"Eight of the bunch rode to town earlier and split up into three groups. They've got the balloon ready to go and the rest are probably loading the loot now."

"Did you see any sign of the Dougherty?" Hilda asked.

"Yeah. It's there too. I believe they'll hit the bank within the next couple of days."

Gramford frowned and munched on a bear sign. "We must tell the marshal."

"Trouble is—if we spook 'em, we may not be able to surprise them at the hideout."

"We've no choice. Got to warn the bank and the law. Marshal Hendrix will inform the sheriff."

Slocum stood. "If MacTaggert will go with me, I can show him where they're located. He can ride back and lead you there. I'll stay. Maybe, I can stop them. Slow 'em down."

"It's a long shot, John," Gramford seemed to slump in on himself with worry. "Don't want anyone killed or hurt. Gold's not worth it."

Slocum patted his shoulder. "We'll take care of it, Bill. Angus! Let's ride!"

22

As the sun came up, Slocum and MacTaggert rode north along Dry Creek until it branched. MacTaggert pointed. "That's Blacktail Creek going east. I've hunted there a couple of times. The Missouri's about ten miles west of us."

"Is it navigable?"

"Not much beyond Fort Benton. Small boats. Why?"

"Always the chance they could take the river."

"The Army's watchin' 'em. Won't go that way."

"That must be the creek that flows into the divide," Slocum replied. "Let's try to get closer."

He couldn't be sure Grace and Argus didn't have lookouts in the hills to spot anyone approaching. By keeping inside the line of cottonwoods along the stream bank, they got within half a mile of the entrance where the foothills of Table Mountain fell steeply to the creek flowing from the divide.

"They're in there. About three miles. They can't go anywhere. That's where they've got the balloon. The mine's inside that mountain. That's where the loot's hidden."

MacTaggert studied the terrain and asked, "How're they

gonna get that Dougherty over those hills? If they plan on using that ambulance, they've got to get it beyond that mountain range and on the level ground east of here.''

"Don't know. I'll work my way back in and see what they're doing. You ride back and tell the others where they are.''

"How soon you figure they'll make their move?''

"They need the Dougherty and at least two other wagons to haul fuel and equipment for the journey. The transfer of the money from the bank to the Texas outfit will be either today or tomorrow. My guess is they'll move in today. Have Gramford find out when the transfer of money takes place. If the robbery fails, the gang will head back here and vamoose in the balloon. They'll have the loot loaded and ready to go. Once they're in the air, we stand little chance of catching them.''

"Okay,'' Angus said, and pulled his horse about. ''Good luck! And stay out of trouble!'' He rode off. Slocum waited until he was out of sight, then rode toward Blacktail Mountain.

He found a gulch on the north side that enabled him to ride east. The ground was rough, full of arroyos and ravines, as if some giant hand had crumbled paper. He figured he'd ridden a little over four miles when the ground cropped and he found himself at a creek. He was following it north when he heard voices ahead of him. He reined in and watched from cover.

The Dougherty, a four-span of mules pulling it, and three other wagons covered with canvas were working their way through the creek bed. The ground sloped sharply upward on both sides to give little room for a wagon trail. Several men rode forward to clear the way with axes. A high hill loomed on their right to form a kind of gulch that channeled the creek north. Five drovers herded horses and mules behind the wagons, the procession moving slowly to curses and shouted orders. Slocum figured they weren't much worried about running into anyone. He followed them for about three miles. Then the procession halted.

He spurred his horse up the high ground to his right but kept off the forward slope. The hill climbed steeply through the warm, sticky air. The sun was a bronze disk overhead that made rivulets of sweat course down his back and chest. When his horse fought for breath, eyes rolling white, sides lathering, he dismounted and hitched him to a tree. He poured what remained in his canteen into his hat to let the laboring animal drink.

Taking his Sharps, he climbed on, pulling himself up by trees, pausing only to catch his breath, then moving on. When he looked down, he figured he was probably twelve hundred feet up. He moved around the hill in a northerly direction until he had the creek below him and the wagons in sight through the foliage of the trees. Far below, men and animals resembled the toy soldiers he'd played with when a boy.

He raised his glasses and saw the wagons had come to the confluence of another creek that ran east through a narrow divide. A thick forest bordered the divide on the north, his hill on the south. The terrain beyond flattened out to a rolling plain twelve or fourteen miles to the east. He saw now what was going on.

The Dougherty and the three wagons would rendezvous somewhere east of the Bridger Range after the robbery. Grace clearly planned to abandon the rest of his wagons. He would take the animals, which he would need as fresh teams on the journey across the Bozeman when the supply wagons followed the balloon. He wondered if Grace had the amount of fuel needed worked out. Probably. So far, his operation had been a success.

Slocum reckoned he'd seen enough to tell him what he needed to know. He worked his way down the hill, being careful not to dislodge rocks. It wouldn't take much to alert the men below. He led his horse, rubbing the animal's nose and cajoling, "Easy, boy! There's water down there. We both could use some."

While they stood in the creek to cool off and drink, he tried to orient himself. If his reckoning was right, he wasn't quite two miles east of the abandoned mine.

He filled his canteen for the long march uphill. He figured they'd climbed close to a thousand feet in the mile it took them to come out where the mine entrance yawned like a black maw just west of them. Below him to his right, the balloon stood tall as a Sequoia—and just as magnificent.

The sight stopped his breath. The huge sphere wavered in the shimmering heat as it tugged at the basket. He had the impression that it wanted to shake off its bonds and fly off. He muttered, "Good, hot day. They can stay up longer and higher and use less fuel."

Men were loading the loot from a wagon onto the basket where the railing opened to form a gate. They passed sacks and boxes, which he assumed held ingots and pokes. Three containers of kerosene were rolled onto the platform and stowed.

How much will that contraption lift, he wondered. Be hell to pay, if they crashed into those mountains.

But Grace undoubtedly knew balloons. Figuring he was in for a long wait, Slocum rode off a distance where he could keep the balloon in sight. He wondered what Grace would do if the gang didn't return.

If Gramford had warned the marshal, and the marshal had sent for help from the sheriff, they might bag the lot. That would include Mary Grace, who could turn out to be a wild card no one had counted on. He doubted the preacher would abandon his wife and meteorologist. She and Grace knew how to fly the balloon. The others apparently didn't. He doubted Grace knew his wife was carrying on with Argus and that Argus was planning to kill him when they had safely delivered the gold.

When the sun was high in the west, Slocum saw dust

and counted ten or eleven men armed with rifles riding west through the divide. Probably to guard the entrance, he thought. He decided to inspect the mine again.

Feeling his way in through the tunnel's blackness, he tripped and stumbled repeatedly. If anyone was inside, they couldn't help hear him. Blind, he found the intersection and turned right. Twice, he bumped his head painfully on the low beams supporting the ceiling. He knew when he reached the room because the floor smoothed out. Groping his way, he bumbled into the chair and nearly fell.

"Hope to hell they left the lantern." He ran his hand over the tabletop and knocked something off that clattered when it fell. His fingers closed over the metal frame of the lamp.

He had to light two lucifers before the wick caught, smoked, then flared to fill the room with light. Its emptiness flew to his eye. He saw immediately that they had stripped the room of everything but the table and chair. The empty shelves reminded him with a painful jab in the belly that he hadn't eaten all day.

He left the lantern lit to make his way back out. He would camp and try to figure what to do next. He stumbled his way in the feeble, dingy light to the tunnel intersection.

He heard the scuffle of a boot, then—

His vision shattered into a million shards of light. Pain shot through him like molten lead. He fought to keep his feet as his head swam in raw agony. His hand instinctively shot to his cross-draw Colt. A blow to the arm sent shocks of blinding pain to his shoulder. Bodies thick with the stink of sweat and beer threw him against the wall. Pigging straps hobbled his wrists.

Half dazed, he was only dimly aware of voices as strong hands kept him from falling. They half-walked, half-kicked him back to the room. Strong arms wrestled him to the ground and bound his ankles. He was then dragged to a sitting position against the wall. When he blinked and shook his head to clear it, lightning bolts of agony scoured him. Slowly, the room came into focus. He was conscious of blood flowing from a wound in his scalp.

The two men who'd captured him stood back to let another figure enter. Jim Argus, clad in his usual black, ducked his head as he came in.

"Got him, eh?" His smile, cold as ever, played over his heavy mouth. "Not your day, Slocum."

Slocum's mouth felt full of sand. He ran his tongue over its inside to wet it. His voice was little more than a croak when he spoke. "Appears it wasn't yours either. Were they waiting for you at the bank?"

Argus crossed his arms over his chest. He didn't look happy. "Your warning got to the marshal. And the sheriff. Killed everyone but Joe and Mary."

"That's a start. Mary's escape ought to make Grace happy."

"I said they didn't kill her. They captured her."

He breathed, "Better and better."

"Not for you, it isn't."

"You said you wanted to kill me. Too bad you'll never know if you could've taken me on the up-and-up."

"I'm not here to play games with you, Slocum. By the way, we brought you company. Bring her in!"

Two other men and Amanda Brockwhite pushed Hilda into the room. Temporarily dazzled by the light, she blinked, then looked quickly about her. Her mouth was open as if to scream, but no scream came forth. Icy fear and despair flowed through him. Not for himself but for the woman. Amanda's face was a cold mask of hate as she shoved Hilda into the center of the room. Argus moved in behind her. Pilon Joe appeared in the shadows, his face wreathed in an unholy leer of triumph.

Amanda ordered, "Tie her feet!" Joe forced Hilda to her knees, then pushed her back so she lay next to Slocum. He quickly bound her legs.

A scuffling noise sounded in the tunnel, a light glowed, and then Theodore Grace pushed his way into the room.

He stood staring at the two prisoners, then rounded on Argus.

"How in the hell did you allow Mary to be captured?"

"They were waiting for us. We didn't have a chance. When rode up to the bank—there they were! The whole damn town! They shot everybody out of their saddles before we could do anything."

"How could they have known we were coming?" Grace, ashen-faced and trembling, stuck his face to within an inch of Argus's.

"Slocum here got word to them." It was the first time he had seen Argus without a smile.

Grace turned to look down at him. "Is that true?"

"How could I have told anyone? I've been here the whole time. Watched you take the Dougherty and the two wagons through the creek bed to get through the mountains."

"So—you knew what we were up to the whole time."

"Pretty much. You'll never get out of here."

"You're still working for Gramford?"

"Yup. Ain't earned my wages yet."

"I'm curious, Slocum. How did you tumble to us?"

"Up in Idaho. A couple of locos tried to take my grubstake. Their names were Zeke Scroggins and Bead Maleau." When Grace frowned, puzzled, he explained. "They kept going on and on about flying. Said they'd belonged to a gang of bank robbers that flew to each job. Said the gang leader, a preacher, had left them behind in the Hoodoos."

Grace nodded. "Those two. I remember. They shot up a bank we robbed in Oregon. Killed three people. Only time we ever harmed anyone. Argus wanted to kill them. I said no. We left them in the wilderness of northern Idaho. What happened to them?"

"I killed them."

Grace rounded on Argus. "Jim, you told me Slocum was on his way to Washington."

"Thought he was." His catlike smile returned. "It's obvious I overestimated his concern for the schoolmarm.'' He kicked Slocum's leg with the toe of his boot. ''He'll very shortly regret not heeding my warning.''

When Slocum noticed Pilon Joe leering in anticipation at his words, his blood coursed like ice through his veins as his fear for Hilda heightened.

''The sheriff will pick up your trail at daybreak,'' Slocum said. He tried to look more confident than he felt. ''You can't fly out of here at night.''

''You're right,'' Argus replied. ''But you're wrong about the law. They won't be coming.''

Slocum's heart slid into his boots.

''They won't be coming,'' Argus repeated, ''because we have the schoolmarm. If they return Mary and allow us to fly out of here, we return Mrs. Hasso. It's as simple as that.'' He beamed, his big teeth reminding Slocum of a swamp gar's. ''When Joe and I got away, we stopped by the lady's house long enough to persuade her to go with us. Needed an ace in the hole.''

''They told me you were dying,'' Hilda said.

''Does Gramford know about this trade?''

''He's the one we parlayed with. Him and the sheriff. Gramford's all for giving us his gold in exchange for the lady. The sheriff's not so sure. There's the loot from the banks we've hit. They want it back. For the rewards. There's a heap of fliers on us. Looks like we've got a Mexican standoff.''

Argus pulled out the chair for Amanda to sit on. She glared down at Hilda, her look cold venom. ''If anything happens to my sister, I'll tear you limb from limb!''

Hilda studied Amanda with contempt. ''And you call *me* a jezebel! I keep wondering who is the biggest whore— you or your sister!''

''Why *you*—'' Amanda sprang to her feet and kicked wildly at Hilda. Slocum tried to fend off her attack with his bound feet. Grace grabbed the irate woman and pulled her away.

Holding his struggling sister-in-law, he demanded, "What does he mean? Whore? You I can understand. But Mary . . ." His look was one of pure outrage and alarm.

Slocum chuckled. "What she means, preacher, is that your wife—or mistress—or whatever the hell she is, sees a lot of your bedroom ceiling over Argus's shoulder."

A snarl like an animal's growl escaped from Argus. Grace paled, his mouth suddenly twisted in speechless bewilderment. "What're you talking about?"

"He's lying!" Argus put his hand on his gun butt. "He's trying to save his skin."

Grace rounded on Amanda, who was listening to the exchange with open-mouthed astonishment. "Did Mary confide in you? She always does!"

But Amanda was reserving her fury for Argus. "You've been bedding that bitch? After you told me—"

"It's all lies," Argus stormed, his face red.

Grace, now thoroughly befuddled, swung back to Slocum, his face contorted with outrage. Slocum wondered if he'd already had suspicions about his wife's conduct. "What do you know about my wife?"

Slocum rapidly assessed the situation. He needed a handle, something to grab on to, if he was to save himself and Hilda. If he could drive a wedge between Argus and Grace . . . "When you were holding your revivals, I inspected your wagons, looking for the balloon. The house on wheels you sleep in"—he quickly described it—"was making odd rocking motions. Curious, I listened. Your wife and Argus were figuring how to get rid of you—while he was hiving her. Seems they agreed they couldn't act until you got them and the loot safely to North Dakota by balloon. After that, with the gold on its way to New York, you would no longer be needed. Getting rid of husbands is apparently old hat to Mary."

"That's a goddamn lie!" Argus again surged forward, hate contorting his features. Grace forcibly held him off.

Slocum managed a convincing laugh of contempt. "Like

I say, they were figuring how to kill you.'' He frowned as if trying to remember.''Yeah—your pardner in crime here wanted to shoot you. Your wife thought tossing you overboard just before they landed might work better.''

Grace's features were transformed from those of a sanctimonious bible-thumper to those of an enraged demon. ''You sonuva *bitch*! It's true—isn't it!''

Slocum twisted the knife. ''Too bad you couldn't have heard the rest of it, Reverend. Seems good old Mary's a gun collector.''

Grace, mouth trembling in his rage, stared at him.''*Gun* collector?''

''She likes Argus's guns. The one hanging by his side— and one hanging between his legs. She told him he's equally good with both.''

The preacher exploded in fury. Unable to get out more than an incoherent, animal-like screech of rage, he flung himself on Argus and seized him about the throat. Pilon Joe and two of the men wrestled him off.

Amanda stood and kicked at Hilda with demonic fury. ''You did this—you Jew bitch! I'll kill you!'' Hilda snaked her body to ward off the kicks.

Joe and two other men grabbed the screeching woman and pulled her into the tunnel. Joe blocked her from getting back in while the other men subdued Grace.

Slocum chuckled. ''Nothing like a family squabble to liven up things, eh, Argus?''

Argus, clearly shaken, choked, ''Get him outa here!'' The men dragged the screaming, raging preacher down the tunnel. His and Amanda's voices, shrieking curses and threats, receded. Argus smoothed his ruffled coat and shirt, shot his cuffs, and ran a hand through his hair in obvious distress. Turning to Pilon Joe, he muttered, his voice shaky, ''Watch these two.''

''Where you goin'?''

''Gotta settle matters with Grace.''

"This ain't no time for us to start fightin' among our-selves, Argus."

He studied the little man with cold contempt. "Just do as you're told!"

Joe's face lit up as he gazed at Hilda. "You gonna give her back?"

"If the sheriff shows up with Mary, yes."

Joe's pinched face was wreathed in a licentious leer. "I like big women." He studied Argus's face, his eyes que-rying.

"She's all yours. But no knife work like you did the others. Don't want blood and body parts to clean up." He shot him another scornful glance, muttered, "You little butcher!" then left.

Slocum's heart sank. He couldn't look at Hilda, who sat expressionless. Joe unbuckled the cross-draw holster from Slocum's waist and laid it on the table. He pulled the .44 from his belt and jammed it into the holster. He unbuckled his gunbelt and laid it aside and unbuckled the belt to his trousers. Then, grinning his unholy grin, he drew his Arkansas toothpick from his belt and ran his thumb along the edge. A thin line of blood followed it.

23

Slocum lay back to ease the strain of the thongs cutting into his wrists. He needed no distractions to jar him from thinking clearly. His throbbing headache was distraction enough.

Joe exclaimed, "Well—look what we have here!" He stood arms akimbo and stared down at Hilda, a leer lighting his weasel face. He bent and traced a finger over her cheek. She tried to shake off his hand. He gripped her jaw and shook it cruelly.

"Before I slit your throat—I'll slit your slit." He grabbed his crotch with his other hand and shook it, a giggling laugh of pure evil coming from his parted lips. "Gonna make you like it, bitch! But you're right. Ol' Mary was a whore."

Slocum said, "She was also your weather expert. You're going to have trouble without her crewing the balloon."

"We'll manage. Just get that ol' gas bag in the air and whoosh! We'll be gone. Like always!"

"Hope it's as easy as you make it sound."

Joe squatted on his heels, lifted Hilda's skirt, and ran his hand along her thigh. Cold fury prodding him like a knife. Slocum strained against his bonds. Hilda's face turned ashen with disgust and loathing. Mouth slack with anticipation, Joe waved his long knife before her eyes and then cut the thongs from her ankles. Grinning his hellish leer, he again ran a hand under her skirt. She snarled and kicked at him.

His face went from a licentious smirk to an angry grimace.

"Kick me, would ya! Ya bitch!" The knife pricked her throat. She froze. A thin trickle of blood flowed from the pinprick. "Oughta slit yer throat—ya lousy whore!"

Slocum steeled himself to try to throw his body in front of the woman and exclaimed, "Don't be a fool, Joe! She's your only way out of here! Kill her and you're dead! The sheriff won't trade for a dead woman."

"Then she better watch her mouth!" The hand gripping the knife wavered with uncertainty, then fell. He stabbed the knife down on the tabletop, where it quivered. He then unbuckled the belt to his trousers and wriggled them off his hips down about his ankles, making the act an unholy, erotic dance. He wore nothing under his trousers. His small erection glistened in the feeble light as spittle coursed down his chin. He pulled her skirt up, grabbed her ankles, and tried to force her legs apart. She grunted and fought him, feet kicking. One foot broke free of his grip and knocked him backwards.

"You bitch! You whore! Always did want to fuck a goddamn schoolteacher!" He again tried to force her legs apart, but she was too strong for him.

Slocum yelled, "You little weasel!" In his desperation, he tried to make Joe angry enough to turn on him.

Furious and frustrated, Joe gripped her throat with one hand and drew back the other in a fist. "Sorry, sweetheart! If you ain't gonna cooperate—then I got no choice. Too bad you won't be awake to enjoy it!"

Shots boomed. The mine muffled the noise, but the gunfire was outside the mine. The noise froze Joe, whose fist was drawn back to hit Hilda. Rattled, he stood and exclaimed, ''What the hell's that?''

More shots, followed by yells. He yanked up his trousers and listened intently. The baffle formed by the tunnels muted the sounds, but a gun battle was going on close by. The gnomelike outlaw hesitated, then scurried out to the tunnel.

Desperate, Slocum thought fast. ''Can you reach that table leg?''

She stretched her foot. ''No.''

''Scoot closer.'' She scooted, her body undulating like a snake's. ''Now try it.'' She hooked the table leg with her toe. ''Pull it toward me! That's it!'' The table skittered toward him. He snaked his way to it until his legs were under it. Raising his bound feet, he tilted the table until the gunbelt slid off and clattered to the floor. Joe's knife lay next to him. Using his body, he shoved it toward her.

''Can you shuck your boots?''

''Think so.''

''You'll need your toes.''

She worked one boot off, then the other. Then the woolen stockings.

''See if you can pick up that knife.''

She struggled, her toes straining to get a grip on it. At last, she held it, the handle between the big toe and second toe on her left foot. He squirmed until his feet were next to the knife.

''Now! See if you can saw those thongs!''

''I might cut you.''

''Jesus Christ! Do it! It's a little cutting now—or a whole helluva lot when that little snake returns!''

She had to balance the knife, hold it, and cut. Twice, the blade clattered to the floor. The third time, she secured the knife between her toes with her other foot and sawed. The knife's razor edge frayed the thongs on his feet.

''Keep going!'' he urged.

She gritted her teeth, bit her lip, and sawed. The heel of the foot gripping the knife, made a scraping sound as it moved back and forth on the dirt floor. She winced at the pain when the grit sandpapered the heel raw. Compassion and admiration for her warmed him. He strained to force his ankles apart. She sawed, her bare legs pumping back and forth, the blade awkwardly held but the cut deep enough now to channel the edge. Again, he strained, every muscle in his body as tense as steel rope. The thong burst.

She collapsed backwards from the effort. He shook his freed legs to get the circulation back. He then rolled forward to his knees, backed up to Hilda's foot, and felt for the blade with his numbed fingers. His right hand closed on it.

The stinging edge of the honed blade cut his palm. Greasy blood made the handle sticky. Swallowing the pain, he maneuvered the blade until it rested against the thong. He worked the knife with his long fingers, grimacing at the effort, and swallowed a curse. "Come on! Damn it! Cut!" More sawing. The blade slipped from his fingers, and he fought to hold it. Catching his breath, he started again. The firing and yelling outside slowly died. He steadied his hand against the side of the table and sawed.

His wrist stung as the blade cut into it. He strained his forearms. A snap—and his wrists were free.

He cut Hilda loose and whispered hoarsely, "Get over there! Out of the way!"

She shook her head and looked about for a weapon. She picked up the iron bar used to secure the door and stood with it in her hands, testing its weight and feel like a cricket player testing a bat. Her face mirrored grim determination.

The door opened. She swung.

The bar hit Joe's face with a meaty *splat*. Teeth and blood splattered. His gun flew from his hand. Slocum threw an uppercut that slammed the big man against the wall. Another punch to the jaw flattened him. He slithered down the wall and lay in a bloody heap.

Slocum paused long enough to grab his gun and belt. Then seizing Hilda's arm, he yanked her into the tunnel.

He almost ran into two men. Both carried rifles. Their surprise and momentary inaction saved him and Hilda. He fired twice on instinct. The bullets slammed the two backwards.

He whispered, "Take a rifle! We've got to get to the balloon." They moved through the tunnel, the noise of their stumbling echoing off the wet walls. Outside, they looked quickly about them. Three bodies lay sprawled in death near the entrance. He had no idea of what was going on. Sporadic gunfire came from his left farther down the hill. He could only assume Argus and Grace were fighting it out. In the distance below them, the balloon hovered, a huge, silent, ghostly shadow.

Argus's faint voice rang out, "Goddamn it, Grace! Listen to me! We can't do this without each other! Truce, man! Let's talk!"

Grace's voice echoed, "Go to hell! You sonuva bitch!"

"Look, you stupid fool! This no time for us to be fighting! Not with a fortune at stake!"

"You were gonna kill me! Remember? Fucking my wife, plotting against me! You want this fortune—you'll have to ride a long way to get it! We're leaving!"

Argus's curse rang off the hills. "Shoot those bastards!" Rifle fire raised puffs of smoke on the hill. Bullets hummed and whined.

"Come on!" Slocum pulled Hilda with him as they half-ran, half-slipped down the hill toward the balloon. Using the few trees for cover, they worked their way to the basket. The sphere towered over them like a thundercloud. Grace and what remained of his crew crouched behind wagons, rifles ready. Gun smoke near the area of the mine entrance and the slapping crack of bullets said Argus and his men were concentrating on the wagons barricading Grace and his men. Neither faction was paying any attention to the balloon.

The man guarding it wore two bandoliers filled with 10-gauge shotgun shells for the Greener he carried. He was crouching to make himself less of a target, his attention fixed on the clouds of smoke on the hill. He turned and stood in momentary confusion while he tried to recognize the couple approaching him.

"What's goin' on up thir?" he demanded. "Who's a-shootin' who?"

Slocum shot him. In the distance, someone yelled, "What's going on?" He recognized Grace's stentorian voice. "Yancy? What was that?" The question was clearly meant for the dead man.

Slocum feverishly worked the bandoliers off the corpse, and handed them and the shotgun to Hilda, admonishing her to keep her head down. She climbed into the basket. He scrambled aboard and opened a container of kerosene. Using the funnel, he strained under the heavy container, tilting it slowly to let the fuel gradually fill up the reservoir.

"Goddamn it! Hurry!" he muttered. He was about to toss the empty can overboard, but thought better of it. He struck a lucifer only to have it go out. He struck another. The wick caught and flared into flame.

He turned the bellows wheel to blow the flame into a roaring, blue torch of heat. A muted shriek sounded as the heat soared up the chimney and into the mouth of the balloon. Slowly, laboriously, the huge bag trembled as it expanded. The ropes anchoring the gondola creaked as they tightened and strained at their moorings. The gondola groaned then moved under their feet.

Hilda ordered, "Faster! More heat!"

Distant voices. "Hey! Stop 'em! Who's in that basket?" Pounding feet sounded.

He turned the blower wheel faster, his shoulders and arms burning with the effort. The furnace flared, the chimney shook. He prayed that a spark wouldn't ignite the skirt. The gondola again lifted, the cables creaked and groaned.

Hilda screamed, "Pull those slipknots!" He grabbed the

first line and yanked it. It popped and threw the basket askew. He yanked the second. The basket again lurched, nearly throwing him to the deck. He jerked the third—and the floor surged upward. He wondered why his feet couldn't get a firm purchase on the deck, then realized it was tiled with gold ingots. A canvas tarpaulin covered them. No wonder, he thought with dismay, the balloon's having trouble rising. The fourth anchor line broke—and the basket lumbered skyward.

Hilda's voice in his ear broke his concentration. "John! They're coming!"

He jerked his head around to where she pointed. Five men ran all out toward them. He recognized the leader as Grace. Pilon Joe, mouth and face bloody, loped along like an ape. All brandished rifles.

He pushed her down. Grabbing the shotgun, he broke the barrels and loaded it. A fusillade of rifle shots sounded, and bullets whined as they ricocheted off the iron furnace. Grace's voice yelled, "Stop the shooting! You'll hit the balloon! Grab the anchor ropes!"

Two men raced toward the dangling lines. Slocum rose and fired. The 10-gauge bucked against his shoulder. One load nearly tore one robber in two, the other sent the second sprawling. Frantic with pain and drenched in blood, the man crawled for cover. Bullets hummed as Slocum ducked. Hilda calmly reloaded the shotgun. A bullet nicked a cable and partially frayed it. He drew his Colt and peeked over the metal rail.

The remaining robbers stayed out of range of the shotgun. From the cover he'd crawled to, the wounded robber fired to help keep Slocum pinned down. Hilda crawled to the blower wheel and turned it. The furnace roared louder. The balloon broke free with a wrenching sound and rose.

Grace screamed, "Goddamn it! They're getting away!" Bullets hummed. One ricocheted off the chimney to leave a deep groove.

As the balloon rose slowly like a lumbering beast, Slocum waited, then stood and shot at three men who were within twenty feet of the gondola. One man screamed and fell. The other two disappeared under it. The platform cleared the tops of the cottonwoods. The stream below dwindled to a line, the trees to green blobs. He broke the barrels and inserted two fresh loads. Then he relaxed, the tension flowing out of him like air. He got up and spelled Hilda at the wheel.

She knelt, bent forward, and murmured, "John!" He turned his head as her lips found his. She clung to him as the gondola lurched in a downdraft, then rose again.

"We made it!" She beamed at him, her teeth white in her face. Her hair stirred like a silky halo framing her face. He kissed her back.

"We made it, all right. All we have to do now is to get this contraption somewhere near Bridger's Rock."

"The wind's blowing the wrong way. The town's in back of us."

"Can you get us up to the next wind layer?"

She bent low to study the compass, then the map.

"Yes. If the wind is different up there. We'll find out soon. Keep that blower going! That'll take us up. Everything looks different up here anyway. We're going over those hills. The wind usually follows the valleys. Bridger's Rock is back of us. We want to stay outside town if we come down."

"Why outside?"

"A balloon will attract everybody around. Crowds could strip us bare of the gold before Gramford can get to us." She frowned as she computed the distance.

"Reckon we got time, then, to pick a spot. What about setting down on a mountain?"

"No, Mrs. Hasso! Pick a spot! *Now!*" The voice spun him away from the blower. Disbelief grabbed him when he saw Grace and Pilon Joe, guns leveled, peering at them from their vantage point behind the railing opposite them.

Both men scrambled over and lowered themselves to the deck. As Joe crept carefully around the column of the furnace, Slocum recognized his missing Colt cap-and-ball in his hand. He noticed Joe hadn't covered the holes of the chambers in the cylinder with grease to prevent a sympathetic discharge of all six charges at once. Grace, gripping his .45, moved carefully around the other side so that the two gunmen flanked them.

The preacher grinned happily. "Obviously, we're the last people you were expecting, eh?"

Slocum slowly raised his hands. "You do have a way of dropping in uninvited, Grace."

"Thoughtful of you to leave the anchor ropes dangling. I'll take your gun, Slocum." He reached out his hand. Hilda put her hand on the valve rope as if to steady herself. Slocum shot a look at her. She stared unblinkingly back at him.

"Why don't you take it?" he said.

"Shoot the bastard!" Joe yelled. "We don't need him."

"We don't need either of them. They're extra weight," Grace said. He shifted to steady his feet. "You've done me a big favor, Slocum. Don't have to share with Argus or the rest."

Slocum wondered if there was a chance in hell he could draw fast enough. Hilda gasped, pretended to fall, and dragged the valve rope with her.

The envelope shuddered as the gondola fell from under them. They were weightless for perhaps two seconds. Slocum, reading Hilda's mind, knew what to expect; Grace and Joe didn't. Slocum drew, his thumb hauling back the hammer, his finger holding the trigger back. When the gun was clear of the holster and level, he lifted his thumb from the hammer.

The Colt cracked and rolled back in his hand. He caught a glimpse of Grace folding in the middle. His Colt roared, the heat of the muzzle blast searing Slocum, the bullet ricocheting off the steel ring and whining upwards.

Slocum threw himself backwards to get Hilda out of the line of fire. Joe's gun came up. A crack—a flash of flame between the cylinder and the barrel. Then fireworks erupted in Joe's hand. All six chambers fired at once.

The cylinder exploded in a flash of flame. The frame deflected four bullets that flew off to either side. The bullet opposite the one under the hammer hit the frame. The gun flew into pieces. Joe yelped and staggered backwards, blinded by smoke and flame. His right hand was a mass of bloody garbage.

Slocum spun back to Grace. Hilda grabbed a struggling Joe.

"Run your hands up me, would you! You filthy little rat!"

With superhuman effort, she lifted his struggling body up and over the rail. Joe grabbed her arm with his good hand, half pulling her over the railing with him. She sunk her teeth into the hand and bit it loose. Joe screeched in agony and got out a single fleeting, strangling cry of terror that faded as he plunged earthward.

Grace, sitting on the deck, tried to raise his gun. Slocum shot him again. He paused to let his heart catch up, then turned to Hilda. She lay slumped against the railing.

"Hilda! Are you all right?" He staggered to where she lay. A dark stain of blood glistening on her sleeve. "Damn! You're hurt!" Cold fear gripped him as he pulled her to a sitting position, knelt, and worked off her coat. Blood oozed from a gash on her upper left arm. Happy relief surged through him that she wasn't seriously hurt.

When her head wobbled, and she looked on the verge of fainting, he steadied himself on the shuddering deck, grabbed a water flask, and held it to her lips. She gulped down the water, letting it dribble down her chin. He cut away the sleeve.

"Looks worse than it is. Not much more than a scratch. They must have a medical kit aboard."

Breathless, she pointed weakly to a cabinet. "In one of those drawers."

He soon had the wound bandaged. She gave a nervous giggle.

"One of those wild rounds hit me when his gun exploded. I'm all right." He helped her to her feet.

While the balloon drifted earthward toward a stand of trees bordering a stream, he quickly assessed the situation.

"Got to lose ballast," he exclaimed.

"We have none. The gold . . ."

He examined the prostrate preacher. "He's dead. That's a hundred and seventy pounds we don't need." He lifted the body and rolled it over the railing. He turned away from watching it plummet to the ground. Heights made him ill, a secret fear he had never divulged to anyone. Hilda checked the fuel reservoir.

"We're low, John."

He wrestled the remaining canister to the burner and filled it. She tried turning the blower wheel, but the movement brought a wince of pain to her.

"Let me do that." He took over. He spun the wheel, the blower roared, the chimney shuddered under the blast of heat—but the balloon didn't rise. It didn't sink, but it didn't rise.

"What the hell's wrong?" he demanded.

She looked up, her gaze searching the vast expanse of silk. A ripping noise sounded overhead.

"There! Look!" She pointed. He saw it. And heard it.

A rip in the fabric near the envelope's equator hissed as hot air escaped. The tear, some four feet wide, slowly widened, the flapping edges of the wound signifying hot air was escaping.

"Must've been a bullet," she exclaimed.

"What the hell do we do now?"

She busily yanked open drawers in the storage box.

"Here it is!" She held up a huge curved upholstery needle and a roll of sewing twine. "Figured they must be equipped to patch tears in the fabric.'' She expertly threaded the needle, stuck it in her skirt, then opened her blouse. She placed the roll of cord between her breasts and rebuttoned her blouse. Before he realized what she was doing, she clambered up onto the railing, shimmied up the load ropes, and worked her way under the load ring. It was a close fit as she slid by the hot chimney.

"What the hell're you gonna do?" he shouted in alarm.

"Just keep the blower going!"

"You're not going to try to climb up there—"

"Have to. That rip's getting wider. We'll go down if I don't sew it shut." She was working her way up the rigging. Every fourth set of load ropes was a ladder. She climbed, wind whipping at her. Numb, he could only hold his breath in fear for her. The ladder, because it angled downward toward the load ring, resembled the futtock shrouds of a full-rigged ship. She swung herself around the ropes so she was inside instead of hanging outside. She climbed quickly to where the rip fluttered and flapped.

He gripped the rail, his neck strained back to watch her high in the netting. Fear for her squeezed his heart like a vice.

24

Slocum was so busy turning the blower wheel he couldn't spare a glance upward to check Hilda's progress. The shifting deck was threatening to make him seasick, and looking up only made it worse. She kept shouting, ''Keep that blower going! Don't stop!'' The wind buffeted and tore at them, and cold seeped into him despite the sweat he worked up turning the blower.

When he did finally look up, he saw she'd managed to gusset the ends of the rip to keep it from widening. When he ventured his second look, she had closed the tear and was drawing the edges together by wide, rough stitches. She had to lean to reach the slash and tug the cord to draw the edges together with the escaping hot air buffeting her the whole time. When he looked again, she was finishing a finer stitching over her rough one. Her precarious perch— one leg wrapped about a load cord while she leaned inward to sew—made him shudder. He didn't want to lose her. Women like Hildegard Hasso came from no common mold. His mouth was gritty-dry, but he wasn't going to drink until she was safely down.

The wind surged and lifted the balloon, making the deck shudder under his feet. He grabbed for the railing and fought to keep his balance. A scream. Startled, he craned his neck to look up.

She hung upside down, dangling by one leg. The leg hooked over a rung was all that prevented her from falling. Her hair had come loose and blew like a banner in the wind. She struggled to grab the load rope, but she had fallen outside the ladder, which sloped away from her. She tried to swing her body so she could grab the load rope, but she was hanging too far out.

His fear of heights vanished in his frantic concern for her. He scrambled up the netting and stomped back every thought but the necessity of saving her. He wanted to look down, but fought the urge. Her skirt had fallen over her face to further confuse her. Her legs glistened white between her dark boots and her skimpy, frilly white underpants. The picture of a circus acrobat hanging from a tightrope flashed before him. He finally reached her and steadied himself against the taut, thrumming load ropes.

With his left foot on the rung, left hand gripping a thick load rope, he leaned out, caught her, and circled her shoulders with his arm. Her flapping skirt blinded him. She reached up, undid the belt, and frantically wriggled and pulled until the skirt dropped over her shoulders and floated away. It caught on a line where the wind held it. Her teeth clenched in a grimace of icy fear, and her breath gasped in wheezing sobs in his ear. Straining to hold her, he drew her to the load rope. She seized it and hung on. He climbed three more rungs to where he was level with the leg bent over the rung. Her skin felt like ice when his hand touched it.

"Can you pull yourself up?" he shouted in her ear. The wind whistled and tore at them.

When she remained frozen, he took her right wrist and squeezed it.

"Let go!" She released her grip on the rope. He pulled

her hand up to the next rung. Slowly, muscles burning, he managed to walk her up the rungs until she could free her leg. They hung in breathless exhaustion, panting, gasping. The balloon rocketed along, the buffeting wind threatening to tear their hands from the lines. The ground four hundred feet below whizzed by under them.

"Let's get down!" he urged. She nodded quickly, lips drawn over teeth clenched with terror. She shook him to get his attention and pointed.

A high, jagged ridge wavered before them. They would soon crash against it. Gathering his strength, he helped her down. When they squirmed their way through the load ring, his hand touched the hot chimney. Searing pain shot through him, and he nearly let go.

When they were again on the platform, he forgot his burned hand in a frantic effort to force more hot air into the mouth. Twice, the wind gusted to make the balloon soar, then flatten out in flight. Twice, she had to grab the lines and hold on until the gondola settled down. It slowly rose.

"We're not going to make it!" she screamed. The ridge loomed closer. The jagged rimrock would tear the balloon to shreds. The precipitous rocky side would plunge them four hundred feet to their deaths. He jerked her to him and pulled her face into his shoulder so she couldn't see death hurtling toward them.

The deck surged upward with such violence that gravity forced them to their knees. An updraft of warm air lifted the balloon over the ridge, which slowly receded behind them. His heart beat again as he slipped to the deck, his arms tight about the woman. The furnace roared, the heat warming them. He fought the urge to lie down and let his heart catch up. Hilda was a familiar, comforting warmth against him. He absently ran his hand over the length of her naked hip and thigh.

"Thanks," she murmured.

"For what?"

"Saving my life."

He shook his head. "You saved both our lives." When he said, "You're a brave woman, Mrs. Hasso," his voice sounded unnaturally hoarse to him.

"Wasn't thinking about being brave. Just needed to sew that rip shut." She gave a nervous giggle, then broke into tears, her sobs shaking him.

He stroked her hair, his fingers kneading its soft mass.

"You're not only a gourmet chef—but you can sew too. You're your own seamstress, I'll bet."

That broke the tension, and they both laughed. He then climbed up and retrieved her skirt.

The wind coursed them over the ground, which she reckoned lay a thousand feet below them. That meant they were a mile and a half above sea level. The balloon climbed steadily. The hills became rolling terrain the farther east they flew, then gradually flattened out into a plain.

Abruptly, the balloon shuddered and appeared to hover. The air was now icy-cold and thin, and he was suddenly panting as if he'd been running. His heart raced faster. Then, the balloon moved.

She read the compass. "We must be at least twelve thousand feet up. We're moving west-southwest. The current's changed."

He ventured a cautious peek over the railing. Far below, the terrain, resembling crumpled green plush, looked unreal. Squinting against the sun, he saw four thunderstorms miles apart, great roiling black clouds, rain a solid sheet sweeping to the ground like giant black brooms. The awesome beauty of it wet his eyes. The horizon was a hazy blur of land and sky that coursed in a faint arc until its ends were diffused and blended in darkness.

"John! We're flying west! Keep an eye peeled for the town." She pushed him gently aside to spell him at the blower wheel. "The cold'll take us down soon."

The updraft buoyed the balloon now, which required only periodic use of the blower. He peered westward, searching, because he had no idea where they were. Or how long they'd been flying.

"John! Look!" She held the map in one hand and pointed with the other. "To the northeast! Almost below us! There!"

He stared. The Missouri running north and south was a stream of liquid fire snaking almost below them. East of it, shrouded in haze, was a town—streets, houses, barns—the roofs glinting in the setting sun like some child's toy.

She pointed. "That's Bridger's Rock, John! See! The school—our house!"

He stared south, and could barely make out another sprawl of human habitation. "That must be Bozeman," he yelled. The dark mass of the Bridger Range loomed up to their east.

She pulled the valve rope. The basket fell from under their feet to make them grab the railing. The air gradually warmed, breathing became easier. Coming up was a stream bordered by cottonwoods. A cabin stood near the stream.

Thoughts coursed through his mind. Gramford was going to get his gold back if everything went right. But what about him and Hilda? Five hundred dollars wasn't much when he recalled what they'd both been through. The balloon could stand losing some ballast. While she was busy with the compass and the valve rope, her back to him, he pulled the tarpaulin aside.

He picked up an ingot in the shape of a heart and set it on the rail. When they were directly over the cabin, he pushed the ingot into space and quickly lost sight of it as it plummeted earthward. He thought he saw the roof splinter, but couldn't be sure.

She hadn't seen him jettison it. Gramford, he told himself, would be just as happy getting 127 ingots as 128. Hell! It would make sense that the gold, in being transferred about as much as it had been, would come up one ingot short. Gramford might not like it, but he'd accept it. He was still coming out the winner, and Slocum would have done his job.

He would ride out with Gramford's five hundred in his poke and find the cabin. With the gold, he would have close to five thousand dollars. Frank James had once confided to him that his brother Jesse had never had more than six thousand dollars in his life despite all their train robberies.

When his conscience stabbed him, he recalled Hilda hanging upside down in the netting. She deserved whatever she could get. Her voice jarred him from his musings with painful force. "How're we going to contact Gramford, John?"

"Don't know."

"We mustn't put down near Bridger's Rock. If the townspeople see a balloon, they'll be all over us. The gold'll simply vanish in the crowd."

"Yeah. You're right! Let's get this contraption safely anchored someplace first."

"You think the rest of the gang'll follow us?"

"Doubt it. With the leaders gone, they'll probably scatter. But we'd better play it safe."

When she wasn't looking, he penciled a small X on the map where he thought the cabin was.

Twilight obscured the landscape and rendered it a series of dark, foreboding mountains and flat, dimensionless plains. Night pushed the sun over the last ridge of hills to the west.

"We'd better go down," she said, and took hold of the valve rope.

He nodded, and partially closed the fuel feed line. They traveled for another ten minutes in silence, the only sound being the wind thrumming the load lines like giant harp strings.

A vast, overpowering loneliness swept over him as he looked out on the endless sweep of sky above, burned red and orange from the setting sun. The same sun that only a few hours earlier had warmed Slocum's Stand in Georgia.

Visions of his home, the war, his rides with the Youngers and Jesse James passed before his vision. What had he done with his life? What was it all about? Up among the clouds, the earth a blur below, he felt his mortality as he'd never felt it before. He would die in some shootout and leave nothing anyone would remember him by. He moved to Hilda and put his arm about her. She, at least, was real.

"That line of trees, John." She pointed. "That means water. We'll try for that."

He strained his eyes and barely made out a faint dark wash against a lighter background. Hilda, he reckoned, had eagle eyes. "See any fish down there?" He grinned. She laughed, and the tension eased.

By now, they'd had enough experience with the balloon to sense its quirks and whimsies. She hauled on the valve to release more hot air. The partially deflated envelope fluttered as the balloon glided downward, the deck abruptly falling from under their feet.

"More hot air, John! Quickly!"

He fed more fuel to the burner and it blew into a roaring flame. The deck came up to meet them. She released more air.

"Like playing the organ at church," she exclaimed with a laugh. "You keep pumping the bellows, and I release just the right amount of hot air. I'm getting the feel of it. Now— if I could just make it boom out a Bach cantata . . ."

The approaching darkness dangerously blurred visibility. The deck hit solid earth with a jar that buckled their knees. The envelope fluttered overhead and threatened to settle down on them like a huge blanket.

She shrieked, "Kill the burner!"

He shut the fuel valve and hit the damper switch. A muted crash sounded when the spring-loaded damper plate doused the flame. He prayed the chimney would cool enough before the envelope touched it. Pain in his burnt hand reminded him of the heat involved as he unlimbered the stilts that supported the mouth, anchored them into the ground, then tied them in place. The huge, wavering black maw gaped down at them.

A gust of wind blew the sagging envelope beyond the gondola where the load ropes, tightening, then slacking, threatened to upset it. He prayed the four stilts would hold.

"Hope that gold is enough ballast."

She murmured, "Envelope's just about deflated. We'll have a time re-inflating it."

"How far are we from town, you reckon?"

"Saw lights north of us. Four or five miles, I'd say. Hope the wind stays calm."

"We got any food?"

"Let me look." She lit a lantern and rummaged through the equipment chest. Holding up two airtights, she grinned. "Baked beans pique your fancy, sir?"

"The West's greatest chef can surely do better than that."

"Go on with you! Light the kerosene stove while I get the fixings." She found a pan, filled it partially with water, and set it on the burner. He used Joe's Arkansas toothpick to open the airtights. Soon, the delicious aroma of simmering beans and boiling coffee reminded him that he hadn't eaten in two days.

He readied the shotgun and their other weapons just in case. But the night was quiet. The faint chirping of insects, the occasional hoot of an owl, and distant howl of coyotes and wolves told them they were alone.

His belly full, a cup of hot coffee in his hand, he sat resting his back against the warm stove. Nights quickly chilled on the prairie. Hilda was a blurred shadow near him. The day's adventures became far away and remote to him, as if they had happened to someone else. Even the picture of her dangling by one leg a thousand feet in the air seemed unreal.

"Woman?"

"You addressing me, sir?"

"Only one of you around at the moment. Come here."

"I'm fixing a bed for us. What do you want?"

"To hold you. Make certain you're alive and well. That this was only a bad dream."

She gave a shuddering sigh. "Come on! I've used what blankets I could find. Won't be like home, but . . ."

He pulled her into his arms and breathed in the aroma of her hair. "You've got very nice legs," was all he could think to say.

A laugh exploded from her. "Here we are in the middle of nowhere. A gang of outlaws are after us—and all you can think of is I have nice legs? *Really,* John!" Her laugh was soft and warm.

"Saw you hanging upside down. Remember? That's what stuck in my mind."

"Not that my life was in danger, huh?"

"That too. Best lay I've ever had, gourmet cook, great seamstress—now a lady with a magnificent set of legs." He hugged her. "Bet you did all that on purpose simply to get my attention."

"If I weren't so tired—and so content—I'd punch you, John Slocum."

The juices were heating in him. He murmured in a shaky voice, "Want to?"

"Want to what?" Her voice was full of sleep.

"You know."

"Do I have a choice?"

"No."

"Then why ask academic questions?"

"You and your damned education! Why don't you speak English?"

"All right. You want me to screw me, you unshuck me. That plain enough for your cowhand vocabulary?"

He grinned, and found the buckle to her skirt with one hand and the buttons of her blouse with the other. "Plain enough."

●   ●   ●

The morning sun brought them drowsily awake. She slipped out of his arms, climbed the railing, and, naked except for her boots, vanished among the trees. He yawned, stretched cramped muscles, and made coffee. Splashing in the creek told him she was bathing. She walked back, hands busily fluffing her mane of hair dry. Shivering, she put on her clothing, then rustled up breakfast.

"We've got to get word to Gramford, John."

"How? Too far to walk. And too dangerous. I'd go, but I don't want to leave you alone."

She sat in silence for a moment. "Where does he have his office?"

"Over the bank on Main Street. Why?"

"Maybe the quickest way to get his attention would be to fly over the town."

He objected. "You yourself said everybody would flock out to see us."

"If Gramford's in his office and hears the ruckus, he'll come outside to see what's up. Literally. He knows about the balloon. He certainly would have enough presence of mind to gather his men and follow us."

"If he could keep up."

"He'll know we're out there. And why. I don't believe we should split up."

"Me neither. Maybe you're right. I'll fill the reservoir. You think we can pump hot air into it when it's on the ground?"

"Grace did. Start the blower."

The envelope filled slowly, climbed off the ground like a fat woman pulling on her clothes, and finally soared over them. He filled their canteens from the stream.

"We're down to one container of kerosene, John. I'll write a note telling Gramford what we need and drop it to him."

"We'll have to be close to the ground."

"None of this is going to be easy."

An hour later, the balloon had climbed to six hundred

feet, and the air current swept them toward the town. Hilda played the valve to drop them to four hundred feet. The lower layer of air pushed them in the direction of Bridger's Rock.

Main Street was easy to see. It was wide and obvious from the air. He wasn't sure where the bank was in the row of buildings fronting the street, but it was, he recalled, on the north side. People ran into the street to stare up at them and wave. He wasn't sure, but he thought he saw Gramford in the street waving wildly at them, his white hair blowing.

They were about two hundred feet up as they glided slowly over the crowd. Hilda had tied a packet with a letter in it to a blanket weighted with an airtight.

He yelled, "Drop it! I think that's him!" The figure, in shirt sleeves, hair white, loped along under them, his arms waving wildly.

She leaned over the rail and yelled, "Bill Gramford!" The figure shouted something as she released the blanket.

It fluttered down and landed on a roof and rolled off into an alley. The figure gesticulated wildly.

"Well, we've done what we could." She relaxed against the rail. "Told him we would put down near Blacktail Gulch. I can find that with your help."

"Then what?"

"We wait. And hope it was Gramford."

25

Slocum hung on as the heat boiling off the roofs and street below lifted the balloon and the breeze shoved it a northeast direction. Hilda spilled some hot air to slow it. He watched to see if anyone followed them out of town. Two horsemen raced after them, but were too far away for him to recognize them. He settled back and enjoyed the cool ride.

When he stared and saw the Gallatin to the south and the Missouri to the west glimmering in the sun, he reckoned they'd traveled some five miles. Ahead of them loomed the entrance to Blacktail Divide between two high hills. They were back where they had started from. She hauled back on the valve rope.

"John! Douse the blower! I've got to bring us down on that level ground by that stream!" She pointed. "If the wind carries us though that canyon, it'll tear us to pieces on those rocks."

The balloon drifted and descended. She skillfully manipulated the valve rope. He hung onto the rail, his heart in his mouth. The ground was coming up too fast for comfort. She loosened the valve rope, and the deck pushed up at his feet. He could almost reach out and touch the tops of the trees bordering the stream as they glided by. The gondola jarred him to his skull when it hit ground. The load ropes creaked and groaned as they dragged at the heavy basket. She tugged the valve open while he unlimbered the stilts. jumped to the ground, and anchored them in place. The vast maw of the mouth sucked and flapped overhead. The breeze carried the envelope away from the gondola to where it draped itself on the ground and fluttered like a dying bird. It was only then that he could breathe again.

A half hour later, three horsemen leading four heavily laden packhorses rode up and reined in. Slocum stood, the Greener loaded and cocked.

"Who are you?" he demanded.

"We're from Bill Gramford. He told us to ride ahead and find out where you landed."

"Don't remember seeing any of you before. Stay where you are!" The men steadied their dancing horses but stayed put. He didn't like it, but maybe it was because he'd been through so much he trusted no one. "Get off your horses!" He gestured with the shotgun.

"Drop the scattergun, Slocum!"

The icy voice froze him. Despair hitting him, he turned his head. Jim Argus stood a few feet away, his nickel-plated Colt glinting from the sun's rays.

Slocum groaned to himself, let the hammers down easy, and laid the weapon at his feet.

"Now the Colt! Easy! No tricks!" He waved the gun. "Now, step aside! That's it."

The three men rode up and slid from their horses.

"George! Check and see if the gold's there." George, young, blond, and agile, leaped over the gondola's rail and lifted the tarp.

"Seems to be, Boss!"

"Good!" Argus grinned. "Don't have much time. Gramford's on his way. Lon! Harry! Get that heater going! Got to inflate the balloon."

"What the hell're you going to do, Argus?"

"Why, take the gold. What else?"

"And how do you aim to do that?"

"Very simple, really. I take Mrs. Hasso, balloonist extraordinaire, and . . ." He shrugged. "We continue east."

Slocum fought for time, his eyes darting, searching for some handhold to change the situation.

"Tell me, Argus. I'm still confused. Are you the one who hired those wolfers to attack us on the road to Virginia City? To take Gramford's scalp? After Mary stole the Dougherty?"

He grinned. "Guilty. Grace didn't want any killings. But I knew with Gramford dead we'd have a much easier time of it. The old coot's worse'n a badger. When he gets his teeth in you, he won't let go. So I hired those animals to bring me his scalp. After Mary had lifted the Dougherty to our hideout. However, you foiled me there too. Grace's big mistake was in not killing all of you when Mary held up the Dougherty."

"Where's Amanda?"

"With her sister in jail. Had to sacrifice her. Too bad!" He made a mournful face and shook his head in mock sadness.

Slocum managed a laugh he didn't feel. "Bet that breaks your heart. You won't get far, though. There's no more fuel."

"We thought of that. Harry! Bring up the packhorses!"

Harry, tall and plump, hauled the laden animals to the gondola. "Okay. Get those cans of fuel aboard."

Harry and Lon unloaded the canisters of kerosene and rolled them to the gondola, but together couldn't lift them over the railing. They strained, muscles bulging on their necks and shoulders, sweat pouring from them, but the heavy cans stayed on the ground. Slocum refrained from telling them the railing had an opening in it.

Argus gestured with his gun. "Help 'em!"

He pretended to struggle with a can. George added his strength.

He was startled to hear Hilda say, "Why don't you open that gate? On the other side?"

Argus smiled at her. "You're going to be an even bigger help, lady. I wondered what our cowhand here"—he motioned to Slocum—"found so attractive in a schoolteacher. Now I see."

He took her chin in his hand and studied her with his intense gaze. "You're not only intelligent but quite attractive. Wonder how I missed that. Well, we'll have ample time to become much better acquainted on our flight to Fort Lincoln." His gaze boldly undressed her.

"I won't go with you."

"Oh, yes, you will. Otherwise, I'll kill your cowpoke here and now."

"You'll kill us both anyway."

"The boys here will dispose of Slocum. Whether I dispose of you depends on how well you cooperate. Meanwhile—get that fuel on board!" He turned to her, his suggestive leer curdling Slocum's belly. He remembered then that she had his hideout. Where on her person, he couldn't guess.

Argus motioned her to approach him. "Reckon I ought to try you out before I commit myself too far."

She sashayed shamelessly up to him and murmured in her throaty voice, "Since I've no choice . . ." She slid her arms about his neck. Slocum, busy wrestling the cans onto the deck, couldn't believe her giggle and then her groan of pleasure. Argus had his hands low on the backs of her thighs and was lifting her skirt.

"Here," she murmured, "let me help you." She unbuckled his gunbelt. He struggled out of his coat. She pulled his suspenders off his shoulders and unbuttoned his trousers. Slocum, fighting to see what was happening, cursed, "Goddamn it! Hilda—what're you *doing*?"

"I'm going with the best man."

Argus rounded on them with a curse. "All of you! Keep your eyes to yourselves. You too, Slocum! The lady and I have some business to transact." His trousers bunched around his ankles. He struggled to keep his balance while he stepped out of them and pulled up her skirt.

Her sultry voice breathed, "Here! Let me help you."

"Can you do it standing up?" he demanded, his voice thick with lust.

Her voice was a throaty murmur. "Any way that pleases you, big man."

Slocum groaned in agony. He couldn't believe what was happening. He might have believed it of any other woman. But Hilda? George and Harry flanked him, their faces wreathed in goatish anticipation.

Harry, spittle dribbling from the corners of his mouth, muttered, "Maybe he'll let us have a piece of her when he's done."

George shook his head. "Stick with yer hand. Look at the legs on her! Naw! He'll keep her."

Slocum got a brief glimpse of Argus freeing his erection from the tangle of his underpants, his other hand pulling Hilda's skirt higher.

"Here! Let me do it." She surged against him, unbuckled her belt, and wriggled free of the skirt that fell to her ankles. Slocum caught a glimpse of the frilly undergarment.

Argus, voice hoarse, ordered, "Get that off!"

She wriggled her hips as she pulled the skimpy garment down to reveal—

The crack of a gunshot froze everyone.

Argus staggered backwards. His face mirrored total surprise as his legs buckled and he slumped to his knees.

She dipped and came up with his .45 in her left hand. Her right held Slocum's derringer.

Slocum dropped his end of the canister and jumped aside as it fell on Harry's foot. Harry screeched in agony and hopped about in pain. George stood paralyzed with shock. Then his hand snaked for his gun. Slocum drove his right fist into George's face, then brought up his left in an uppercut to the belly. George gasped and went down. Slocum drove his boot into his face.

He spun as he heard a noise behind him. Lon shoved him roughly aside as his .45 came up. An earsplitting crack—and Lon went over backwards, his heels drumming the ground in his death throes. Hilda stood expressionless with the smoking Colt in her hand.

Argus, staggering to his feet, held a derringer in his right hand. His features twisted in demonic hate. "You filthy bitch! I'll . . ."

The tiny pistol came up to level at Hilda. Slocum wrestled the gun from George's hand.

"Argus! Here!"

Startled, he half-turned, his chest oozing blood. Eyes blazing, he jerked off a shot at Slocum. The bullet slapped at his coat sleeve. Slocum released the Colt's hammer. A click as it fell—on an empty chamber.

Argus, steeled for the shot, grinned like a demon from hell. He steadied himself as he aimed. Slocum hauled back the hammer, the cylinder clicking into place. He pulled the trigger, knowing he was too late—

The gun in Hilda's hand spat flame. The crack deafened him. Argus staggered under the impact of the 255-grain bullet. She fired again. The bullet tore bits of bloody flesh and white shirt from his shoulder. He went to his knees. The gun in her hand fired a third time. Argus settled in death, eyes glazing over.

Slocum brought his gun down on Harry's head with a meaty splat, and he collapsed with a sigh like a punctured bellows.

Slocum stood for a moment to get his breath and let his heart slow down. He stared at Hilda, who looked ridiculous standing with legs naked from waist to boots. George was right, though. She had damned fine-looking legs. He staggered to where she stood, her right hand still holding the .45. She let it fall and came into his arms. Collapsing against him, she sobbed hysterically, "That filthy bastard! His hands—"

"It's all right," he managed. "He didn't—"

"I want a bath. Now!"

"No time, Hilda. Help me tie these two up."

She pulled the frilly pants up and helped him, hands shaking.

"Where the hell did you have that derringer?"

"Where do you think?" She was firing up, cheeks reddening.

"You kept it—in *there*? In your—*drawers*?" He stared at her in disbelief.

"Why not? Not nearly as big as the cannon you're constantly prodding me with." She glared at him, mouth tight with anger.

He pointed to the stream. "Go on! Get your bath. I'll watch things here. Gramford ought to be along soon."

She hung her head, picked up her skirt, and walked slowly to the stream. He recalled how she'd looked that night on the Madison when she'd gone to bathe. Her walk had been strong and purposeful. Now, she walked like an old woman. Compassion for her flowed through him as he thought with proprietary pride, "Hildegard Rebecca Bruckmann Hasso. You're one hell of a woman!"

She was braiding her hair when the clatter of wagon wheels and the drumming of hooves grew louder. Slocum readied the shotgun. When the lead rider hove into view and Slocum caught sight of white hair flowing below the black Montana hat, he waved and yelled, "Bill! Over here!" Which wasn't necessary because the partially deflated balloon dominated the landscape. Slocum's belly lurched with apprehension when he noticed Sheriff Griswold with two deputies, their stars catching the sun's fire.

Gramford dismounted and waved the wagons to form a circle.

"There'll be a crowd here shortly. They're streaming out here in anything on wheels. Worse'n the gold rush. How are you, boy!'' He shook Slocum's hand as if it was a pump handle. He then embraced Hilda and gave her a solid kiss on the cheek. ''Couldn't believe it when I heard the ruckus and went outside.'' He stumbled against Argus's corpse. Drawing back, he exclaimed, ''That bastard beat me to it, I see. You killed him. Good! He's wanted for murder. Save the cost of a rope. You men!'' He gestured at those nearest him, ''Throw this bunch into the buckboard. They're wanted! Angus! Unload the gold!''

He turned back to Slocum and Hilda, his face rigid with suppressed feelings, and blurted out, ''You don't know what this means to me. Getting the gold back. I feared riots from the prospectors and miners. It was a close thing.''

He gripped Hilda by the arms and shook her in his enthusiasm. ''You two did it—my God! When I think—'' His voice suddenly broke as emotion swept over his face.

Slocum didn't want to hear his gratitude. He wanted only to stretch out in Hilda's bed and lose himself to sleep. Never had he felt so drained. She didn't appear much better off. He didn't even care about Gramford's reaction when he found an ingot missing. They sat and waited until Angus checked off the last ingot.

''One hundred and twenty-seven, Mr. Gramford.''

Silence fell over the group. Gramford looked at the tally sheet, then at Slocum. Hilda was also staring at him.

''We had trouble staying aloft,'' he began. ''Needed to dump ballast. Thought we were going to crash for sure. Threw over one ingot. An updraft saved us.'' When Gramford merely nodded, he secretly congratulated himself for landing on his feet.

Gramford pulled out a Havana. Biting the end off, he let Angus light it for him. Puffing blue smoke, he said, ''Guess we're lucky we didn't lose more. Don't know where you dropped it, do you?''

''We were up probably a thousand feet.''

The mine owner was silent for a moment. ''Well—to be

expected, I reckon. With all the excitement going on, we came out lucky.''

Slocum avoided Hilda's gaze as he told the sheriff, ''I think most of the bank loot's in those chests.''

Sheriff Griswold nodded and directed his deputies to retrieve the bags of money. When he finished tallying the loot and a deputy recorded it, he announced, ''Looks like it's all here. Stop by the marshal's office tomorrow. It'll take us a bit to sort this all out. My God! There's even sacks here from banks in California alone. If there's a reward—''

''Give it to Mrs. Hasso. She shot it out with Argus. If it hadn't been for her, I'd be dead.''

He ventured a quick glance at Hilda, who stared stony-eyed at him as if he were a stranger.

He rode back in silence with her. He didn't know if she knew about the missing ingot and was angry with him—or if she was simply as tired as he was. She prepared supper in sullen silence, and that night, when she turned her back on him in bed and refused to allow him to touch her, he knew he'd run his course with her.

He arose before dawn. Searching among her belongings, he found her map, gathered up his gear, and without putting on his spurs, walked on silent feet to the henhouse. He put his poke in it under a laying hen where she would be sure to find it. He would ride out before she knew he was missing. Moses watched him, tail wagging, butting him with his nose to have his ears scratched.

He stomped hard on the guilt trying to force its way up from the cellars of his mind. He'd been with her too long. She nearly had him snubbed up to a post so she could break him. He shuddered at how close he'd come. If he rode hard, he could make the creek and the cabin by nightfall. Saddling up, he climbed into the kack, and left her house behind him.

Main Street loomed before him like a pale ribbon in the pre-dawn glimmer. No lights showed in the George Hotel, where Gramford was staying. He assumed Gramford had the gold safely under lock in the bank, his men guarding it. Soldiers from Fort Ellis would escort it to Fort Benton. He wouldn't bother to collect the pay coming to him or the five-hundred-dollar reward. He would simply disappear.

Well, he thought, that was all behind him. Gramford, the gold, Hilda . . . He reined in his horse with such force, it nickered in protest. He winced. Damn! What he was doing was no way to treat a woman—much less a lady. One who had saved his life. She deserved better. So did Gramford—though he had nothing to complain about. He'd gotten back his fortune.

Slocum knew that riding out without saying good-bye was tantamount to admitting his guilt over the missing ingot.

But, he reasoned, Hilda was better off without him. "I can only bring her misery," he told himself, but his words sounded hollow even to him. He spurred his horse into a gallop and put Bridger's Rock behind him.

He reached what he figured was the creek that evening, though it was difficult to tell on the ground. He'd had a hawk's-eye view from hundreds of feet up.

He hobbled his horse and spent a sleepless night, in which he tossed and turned and provided a feast for mosquitoes. He'd never remembered the ground being so hard or his bedroll so uncomfortable. Worse, it drizzled toward morning. Wet and cold, he tried to start a fire. His morning coffee tasted like horse piss. He spat it out in disgust. The jerky wasn't much better. Two hours' search in the rain turned up the cabin.

He started at the deserted log ruin and rode in concentric circles, moving farther and farther out, like a ripple in a pond. He found the ingot embedded in the ground fifty feet from the cabin. The ground was smooth with short, burned grass. Anything unusual stuck out.

He hefted the hunk of metal before placing it in his saddlebag. Nearly four thousand dollars at sixteen dollars an ounce. More money than he'd seen in his life. Stolen money. No—not stolen. He reasoned aloud: "Gramford knew the kind of man he hired. He knew I'd robbed trains. Knew I'd killed the Yankee judge in Georgia. Knew I'd ridden with the Youngers and the Jameses. Most of the men I killed needed killing. Most drew on me first. If Gramford couldn't accept a man like John Slocum cooking him a chateaubriand, placing it on his plate with all the fixings, but cutting off a wee bit for himself in the kitchen before he served it, well, then he was a fool. He's lucky I was content with only one ingot."

He laid reverent hands on the saddlebag and the wealth it contained. He stared toward the mountains to the west. In a week, he could be in California. Or Oregon.

Hilda's face with its look of disappointment and disbelief flooded his vision. Helpless to stop himself, he pulled his horse about and rode back to Bridger's Rock.

His turnip said eleven o'clock when he entered her yard, the stars bright as candles in the black heaven. The night had turned cold. He unsaddle his tired horse, led him into the stable, and lit the lantern. Moses set up a spate of barking until he called softly to him. Moses licked his hand, then sat and watched while he rubbed down his horse and gave him water and grain.

Saddle-sore, he went to the back door and opened it to a kitchen dimly lit by a candle. Hilda, hugging her nightdress to her, Argus's fancy .45 in her lap, stared at him from shadow-dark, expressionless eyes.

He thought fast. "Didn't figure you'd wait up."

"I didn't. Moses woke me."

"Good watchdog," was all he could say. He wondered if his grin was as lopsided and stiff as it felt.

She stood, the gun hanging from listless fingers. "Thought you might be a burglar. You hungry?" If some kind of turmoil was roiling inside her, he didn't see it. She was a woman who could stand barefoot on hot coals and never blink. Without waiting for his answer, she put the coffeepot on and some stew. Fresh biscuits came from the bread box, butter from the root cellar.

He wondered if he dared to put his arms about her, but decided against it. Instead, he plunked the saddlebag on the table. Its weight made the table legs creak in protest.

"Got a present for you."

"Oh? What?"

He pulled out the ingot, which gleamed richly in the candlelight. He tried to look pleased and proud of himself. To his chagrin, she merely glanced at it and went back to loading currant jelly on his bread.

"You found it, eh?"

"Yeah." He didn't miss the flash of relief in her eyes as he hefted it in his hand, marveling at how heavy eighteen pounds was. It was twenty troy pounds, not quite as heavy as avoirdupois weight. Nine-tenths, if he remembered correctly.

Either way, it was a lot of wealth. "This is for you. Buy a lot of books."

"No."

Deflated, he demanded, "Why not?"

"Because it's Gramford's. And not yours to give."

Anger with her welled up in him. "You're my judge?"

She shook her head as she placed the bread on his plate and filled his coffee mug. "No. You're your own judge. Sit! Eat!"

He wished his pride was stronger so he could tell her to go to hell, but he was hungry and tired. And the food smelled delicious. She always managed to do something to distract him. Such as serving a mouth-watering meal so he couldn't think clearly. Or draining him in bed to make him so tired and content he was happy to fall asleep.

When he finished eating, he ignored her protestations and slept in the stable. That way, he figured, her warm, friendly body against his wouldn't change his mind. If he left in the dawn's first light, he could be thirty miles on the way to Fort Benton by nightfall. He'd take a riverboat to Fort Lincoln and be in New Orleans in two weeks. Four thousand would be more than enough to buy back the old homestead in Calhoun County in Georgia, rebuild the house and barns, live like a Southern gentleman.

He got as far as the George Hotel. Gramford was in the dining room, breakfast before him. Angus, his foreman, sat with him. Smoke from their Havanas formed a rich blue aura about their heads. Slocum, the saddlebag slung over his shoulder, strode over to their table and nodded.

"John! Figured you'd be in Idaho by now." The mine owner smiled—which must've cost him considerable effort, Slocum thought. But he was a gentleman. A real gentleman.

Slocum nodded and murmured, "Bill, Angus."

Angus nodded, a guarded smile playing about his mouth. Slocum laid the bag on the table. The weight made the coffee cups jump in the saucers. "The missing ingot. Found it."

Gramford betrayed no surprise, though Angus did. The old man opened the flap and looked in. Slocum felt he had to explain.

"Rode back to where I figured I'd dropped it. Took a bit to find it. Hildegard told me you were here. Figured I'd catch you before you left this morning."

Face expressionless, Gramford presented his cigar case to Slocum, who hesitated, then took out a Havana. Might as well enjoy it while you can—you stupid idiot, he thought. You'll be riding to the chuck line again after tomorrow. That's what comes of getting in too deep with a woman. No—with a lady. Ladies'll be the death of you yet.

He gazed wistfully at the fortune lying before him, irretrievably lost to him now.

Gramford murmured, "Angus, take charge of this. Put it with the others."

"Right, Mr. Gramford." Angus gulped down the last of

his coffee, gave Slocum a long, puzzled look, and picked up the heavy bag. He nodded and left.

"Good man, Angus," Gramford remarked absently as if feeling the need to say something. He motioned to the chair. Slocum, feeling as if twenty tons had been lifted from him, slumped into it. "You're a good man too, John. Fate smiled on me when I hired you."

"Hilda's the one you should be giving the praise to. She's a good woman." He thought with bitterness, Damn her honest-Abe hide!

"She is. Hope you realize that." He pulled out a small leather bag from his coat pocket. "Your money's in there with ten additional double eagles." He shoved the bag across the table. "Want her to have two hundred dollars. Schoolmarms don't get paid much. Give it to her. That is, if you plan on seeing her again."

"Thinking of riding to Georgia. Going home."

"Long way, Georgia. If you'd rather, I'll ride by—"

"I'll take it to her." He pocketed the bag.

"If I ever need to get hold of you again . . ."

"Ask the widow. She'll probably know where I am."

Gramford carefully flicked his ash into his plate. "Yeah. Reckon she will. Sometime I might want you to work for me again."

"I'll think on it."

"By the way, I have Joe's sample case. Found it in the Dougherty. No one's claimed it. Full of fancy French lingerie. Good stuff. Maybe the widow could use some of it. It's at the desk. Tell 'em I said to give it to you."

"I'll take it to her." He pushed back his chair and stood. He reached over and shook Gramford's hand. "I'll see you."

"Wouldn't be surprised." He released Slocum's hand and fixed him with a firm stare. "There's gold out there, John—and then there's gold. Real gold. Trouble is, it takes a real man to know the difference. Take care of yourself, son.''

''Adios.'' Slocum turned and walked to the desk, picked up the sample case, and strode out of the hotel.

26

Slocum sat outside Mier's Saloon, beer in hand, trying to figure where he would go. He'd drop by Hilda's when she was in school and leave the money in the barn in a nest under a laying hen. Along with the sample case. A loneliness he'd never felt before pervaded him. He was about to stand when he recognized Hilda's buckboard coming down the street. It passed him with a clatter.

She sat straight and proud like a queen, reins in hand, her funny hat perched on her head. He edged back into the shadow of the porch so she wouldn't see him. He watched as she stopped on the other side of the street in front of Dr. Zimmermann's.

Puzzled, uneasiness edging into him like a norther, he sat back down and waited. A half hour later, she came out, followed by the doctor. They talked briefly, and she climbed into her buckboard.

That was the second time he'd seen her visit Zimmermann. What the hell was wrong with her, he wondered. Uneasy now and concerned, he loped across the road to catch her before she left.

"Hildegard?"

"John? What're you doing here? Thought you would be halfway to the Musselshell." If she was surprised to see him, she didn't show it.

He gripped her mare's bridle. "Why're you at Doc's?"

"Stomach's been acting up."

"What did he say?"

"Nothing serious. That it would go away. Eventually."

He stood in awkward silence for a moment, not knowing what to say, the familiar aroma of her mixed with that of the mare filling his nostrils, his guilt hammering at him. Handing the reins to her, he asked, "Can I see you home?"

"Thought you were drifting."

"I am. But I could see you home."

"Don't think that's a good idea."

"Yeah. You're probably right." When she said nothing but stared stony-eyed straight ahead, he muttered, "Reckon I'd better ride out." He stepped back and touched his hat.

"Good-bye, Hildegard. It's been a real pleasure knowing you."

Her look was one of cold anger. "I just hope I lived up to your expectations. Good-bye, John." She shook the reins over the horse and rode off, the clatter of wheels sounding like loneliness itself.

Her cavalier dismissal of him filled him with anger and hurt. Hell! He'd been with her—how long? She might as well have said nothing. Was that all he'd meant to her? Damnation!

No matter. He would ride out in the morning. With luck and no Sioux, he could make Fort Benton in four days. Be in Fort Lincoln in three. In a month, he'd be in New Orleans and on his way to Georgia. With six hundred dollars in his poke. That might buy back Slocum's Stand, he thought. If he changed his name and no one recognized him. Perhaps no one would after seven years.

He stayed that night in the George Hotel. Its bed wasn't

as comfortable as Hilda's. Breakfast tasted flat. He thought of approaching Dr. Zimmermann and making him tell him what was ailing Hilda. But the doctor would tell him he didn't discuss his patients with strangers. He stewed until noon, and remembered it was Sunday. He picked up the gray at the livery stable, then rode over to her house. She answered at his knock.

Her face betrayed nothing when she stood in the open door. "Damn, she's a pretty woman," was his first thought.

"You're back," she exclaimed softly, pleased, "Come on in." She stepped aside to let him enter. He removed his hat and stood feeling like a schoolboy in his embarrassment. Her sleeves were rolled up over flour-white arms and hands.

He sniffed. The mouth-watering aroma of baking came from the kitchen. "Is that apple pie I smell?"

"Apple, blueberry, two mincemeat, and four loaves of bread."

"You gonna eat all that yourself?"

She watched him from expressionless eyes. "The mincemeats are for the children tomorrow. For a treat. And yes, I may eat the blueberry all by myself." She was silent for a moment, then added, "I'm hungry these days."

They stood in awkward silence for a moment. Then he said, "Look! Hilda—I told you in the beginning I'm a drifter."

"I know."

"Told you not to count on me."

"Never have."

"I never promised you anything."

"No. You were straightforward with me."

"Told you I'd ride out—sooner or later."

"Figured you would. You've ridden out three times in the last three days. You're getting lots of practice."

"Came back because I forgot something." Before he could stop himself, he dumped the bag containing thirty-five gold double eagles on the table. The coins rang, spun, and settled in heaps of dull yellow.

She didn't waste a glance at them.

"What's that for?"

"For services rendered."

Her open palm cracked across his face so hard stars flashed in his vision. He staggered backwards, his nose full of flour that set him to sneezing violently. The blow stung his cheek like fire, and the flour dust half-blinded him. Hilda's face twisted into almost hawklike fury as she stormed, "How *dare* you! You miserable sonuvabitch! You think I'm some whore you have to buy? You *bastard*!"

He grabbed her arms to stop her from hitting him again.

"Ease off, woman! I didn't mean it that way!"

"You're hurting me!"

He released her and stepped carefully back. "Damn! You're worse than a cow whose calf's just been branded." They both stood facing each other, their harsh breathing preventing talk. Finally, he said, "Gramford gave me the money to give to you. For helping us."

"I'm not a *whore*!" She choked on the word.

"Never said you were."

She stood stiff with indignation. He reached out and touched her arms. Gently, this time. When she didn't push him away, he pulled her into his embrace. She remained unyielding as a ramrod in his arms, then relaxed against him.

He put his nose in her hair and breathed in the lilac scent of her. "Brought you something else," he whispered, and reached out for the sample case.

"What?" Her voice was sullen.

"Gramford found Joe's case."

She looked up at him, puzzled. "Joe?"

"Joe Jayco. The female-underclothing drummer."

She put her face into his shoulder and gave a sad little laugh. "Poor little Joe."

"Nobody's claimed his samples." He stepped away from

her and opened the case. "Bill thought you might have use for them."

She fingered the tumble of smoky silk and laughed. "Good heavens! He must've been supplying all the hurdy-gurdies from here to California!" She picked up a lacy red and black French corset and held it to her.

He remarked, "Doesn't cover much, does it?"

She grinned and blushed. "Not supposed to."

He picked out a handful of black silk stockings that felt soft as air in his hand. "Look at these shoes." He held up a black pump with a three-inch heel. He pulled her to him, corset and all.

When she saw his look, she made her lips a round, firm *"No!"*

"Yes!" He kissed her.

"No! No! *No!*" She struggled feebly in his grip. "You're *hurting* me again! Let me go!"

He silenced her with a kiss, nibbled her ear, and whispered, "Yes, I will. Go on in and change."

"John Slocum—if you think for one moment I'm going to parade around in front of you in these—*nothings!* I'm not some dance-hall girl—"

"Can't wait to see what a schoolmarm looks like in these getups. Go on!" He walked her backwards to the bedroom and thrust the stockings and shoes into her arms. "Change. Meanwhile, I'll help myself to coffee and see what I can do with that apple pie while you demonstrate the latest in French—what's the word?"

"Lingerie. And I won't do it! If you think I—"

He again silenced her by fastening his lips on hers. Finally, breathless, she pulled away and gasped in breathless agitation, "John Slocum! Everything they say about you is true, isn't it? You're the most evil, rotten, undependable, licentious, lecherous, goatish satyr God ever put on this earth!"

He grinned happily and kissed her again. "Figured if you put up with me long enough, you'd come to see my good points."

If you enjoyed this book, subscribe now and get...

TWO FREE

A $7.00 VALUE—

If you would like to read more of the very best, most exciting, adventurous, action-packed Westerns being published today, you'll want to subscribe to True Value's Western Home Subscription Service.

Each month the editors of True Value will select the 6 very best Westerns from America's leading publishers for special readers like you. You'll be able to preview these new titles as soon as they are published, *FREE* for ten days with no obligation!

TWO FREE BOOKS

When you subscribe, we'll send you your first month's shipment of the newest and best 6 Westerns for you to preview. With your first shipment, two of these books will be yours as our introductory gift to you absolutely *FREE* (a $7.00 value), regardless of what you decide to do. If

you like them, as much as we think you will, keep all six books but pay for just 4 at the low subscriber rate of just $2.75 each. If you decide to return them, keep 2 of the titles as our gift. No obligation.

Special Subscriber Savings

When you become a True Value subscriber you'll save money several ways. First, all regular monthly selections will be billed at the low subscriber price of just $2.75 each. That's at least a savings of $4.50 each month below the publishers price. Second, there is never any shipping, handling or other hidden charges—*Free home delivery*. What's more there is no minimum number of books you must buy, you may return any selection for full credit and you can cancel your subscription at any time. A TRUE VALUE!